JIBBA AND JIBBA

Other books by Daniel Donatelli

MUSIC MADE BY BEARS

OH, TITLE!

JIBBA AND JIBBA

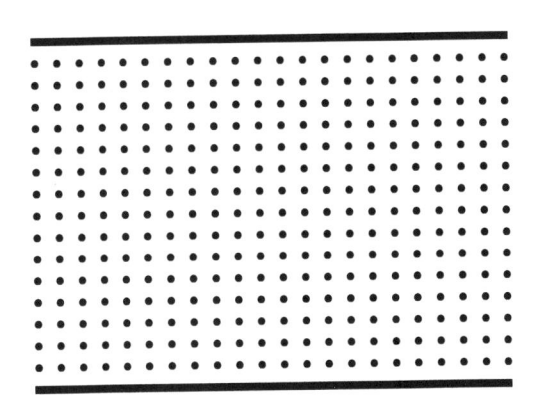

DANIEL DONATELLI

H.H.B. Publishing, LLC

Copyright © 2011 by Daniel Donatelli

All rights reserved. No part of this publication may be reproduced, stored in a retrieval system, or transmitted in any form or by any means, electronic, mechanical, photocopying, recording, or otherwise, without the prior written permission of the publisher.

This is a work of fiction; all characters and events in this novel—even those based on real people and real events—are entirely fictional.

Paperback ISBN: 978-1-937648-04-6
EPUB ISBN: 978-1-937648-05-3
Kindle ISBN: 978-1-937648-06-0
PDF ISBN: 978-1-937648-07-7

Published by H.H.B. Publishing, LLC
Henderson, Nevada

Design and layout by M. Wang

Manufactured in the United States of America

www.hhbpublishing.com

"Screams will soon claw my mouth apart."
—*Vladimir Mayakovsky*

JIBBA

"Hello, you've reached Roland McArthur's message service. I am either on the phone or away from my desk at the moment, but if you leave your name, number, and a brief message, I will get back to you as soon as possible."

Jeezus Krist, I thought, *none of these executive pricks are ever at their desk.* I suppose as a big executive type your phone rings all day, so as everyone knows in this casual-dress, diabolical-cubicle atmosphere, the best thing to do is avoid work.

My phone hasn't rung in days.

I'm the dipshit who rings all the phones.

A temp.

A temporary employee. You know, the expendable type. Here today, gone Corona.

They put me in front of this phone and this computer and I'm supposed to use a "Lotus File" to retrieve the number of every Chief Financial Officer in the greater Milwaukee area. (I don't even live near Milwaukee, so you tell me.)

I am the reason Jonathan Dyba and Christopher Laster are out calmly but assertively correcting other employees—people like me, the poor bastards—instead of actually doing their jobs by fielding the calls on their overflowing voice mail, from people like me, poor bastards.

What I'm supposed to do is tell all these corporate-exec assholes about the "great benefits" of signing up for one of our Executive Breakfast Briefings—a consortium where members of struggling or newly formed companies, this time from the Midwest, gather together to drink barrels of coffee and discuss but not understand such nonsense buzzwords as "Financial Web Enablements" and "Global Solutions."

Cigarettes will be smoked, prescription glasses will be cleaned with pressed white dress shirts, ankles will be placed on suit-pant knees, and the Chief Financial Officers of various corporations will take part in an interactive forum where everything is an acronym.

If I call a CFO and he has quit or been fired, he is "NLWC" or No Longer With Company.

There are acronyms for everything around here.

LF—Lotus file; VM—voice mail; LM—left message; CB—call back; NI—not interested; NTD—notified; JP—just purchased; WP—wrong person; BZ—busy.

I should abbreviate my kid's name. If I had a kid.

My "boss" hasn't learned my name yet. In her eyes I am "Temp 4," so I just refer to myself as "T-4" to fit in and sound professional. ("T-4's back from his lunch break!")

The script is right in front of me. It is my turn to LM on Roland McArthur's VM so that I can mark on my LF that he has been NTD about our EBB. Fuck me.

I work next to four other temporary, expendable, unskilled employees who have called Mr. McArthur at least four times before me. I'm pretty sure he's avoiding us.

But it's my job to let him know that we're still "eager to hear from him" and that "we are very excited about the new software available." I am to say this with a smile in my voice, or WSIV.

I guzzle a huge hot gulp of coffee and begin.

"Good morning, Mr. McArthur. This is James Bentley calling on behalf of the Alpha Corporation, and we'd like to extend to you an invitation to our Executive Breakfast Briefing at the Marriott Hotel in Milwaukee on the morning of December ninth.

"This will be an interactive forum in which we will discuss and demonstrate Alpha's management solutions and e-business technology within the financial arena. We will be discussing self-service applications, automated report distribution, and online analysis, amongst many other rewarding topics.

"Basically, the conference is a really nice way to stay current with the latest industry news. There is no cost to you, and breakfast will be served.

"We are preregistering attendees by phone, so if you can

let me know either way, that would be greatly appreciated. I can be reached at—"

What a load of bullshit. First off, the guy never calls back, probably because he's too busy deleting all his messages.

I speak to secretaries or whatever they call themselves these days and ask to speak to the Big Guy. She asks my name and cause. I state them, she tells me to hang on one minute please, and then she comes back and says that at the moment he's "in a meeting" or "away from his desk," so I am patched through to his VM.

Every now and then I'll catch one of the CFOs at his desk. By this time I've called the office so much we're on a first-name basis. They field my call and in the middle of my spiel almost shout (but usually they keep their composure) "Not interested! *N.I.!*"

I can smell the coffee on their breath over the phone, and I can see their face turn red as they now hear a live version of the speech they've erased countless times before. I can feel the stress reach that troubling vein in their neck and hear their pulse rise from the hatred they have for me and my cause.

I smile.

I think about a young rap star saying, "And to think it's just little old me: Mr. Don't-Give-A-Fuck still won't leave."

"Not interested, *Thankyou.*"

But I must press on. How could you not enjoy angering somebody who makes five times more than you, with benefits, and who probably passes you in a red sports car after work, model SX69, just made for dirty old men to get head from cotton-candy-brained whores?

"Is there any particular reason, Mr. McArthur?"

"I don't have time for this, okay?"

"Sir, are you, or will you be in the future, willing to learn more about Alpha Corporation's financial management solutions?"

"No—not at all."

I can hear his breathing getting heavier.

"Thank you so much for your time, sir. Have a great da—"

I don't even get so much as a goodbye before he hangs up, after all that time we spent getting to know each other.

I smile.

I hate my job.

* * * * *

I NEED to work it out. I need to discover something important I may have forgotten. You never know what you might dredge up, you know.

So I'm just going to blast it all out, shotgun-style, and investigate each grain of buckshot midflight. I have to believe that one of them has something to tell me.

I need one of them to hit something important.

* * * * *

AREA TEMPORARY Employment called me in the morning on some early December day and was wondering if I was seeking a job. As it was, I was.

I was home for break from college, and my mom was yelling at me to get a job.

I've had all sorts of jobs—sandwich-shop guy, umpire, sporting-goods clerk, janitor, mechanic's assistant, etc.—and haven't been very charmed by any of them.

"You've had dozens of jobs before," my mom said.

"I know—they've all sucked."

"But you have to work. You can't be going to school and not work. You need to earn spending money, honey."

"I know, Mom, but aren't I going to school so that I can get a job when I get out? How does it work the other way?"

She gave her familiar shrug. "Listen, I'm heading out to do some shopping and I need you to wait here for a call from Aunt Joan. She's calling with information about how grandma's surgery went."

"Sounds like a stomping good time, Mom. Barron is coming over and we're probably going to do some drugs and play with Dad's gun. Is that all right?"

She laughed. "Don't make me nervous, honey—please just make sure you get that call from Aunt Joan."

I hate Aunt Joan. Well, I don't hate her, but there's nothing I like about her. She gives me money sometimes for my birthday. That's not bad.

Mom left.

I called Barron and he came over.

Then we got high.

We goofed on infomercials. We traded thoughts on the women we saw as we jumped from station to station. There's not much to do in the cold 'burbs.

I am the average American, kind of.

I have seen *American Beauty*, *Titanic*, *The Godfather*s I and II, all of the *Rocky* movies, all of the *Die Hard* movies, and I left each theater a better man. Sometimes I have dabbled in independent films to make myself feel cultured, but most of the time I'm wondering why someone won't just turn on some lights and say what they mean.

I have a sick problem with killing myself off with over-the-counter drugs or vices or abuses. I kill my stomach with coffee and aspirin; I kill my brain with drugs, booze, and the devastating poetry of volatile madmen.

My friends are also drug addicts.

My brother, too.

My parents are Holy-Hyper Catholics, but I myself plan to recant on my deathbed.

I believe in God because I was goddam forced to believe in God.

I believe in myself because I have proof, though it's not much at all.

I am a lazy worker, and my boss knows it.

I am a lazy parishioner, and my mother knows it.

I am intelligent in school but apathetic in class, and my teachers know it.

I am because I am afraid not to be.

Right?

*****

My mom stomped snow off her boots when she walked in.

This served as a sign for the brothers—me and my fucker older brother—to get upstairs and unpack the groceries. We did this as children, so excited to see what new snacks she had bought us. And now even as we neared adulthood we still came running when she stomped her boots—call us the Pavlov dogs.

Even Barron comes running. He's practically lived at my

house since we were about three. We babysat for him and I think he loves my mom more than his own. I don't blame him. And it's all right because I love his mom, but in a physical attraction sort of way. His mom's a piece of ass. Wow.

My mom stomped her boots on the carpet by the door, brushing snow off her coat, and Barron and I came running, baked out of our minds.

"What are you boys up to?" she asked, happy to see us.

"Nothing, really," I said staring at the ground, to avoid eye contact.

"Yeah, not much at all," Barron said picking up my cue.

"James, honey, why are your eyes all red?"

I saw Barron bite his lip to keep from laughing.

"I don't know," I said. "My allergies are really bad today."

Barron laughed.

"Yeah," he said, "he was just sneezing for like five minutes," he told my mom, grabbing some toilet paper and carrying it to the bathroom. I could hear him laughing when he was out of my mom's sight.

"Oh, okay. Well, don't worry, honey. I got your prescription refilled this afternoon."

"Thanks, Ma."

I carried a bag to the table and unloaded it to the faint sound of Barron's giggles.

And we put away the groceries, occasionally laughing at all the little things that are only funny if they're inside jokes or you're high. A combination of both was deadly. Luckily, my mom thought of me and Barron as her little angels, and she would never suspect either of us of smoking that horrible stuff.

After we'd put away all the food, Barron and I went downstairs to finish our game of table tennis.

"Have you ever hurt anything intentionally?" he asked me, nonchalantly, like it was an everyday question.

"What? Why would I do that?" I asked, serving the ball.

He caught it. "Because it's really fun."

It was then that I could see the whole story. I knew it without him needing to tell me. I knew it because I also knew that soon I'd be hurting things intentionally too.

* * * * *

"Everything that happens happens one step at a time," Barron told me while I was driving him to school one day in high school a few years ago. "You're not famous nationally because you've never been famous locally, or even fam-ally."

"I see what you're saying," I said, voice groggy—it was much too early for school. I just wanted to fall asleep at the wheel.

"It even works in circles, man. Most of the time, that's when it happens. You become famous in a little circle and it runs like a drop of rain hitting a puddle. The size of your ripple depends on the size of your puddle.

"For example, you're actually kind of locally famous for baseball. You got all those awards last year, and if you ask any serious coach or player in the area, they'll know who you are, but that's just bragging rights with other baseball players—other people in a very specialized circle. Like, who's your favorite writer?"

"Mayakovsky."

"All right, so pull up to that guy, see him over there, packing those leaves into that bag, pull over to him."

"No, man."

"Just do it, kid."

"I get it, man."

Barron laughed. "Just do it, fucker."

"Fine."

The man bagging the leaves saw us pull up next to him, and I could see the old-man-fear-of-teenagers in his eyes.

Barron leaned out of the car. "Excuse me, sir. Have you ever heard of Vladimir Mayakovsky?"

The look of fear sat on the man's face. He said, "No, no, sorry. Are you him?"

Barron laughed.

"Yes, indeed, I am," he said. "I'm a cloud in trousers!"

I pulled away and called out "Sorry!" to the guy.

"See what I'm saying, man?"

"Not really."

"Being famous is more than art, or artists, or working hard. So what if you can write? What's it going to do for you? Or the next guy?"

"Barron, it's not about being famous."

He waited for me to continue.

"First off, I don't even like attention, and either way I know my limitations. Hell, even David Foster Wallace said a famous book gets about as much attention as a local TV weatherman."

"Who's that?" Barron asked, smiling like a bastard.

"Exactly."

"So what are you saying then? Use your words, kid," Barron said.

"I'm saying . . . I like to write. Like, I need to. My brain sucks, but I like the way my thoughts come out when I write them. It's like art therapy, or something. That's it."

"That's it?"

"Yeah, man. I guess."

"I don't know about you, Jibba. You're a strange guy," he said shaking his head.

"I'm too tired to argue," I said looking into the cold face of a still-dark morning, "with a monkey."

* * * * *

EVERY DAY at work around noon we are given an hour break for lunch. The building I work at is ancient and huge, but not all of it is owned by these Alpha fuckers. The first floor is owned by a deli, a dance studio, and an art store (utensils 'n' canvases 'n' shit).

Situated above all that is four floors of Alpha-owned cubicle cages—a labyrinth of insipid terror, intertwined like fucked-up funhouse mazes.

The word fun is a misnomer.

MN—misnomer.

So at lunch I head down to the deli to get a quick sandwich, head next door to the art store, and go in the back to see Cornelius.

Cornelius owns the place.

I met him when he caught me smoking up in the back of the building one day. He asked for a hit. I laughed and we got stoned. We've hit it off ever since. We talked about how the word canvas came from cannabis, man.

Now every day while I'm kicking it with Cornelius, a busload of high-school girls is dropped off at the adjacent dance studio. And every day, while they change in the changing room, Cornelius and I peek at our little hot-bodied dancers taking off their clothes, all of us laughing and having a jolly old time.

Cornelius claims he "accidentally" found the peephole when he was trying to hang a shelf up in the office. He says the hammer-and-nail went right through the wall, and then—"miraculously, dude"—there was a similar hole on the other wall in the girls' changing room that "must have always been there."

UB—utter bullshit.

I guess you have to look out for whatever advantage you can find these days.

Cornelius hung this framed painting of some dogs playing poker on the wall, which makes it look like the hole is only on the other side of the wall. Surely nobody could be looking through the other side—there's no light showing through, *heh heh heh*.

The key to not getting caught was to stand as close to the wall as possible while taking the picture down. Don't let any light through the opening. And then you press your face against the hole and feast on the naked, beautiful, trim, self-conscious teenage girls.

It was them you thought about as you masturbated during your two o'clock break.

Everyone always smiled at me after that break. And I always smiled back. It was a fun time for all. Maybe they all handled themselves wherever they were while I was handling myself in the bathroom.

The rest of the day goes by as thoughts of those beauties soar through my head, through my hand, into the toilet.

If you follow.

I'm not a chronic cranker. I don't feel like I have a problem. Well at least I hope not. My old psych teacher would call that an unsolicited denial.

Usually two o'clock was the only time of the day I let 'er rip 'round then. But I have friends who do it hourly. I have a friend who can break off twelve nuts in a day.

I respect and admire him.

It was during one of these "viewings" (as we liked to call them, to give ourselves some class) that Cornelius turned to me and said, "I need you to do me a favor."

* * * * *

Before you enter, while you're still outside—where everybody can see you—a man wearing a leather vest and a pair of extremely tight jeans asks each of you for two dollars, and you oblige. The place is so gigantic it's got a goddam cover charge.

He gives the "okay" sign with his hand just low enough so that your eyes are drawn to the massive bulge in his pants. Gigantic, indeed. You have a begrudging, newfound respect for him.

"Thanks," you say, entering the adult shop.

After you're well into the ol' smut shop, Barron turns to you and says, "Holy shit, did you see that guy's bulge?" and he says this with such incredulity it makes you laugh.

"Yeah, man. Impressive. I bet the Pentagon keeps tabs on that thing."

"Definitely impressive, fag, haha."

You notice a movie with a plain black cover titled, "*Blast My Ass With Cum*," you say to Barron.

He laughs. "Let me see that."

He's pissed because the box doesn't have any pictures.

"I'd buy this, man," he says, "but I don't want to accidentally get any more of that hairy-bush, foreign, uncircumcised '80s fuckin' bullshit."

You laugh because you understand, because it's true.

You keep walking around the store, noticing the bright contrasting colors of the shelves and tiles and walls. Big red shelves and harsh yellow walls grabbing your attention, and smooth purple tiles like a warm ocean of lust. How corny.

"How much did he say it would cost?"

"He said the 'good ones' were about fifty."

"Damn. How much did he give you?"

"One former President Dr. Benjamin Franklin, Esquire."

"A hundred bucks? This city's full of morons; who the fuck is buying *oil paint* here?"

"Something tells me he does more than just sell paint."

"No shit?" Barron says.

"Yeah," I say. "In fact, he told me—he sells weed."

"Oh, sweet," Barron says, "So why do you think he wants a 'fist'?"

"Must be a pretty sick fuck."

"Definitely."

"But you'll have that."

"Oh, indeed."

So you pick out the best and biggest 'fist' you can find.

SB—sick bastard.

BTWAHN—but, then, we all have needs.

You carry it up to the counter and plop it down like you've done this a thousand times—like you purchase large, expensive, painful sexual equipment on a regular basis and by now are numb to its corollary embarrassments, and are maybe even vainglorious about it. Prideful.

The pear-shaped, dough-skinned man behind the counter gives you a crooked eye. And to make things worse, Barron says, "I can't believe your dad took our other one! Remember when he *sniffed* it?"

The man holds the 'fist' up to look for a barcode he could scan. It sort of looks like a sword in his tiny, pudgy hands.

"Seriously, though, Barron, I think your mom is going to love this. I just can't wait to see *the look on her face*."

His mom is too sexy.

MILF—mom I'd like to fuck.

The doughy man-pear says it'll be fifty-two-thirty-five.

"Do you have any ID?"

"You need an ID to buy that thing?"

"You need an ID to buy anything in this store."

"Wow, an ID to buy the 'fist'—yeah, I got one. Keep your panties on."

"I will."

Barron and I look at each other. I wouldn't put it past this guy to be wearing women's underwear, but the mere thought of that man slipping on some pretty pink panties makes my stomach churn bile. I see Barron has that thinking look in his eyes and know we're on the same wavelength.

I almost always knew what Barron was thinking.

TBA—twins born apart.

Barron shakes his head vigorously and mutters, "Sick, man."

Mr. Teddy Pear smirks and gives me my change, and we take off right out of there. I'd had enough of that scene.

Barron says goodbye to the Bulge, and we head to my car.

"Check out what I got," Barron says, unjocking a movie-sized box.

"*Blast My Ass With Cum*," I read aloud and laugh.

So there we were, just like old times, walking to my car—me with the 'fist' and Barron with a stolen raunchy black-box porno movie.

Ah, young Americans!

* * * * *

"Now, Jibba, over the course of the last few weeks you've become a trusted friend, so I don't want you to feel weird about doing this for me. But I'm not comfortable, right now, telling you why I needed you to buy that for me, so in trade I offer some KB for the rest of my change and the, um, object," he said and laughed.

KB—kind buds.

"Hell yeah I'll go for that. Throw in that orange bong over there and I won't tell anybody else either."

"You're a shifty bastard, Jibba. That's why I like you. It's a deal."

"Thanks, Corn."

I looked around his office, noticing things I'd missed before, like his straight-off-of-Bill-Gates'-desk laptop computer and other interesting, cold, sleek electronic equipment. You tend to miss those things when you got titties and buds on the brain. Eventually, as always, the mind needs more.

"You plan on crippling the Internet with all that shit or what?"

"Yeah man, do you go online?"

"Yeah, it's the only way I can communicate with my cousin Frue. He's in the service overseas. We send emails all the time."

"Here, let me give you my address, then."

"Take mine, too. Always love catching up," I said pulling the dog picture off the wall.

* * * * *

THERE IS a big shining universe of ways to hurt yourself. You just have to want it to be there.

Maybe it's pain that makes the drugs feel even better, like getting into a hot shower on a cold morning.

It's just that for me and Barron it's always felt like every step up was a step down, and the other way too.

* * * * *

MY FUCKER older brother said he wondered why everything that gives you a buzz is bad for you. Alcohol, cigarettes, weed, cocaine, pain pills, hash, heroin, methamphetamines, narcotics, even overeating—all give the wickedest buzzes.

Even better after you massacre yourself.

I told him that it depends on your definition of bad for you. I know people who are in far worse condition than me who never touch drugs. Orca-fat people. Pear-shaped men who sit all day typing at some computer, filing some file, wearing women's underwear to smut shops. Men who work in coal mines. The religious. The secular. Everyone frowning alone in their motor-caves.

Drugs aren't the problem. Buzzes aren't the problem. Fat people aren't the problem. Those problems are merely responses to the problem. But the problem is I don't know what the problem is. I just know we all judge the effect rather than try to cure the cause. The desire to feel "wicked buzzes" comes from people trying to heal their existential pain, which I think is the real problem that should be addressed and corrected. Too bad it's goddam impossible.

People do drugs to make themselves not themselves anymore, or where they are not there anymore. Lots of people want to exist on another plane. Hard work and dedication can bring happiness and fulfillment, maybe; I know that much is true, but even more so, drugs can give you euphoric happiness without all the work. The thing is you have to choose your battles. While hard work leads to happiness, you have to suffer at the beginning for a long time. And drugs lead from happiness to addiction—you have to suffer at the end.

But who looks that far ahead?

"I feel like you're taking the side of the addicted."

"In a way I am," I said.

He looked at me with that fucking condescending look of his.

"I just think some people would rather face one simple addiction than the harsh, complex realities of their lives," I said.

"Oh yeah, I forgot how much life sucked."

"You're telling me you don't see the desperation behind some people's faces? It seems like everybody is withholding something. Hoarding it for their own. I think they want to uncap the id, but they feel like they can't or shouldn't. I say fuckin' let it fly."

"There you go," he said. "Let's have everyone 'uncap the id'; everything will work out that way, huh?"

"It might not work out, but it'll be better than this shit."

The phone started ringing.

"Try not to take yourself too seriously, Jibba," my brother said as I walked to the phone. "You're not as smart as you think you are."

It was Barron. He said he had a good idea.

* * * * *

"SO WHAT'S this good idea?"

"You'll see."

Barron drove out to the middle of nowhere, just a giant field that seemed to have been logged semirecently. The area was just this huge bald spot in the rich forest surrounding the interstate hillbilly road we were driving down. I remember the sound of birds and urban static off in the distance—that whirring sound over in some direction when you're out in Buttfuck. The sky was bright like the center of white fire, hard to look at. You squinted through sunglasses.

Barron had a backpack with him and unslung it off his shoulder and set it on the ground as I sat down on a large rock.

"What's that?"

"This," he said, opening the bag, "is a paintball gun."

Once again, I knew the story before I heard it.

RN—run now.

I took off.

"Three!"

At least he's giving me a head start, I thought, jumping over a small shrub, remembering to run in zigzags.

"Two!"

Why am I wearing such thin clothes? I should have seen this coming!

"One!"

It's a matter of adrenaline. Maybe that's what we were after. Maybe that is the drawbackless high. I ran hard. I ran for survival. Gazelle and Cheetah and Wind.

"Here we go, kid!"

I heard/felt something whiz by my ear. *Holy shit*, I thought, *he's going for head shots*. I kept low. Darwin would have been proud. He's dead, though.

And then my neck exploded. I went down hard, rather dramatically. I was afraid to touch the spot, afraid I'd feel my own spine, afraid of going paralyzed. The numb searing feeling so sweet, adrenaline rising and fading, pain my god.

Another pellet blasted into and exploded on one of my ribs.

"Fuck!"

Barron laughed and walked up next to me.

"You piece of shit . . . this fucking kills."

"Yeah, yeah. Tape an aspirin to it. Your turn."

I got up slowly while Barron wiped some paint from my neck. He handed the goofy-looking gun over to me. "You ever shot one of these before?"

I put the barrel an inch from his thigh and pulled the trigger. Almost instantaneously the paintball exploded on his leg and he jumped into the air.

"Fuck, man!" he yelled, hobbling like a pansy.

"Now I have, fucker. Head shots, man?"

"It was funny," he said, rubbing his leg. "You should have seen how scared you were."

"Three," I said.

"Two."

Barron took off running. I shot at him. Three pellets hit right between his shoulder blades. He fell to the ground, wincing and laughing.

"You didn't say 'One'!" he yelled from the ground.
"So what?"
"So, like, it's like a *rule*, man!"
"No, it isn't."
Barron laughed again. "Now you're learning, kid."
What Barron called learning my brother would call . . . well, he wouldn't call it learning.

* * * * *

BJ_Lover6969: look at my dad for instance, do you think that cocksucker even knows how old I am? If I'm alive? Fuck no! he doesn't send my mom any money, doesn't do shit for either of us

Jibbawocky: I know, why are you telling me this?

BJ_Lover6969: because I want you to know why I want to be known

Jibbawocky: who doesn't want to be known/famous though?

Jibbawocky: besides me

BJ_Lover6969: will you just hear me out

BJ_Lover6969: or read me out or whatever

Jibbawocky: ya

BJ_Lover6969: like I was saying, I want him to come back to me, saying he regrets all we missed doing together and going down his laundry list of excuses and why he regrets everything he did and missed.

(I can't relate to Barron. Though my dad and I haven't had a conversation last more than three minutes in the last nineteen years, I know he's here. I know he loves me. But, like Barron, I don't really know him. So I guess I can relate after all.)

Jibbawocky: you're a sick dude man

BJ_Lover6969: I know

BJ_Lover6969: so why don't you want to be famous?

Jibbawocky: well whats the point I don't need to be famous to be happy

BJ_Lover6969: that's pathetic

Jibbawocky: so's fantasizing about making your dad cry

BJ_Lover6969: yeah

BJ_Lover6969: whatever
BJ_Lover6969: meat any new ladies lately?
Jibbawocky: haha not yet
Jibbawocky: what's up with courtney?
BJ_Lover6969: I dind't tell you? she caught me cheating on her
Jibbawocky: ouch. I thought you loved that one
Jibbawocky: damn shit changes in ten weeks
Jibbawocky: what were you doing?
BJ_Lover6969: making out with Ashely baker
Jibbawocky: ha damn! At least you oulda cheated with someone decent
Jibbawocky: what were you thinking
BJ_Lover6969: I was drunk, and high, popped 2 dexes earlier, twisted
BJ_Lover6969: totally fucked
Jibbawocky: no, now you're totally fucked
BJ_Lover6969: yeah
Jibbawocky: haha you idiot
BJ_Lover6969: shut up bitch
Jibbawocky: haha
BJ_Lover6969: are you going to the basketball game tonight?
Jibbawocky: Yeah, whos driving?
BJ_Lover6969: I will, don't feel like drinking tonight
Jibbawocky: aight
BJ_Lover6969: buncha beautiful babes gonna be there jibba
BJ_Lover6969: so get yr dick ready
Jibbawocky: yeah
BJ_Lover6969: hoo-wee!
Jibbawocky: later man, I gotta go do some push-ups so I'm all primed
BJ_Lover6969: haha peace

* * * * *

Sender: Jibbawocky@aol.com
Recipient: tsquir@us.navy.efil.mil

Frue,

What's going on, man? How have you been? What's shit like

over there in the fuckin' Indian Ocean? Does it smell? Is anyone else out there besides you guys? Do any of those other countries have boats?

Anyways, my mom tells me to tell you she's sending cookies. She just needs to know how much she's allowed to send. I hear the military has high levels of cookie limitation. Fuckin' Uncle Sam. Can't imagine what it's like having that sour bastard be my boss.

Sorry I haven't written to you in so long. I'm back from school for like six weeks and I've been working and chillin'. You know how it goes.

I was thinking about the time you and I were playing in your old treehouse fort the other day. Remember our sawdust sneeze and how hot it would get up there? And on long summer nights playing we'd sleep out in the air just telling stories and playing with our action figures? Damn I miss those times, Frue. Remember when you brought those two girls up there that one night and we played truth or dare? Oh man I still remember having to kiss that ugly girl, haha, she was so ugly, with that mustache. It felt like I was kissing Uncle Larry.

I still have the blanket I slept on all those nights. How the cool breeze would whip through the little curtain we put up on the window, how from where I always slept I could see through a big crack in the ceiling and I'd just lie there and stare through that crack and think of the stars burning cold and alone out there.

I remember it was up there that I first had that thought, how everyone loves the stars but the stars were too far away to know it. It feels so sad, even though it's bullshit.

Frue, I don't want you ever feeling that way. Even though you're far away, everyone loves you, and we want you to know it. Like my mom's cookies.

All right dawg, I gotta get going to sleep. I have to wake up for my shitty job tomorrow and had a fw drinx tonihgt. I'll tell you about it all sometime. Take care, big man.
~~ Dr. James 'Jibba' Bentley, of the London–Stratford Jibbae ~~

* * * * *

MY BROTHER calls me up to meet him at the high school for some basketball. I was online with Barron at the time. He was thinking about coming along but decided against it. He used to be the best athlete I knew, and then after school he just gave up on all of it.

So I drove my old piece of shit car to the school gym, cussing out my dad to myself for never fixing the radio.

But it was snowing pretty heavily and the inch of accumulation on the roads along with my bald tires and rear-wheel drive monster transmission made the trip about as dangerous and exciting as driving around with Barron's psychopathic one-armed grandfather.

I was sliding every turn imagining I was taking part in some romantic comedy where the humble hero has to get to the chapel so that he can tell the bride-to-be that he loves her and shouldn't marry the jerk fiancé who only wants her for her father's business.

DG—delusions of grandeur.

Alas, no wedding, no love, just my brother. But the trip made the trip worthwhile.

After a few games of whupping on my brother in one-on-one I decided to go for a run on the indoor track.

Running and writing are two of my four greatest releases now. One of them used to be baseball, but I am retired, and I just don't like talking about it, though I'm fucking sure I will at some point.

After a few miles I decided to stop. My brother was taking off and the only other person left in the place was this cute girl I'd noticed earlier. Unfortunately she'd been heavily flirting with my old baseball friend. I didn't feel like putting the moves on someone else's girl, so I passed up my chance to play the role of the postgrad alumni underfuck who still hits on all the high school girls.

I remember she looked so young, but definitely good-looking. Definitely worth any effort I could've put into it.

WKA—weed kills ambition.

So I walked out after catching eyes with her before I took off. I smiled. I might have seen her smile, but I wasn't sure because it could have just been my imagination.

"Get off it, bro. She's too young, young man." My brother scared me, standing just outside the threshold of the door.

"I know, but I can still look," I said and laughed.

I felt like Cornelius. Shit, I felt like me—a 'fist'-less Cornelius.

"You worry me sometimes."

"Thanks, *Dad*."

"I'm being serious. Don't be a smartass or I'll smack your fucking face."

I felt a change of temperature in the room and decided to drop the subject and just admire some pictures on the Wall of Fame. This was a big long hallway with plaques and pictures of the best athletes to go through the school.

I was on that wall.

My brother wasn't, though he should have been. I think he's still bitter about it.

Fuck you, dick, I thought, but I did not want to fight my brother. We had one of those love/hate relationships.

Most of the time, that asshole makes me want to hurt things . . . intentionally.

* * * * *

BACK IN high school, Barron was a bad kid. Well technically not really but he just never went to class. He'd always get a ride with me to school and then he'd just disappear for the rest of the day until I saw him in the locker room during study hall. Kid played hooky like Bach in a fugue.

Meanwhile, I was the smartass of my classes. I'd make fun of people on a whim. I'd never read the required reading or do the required doing. I guess natural intelligence and good genes (or low federal scholastic standards) got me my 2.9 good-enough-to-go-to-state-school GPA. I always knew where my teacher was coming from, and that made me lazy, and sad. I just never studied—not what they were teaching, at least.

I slept in class.

I never worked hard on tests.

I stared at nerds to fuck with them and I stared at girls and wished I was fucking them.

I never hid any of this. The teachers hated me, or they loved me—it depended on whether they liked the feel of my poisonous barbs.

But now I feel like I need to complain because my state college has long winter breaks—long enough to make me need to get a job fucking with corporate executive dickbreaths.

Looks like I graduated into this job. Fuck those fucking fuckers.

Locked in a cubicle, you notice similarities to what it must be like in an insane asylum—the padded walls, the uniformity, the maniacs, the QUIET.

I find myself wanting to paint natural landscapes in Wite-Out on my computer screen. But what I and my job really need are some pills, like in the asylum.

And to think I swore I'd never take drugs.

D.A.R.E. worked for a while. But eventually kids (I) come to an understanding that drugs make you feel great too. All I ever knew about heroin was that it caused holes in your arm and made some model's face get all ugly. Fuck that. I finally read the truth in *The Basketball Diaries*, about the danger, yes, but the *beauty*, too. People wouldn't do it if there weren't any beauty.

I've never done heroin. I don't need that kind of addiction.

What D.A.R.E. should have been doing was teaching kids which combination of drugs will get you killed at a rave. Or which drugs make you suicidal. Or how alcohol is just as deadly as any of those other sexy drugs.

How to handle an overdose.

How to know when enough cocaine is enough.

How to fool drug-sniffing dogs at the airport.

(Take the bag of weed and wrap it in as many Ziploc bags as possible, then stuff the bags into a quarter-empty jar of peanut butter. Smother the outermost bag. Reseal the peanut butter jar with glue or an iron. Put crackers in your carry-on, along with the "peanut butter," and make sure you're in an earnest, polite conversation with a fellow traveler when you go through all the checkpoints. The key is to behave in the most forgettable way possible. Now everyone back at your dorm knows how good your hometown's weed is.)

In college you are educated on your dollar, so you actually try in class.

You don't try at work because you know you will be trying in school. Gotta dole out your effort. Otherwise, you're just pushing against the wind.

So you sit there, at some mass-produced cubicle, feeling expendable and functionally crazy, counting the minutes until lunch, until a nice little deli sandwich, until Cornelius, until smoking, until naked dance-team teenage girls . . . until fucking *anything else*.

* * * * *

HER NAME was Samantha. That younger girl on the track (team), her name was Samantha. She was a junior and three years younger than me. I mention her because I was thinking about her, and she had a big role in getting me into this mess.

And in no way do I mean to say that the mess I'm referring to now is my all-encompassing mess, by any means. So I guess I should say she just got me into another mess. Which all lead up to this particular and overwhelming shituation.

I'm nothing but a prisoner locked in a cubicle on trial for my own begotten influences.

You see, it was Samantha who called me first. Apparently she saw me running, or maybe she recognized me when I smiled and identified me as a Guy On The Wall Of Fame. Either way she found out who I was and got my phone number somehow.

Samantha is a beautiful girl. I'm not going to lie and say I didn't think the typical teenage male thoughts when I saw her, because I did. Everyone did.

She had that aura of sexiness about her that just couldn't be ignored. And she called me. She wanted to go out for coffee or something. Now I never turn down a lady, especially this stripper-lookin' specimen, so of course I agreed.

Then she hung up and I fell back on my couch, put my hands behind my head, and winced at the pain in the back of my neck.

Nice!

* * * * *

THIS STORY keeps coming back.

Barron and I were playing Wiffle ball in my backyard. We were twelve.

On a sunny summer day I threw a Wifflecurve right into the strike zone and just as Barron swung and connected there was a loud explosion.

"HOLY SHIT!" we both screamed.

For the briefest of moments, I thought Barron's connection had caused the explosion. I almost pissed myself.

Apparently, as I was working my fingers for just the right grip on the ball, a squirrel was chewing through the thick rubber at the pivot point of two power lines. As I was delivering the ball it kept chewing through. And when Barron connected, that furry little guy's teeth sank right into that powerful river of energy—

BOOM!

"Did you see that?!"

"No, I was pitching."

"No, I mean there. I saw something bounce off the side of your house," Barron said running over to our little backyard garden.

"Wow, look at this!" he said picking up a blackened squirrel leg.

"Put that down!" I shrieked, obviously a little more shaken up than Barron.

"No, look at it. It's like a chicken wing."

I remember looking at the smoking remains of the squirrel's leg. The fur was all black where it was usually rich and smooth and brown. I remember this bit of sadness passing over me.

"Here, Jibba, take a look!" Barron said and tossed the black, dead leg at me.

I shrieked again and jumped out of the way.

Then we both crowded around it, just staring down at the poor deceased animal's leg.

"Have you ever thought about it?"

"Thought about what?"

"That."

Oh.

"No."

Until that day, I'd never been there when something died.

* * * * *

THE FIRST time I hurt something.

After Barron asked me that question over our game of table tennis, I realized what I was now entitled to do. I remember feeling this wary excitement.

After all, it was Barron who had made me into what I am today. It was Barron who basically kidnapped me and dragged me to a ski resort, tossed a snowboard on my feet, and shoved me down the mountain.

I remember one run, when I actually got a little speed under my locked-in feet, with cold biting wind a long slap across my face, he yelled for me to try to turn. I had no idea how, but I tried anyway. It felt like I was in a different world, where the laws of friction and gravity didn't make any sense. I tried to turn.

The next thing I knew there was a "**SCHUCK!**" sound, a puff of snow, and a jerking at my knees, and I remember thinking *Oh, fuck*. I took the fall hard. First I got slammed down on my ass, knocked the wind out of myself, and then my knee came up and cracked into my forehead. I saw a flash of red I thought was blood but was actually my jacket as my own arm slammed across my face. Much harder than the wind. Then the shock of ice crystals and the annoyance as they melted and dripped down my neck and back.

After finally rolling to a stop halfway down the trail, Barron rode over, laughing. "See that, you bastard?! How'd you like that?"

"Holy shit! . . . That was fuckin' awesome!"

"Fuck yeah it was!"

And thus our sick fascination started.

* * * * *

I CAN'T say exactly what we were trying to do or accomplish. I remember it was something like Catholicism, which is my born-into religion. Receive your salvation through your personal damnation, punishment, or death. Pain is penance. Except we had no real purpose, or cause, except maybe those same stakes. We hurt ourselves for the rush, for the defacement of God's property, for all sorts of reasons I don't fucking know.

"Remember what I said about life's little steps?" he said, offering me a hand. "Well, there you go."

I took his hand and stood and laughed. Shakily I rode the

rest of the way down. I had a plan.

I took the lift to the top of the hill, my face a little red and still stinging and slightly bleeding, my ass sore like prison sex.

I did a jump-start down the hill. At this point I was able enough to go straight without falling, so I had to line myself up just right with the kicker I saw some skinny kid building earlier.

I rushed at it, gaining speed, barely breathing, staring eyes focused on the four-foot incline. When I hit it I jumped wildly and threw my body in every direction possible. While in the air, no idea where the ground started and the sky ended, I felt the innocence and power of youth so sweet in the bliss of the rise and fall. I felt freedom, body and mind, my mind floating on a simple thought, a peaceful feeling, and my body floating through the making-way air. And then the two snapped together in an instant as I collapsed to the ground, nearly breaking my everything.

"Holy shit!" Barron said coming to a sliding stop behind me. "Good fucking idea!"

And that's how it went for a long time. We'd find ways to hurt ourselves everywhere. It was never about malice, just fun. Just a stinging buzz, an excuse to steal painkillers from old people. It was good fun. A good time.

We'd wear these thick rubber bands, pull them as hard as we could on one side, and let them slap down, breaking blood vessels, bringing blood. Sometimes Barron would push bits of soap into the tip of his dick so it burned when he pissed.

I've done that, too.

It burns so bad.

It's fucking great.

* * * * *

"CORNELIUS, I have to ask . . . I'm sorry man but why did you need me to buy you that fist?"

"Jibba, you said—"

"Yeah I know but I smoked all that stuff so the deal's off," I said and laughed like a scumbag. "But if you don't want to tell me, it's cool. I just think it's weird."

"Jibba, it's—Can you keep a secret?"

"Usually."

"Okay, we'll see I guess. You see, Jibba, I'm sort of a renaissance man. I own this store—well, I inherited it from my grandfather—and I do a bit of dealing on the side, but my real passion is art itself. I'm actually a rather respected artist, sort of, not really, but kind of. I don't tell anyone because they don't need to know, and I don't want anyone asking me any questions when they come here. I don't have any answers, you know? All of a sudden they want to get all deep and talk about Mozart or some shit."

"He was a composer."

"Still an artist."

"Right, so what does Mozart have to do with the fist?"

"Well, I don't paint on canvas. My deal is I make art out of objects. Would you like to see what I did with the fist?"

"Maybe."

He laughed and pulled it out from the bottom drawer of his desk. I could barely recognize it. The once-black "skin" had been painted a cosmic array of reds, whites, and blues. It almost looked beautiful, though that word seems a bit perverse for that object. It had been glossed, and the colors meshed together so well, simply and compellingly.

"That's amazing, Cornelius," I said, engrossed with the fist. "I'm impressed."

"Do you get it?"

"I could ask you the same thing, right?"

"Don't be an asshole. What do you see?"

"Besides an obvious talent on your part, I see the strong fist of national pride—or rather the strong fisting."

"Ha. I like that."

"Well I'm sort of artsy myself, and I don't tell anyone either."

"Oh? What's your medium?"

"Poetry."

He laughed. "Can I read some? I have a friend in the word biz."

"Sure. Anytime. But, let me ask: why did you need me to buy that thing?"

"You think I want to be caught buying a giant prosthetic sex fist?"

I laughed. What a jerk I am. To think I was thinking Cornelius was getting his jollies with it. I shudder to think about the people who use those fists for purposes other than making avant-garde art with them. Or maybe not. Maybe some men and women have huge sex openings. It happens.

GV—giant vagina.

* * * * *

I'D JUST gotten off the phone with Samantha when Cornelius called. He told me I needed to go over to his store tonight around eight.

My mind reeled with possibilities. I didn't want to do it but what the fuck, you know? It was a good excuse to go out with Samantha. So I took her down to the art store I'd been telling her about—telling her about how the owner would smoke me out and how good he was at art. I didn't tell her about the fist, though.

She was eager to get out of her house and into my car. She looked great. I really liked her and it was too bad I was going back to school in less than a month.

The drive takes about twenty minutes but Samantha'd made a music mix so it was all good. You know how girls can get with that type of thing.

When we got there Cornelius was standing outside his shop, apparently pretty excited to see me.

"Jibba! Glad you could make it. And this must be Samantha. Pleasure to meet you. I'm Cornelius. How are you?"

"Good," Samantha said, blushing.

"Jibba, I wanted you to see this. It's my newest piece."

"Sure," I said. "Definitely." Samantha didn't look that comfortable, and I didn't really blame her. We were all pretty new to each other.

Cornelius took us through the front of the store and to the back. I liked the way that it felt in there, all those blank canvases and the implements with which to give them transcending value. A store of aesthetic potential. A possible universe in every corner.

And when we headed to Cornelius's personal office with the Dog Card picture hanging so awkwardly in place. I looked at it and then at Cornelius, relieved, and he winked.

"Here it is," he said, holding up a car bumper with scandalous abortion bumper stickers painted on it.

A white one with blue letters that had a drawing of a pregnant woman and a coat hanger, with a caption that read, "Don't get hung up on the little things."

And "Children: an easily curable STD."

And "My aborted child would have been a total slut at Richfield Middle School."

"Oh, my God, that's horrifying," Samantha said and shuddered.

Once again I couldn't help but notice Cornelius's high-quality painting skill. His drawn-on stickers looked so real. I had to tip my hat to him, despite Samantha's nearly having been rocked to sobs.

"You've made another beautiful-terrifying piece of art, Cornelius. Kudos to you."

Cornelius smiled. Samantha grabbed my hand. That was nice.

"It really is a piece of art," I said, "and such a statement too."

"Thank you. The reason I called you all the way down here is because I need your help. Actually I need your advice. I'll just cut through the bullshit and ask: are you under the impression that my work is good?"

"Cornelius, I just told you—"

"Just answer the question."

"Yes. I think your work is great, from what I've seen."

"Do you think I should take all this to New York?"

Without thinking I said, "Yes—definitely."

"That's what I thought. Well, that settles it. I'm leaving after Christmas. I'm getting the fuck out of here. Just wanted to share the news."

"That's great, Corn!"

"Yeah, I'm excited too. I really feel good about it," he said with a nervous smile.

"Well I think you'll do great," Samantha chimed in, adjusting her hand in mine. "At first I was a little shocked, but this is really well done, and art's probably supposed to shock us, right?"

After some more chitchat, Samantha and I peeled off and headed back to her house.

"He seems nice," Samantha said as we topped her street. "He's kind of creepy, but he seems cool. It's too bad he's leaving."

"Why?"

"I'd totally fuck him," she said and laughed. "Just kidding!"

"You'd better be, ho, or I'll throw yo' ass out this movin' car," I joked.

By then we'd pulled into her driveway. We said goodbye and I drove away feeling contented—good about myself for a little bit.

I needed some pain.

* * * * *

THIS IS how you steal drugs from the elderly. It was all Barron's idea, and mine.

First you mass-produce a handsome handout that says "Catholic Youth Help League" across it in big, bold, Christian lettering. Then you put "Brothers James and Barron are able and willing to help you with day-to-day chores if you are suffering through any pain."

Pain means doctors. Doctors mean drugs. And we all know what drugs mean.

"So if you ever need any help at all, please call us at" and I left Barron's cell-phone number. "This is a number where we can be reached anytime, day or night."

Old people go to bed early and wake up before school starts so that was no concern of mine. It was Barron who skipped classes during an emergency situation with one of our "clients."

The old folks said that it was just the sweetest thing. You can get away with it if you dress nicely and smile enough. What they didn't realize was that our "free" service actually cost them quite a bit in pills. But it wasn't like we just swiped the whole bottle; that would have looked obvious. We'd take two pills here, two there, you know.

There are a lot of lonely old people out there. There was no malice behind it. We weren't trying to harm them. It's just that we wanted drugs. We needed drugs. Did you know that you only need like two beers after popping one of those beautiful bas-

31

tards?

We felt great. Getting showered with thank-yous and tons of free food. Sometimes old ladies would call us over just to give us some pie they'd baked. And of course one of us might make a bathroom visit and walk out with three, big, white happy-makers.

She probably forgot she took them in the middle of the night when her back was hurting.

Barron was carrying a pan downstairs once when he "accidentally" tripped and rolled and tumbled all the way to the basement. The woman was so overwrought with sorrow that she handed him an entire bottle of Codeine and said, "Oh, I hope you're okay, I just feel terrible about this. Here, take these. My coverage gives me an open prescription."

"Thirty-two fucking pills, man!" he said to me, looking up from the poured-out bottle on my kitchen table. There was a huge bruise across the length of his forearm. "Fucking jackpot. I got Las Vegas in my *pocket*, bro!"

It's called two birds with one stone.

Hurt yourself and receive drugs.

I smiled at the simplicity of it all. The old woman smiled at the kindness of it all. Barron smiled because he'd just popped four painkillers and his eyes were glazed over with cosmic reverie.

It feels good to help.

* * * * *

YOU SMOKE weed at seven-thirty in the morning on your way to work just to make it through the god-awful morning. You stare at your computer screen and think about Samantha for twenty minutes at a time. Then you call some CFO and start laughing in the middle of your speech because it's the third time today you've called and the kid next to you just had that look of total defeat wash over his face as another exec told him he wasn't interested.

He must take this shit personally. He carries the persona of a defeated man, and he's not that much older than you.

Mostly you laugh because you're baked. No need to worry about getting fired; those pricks probably never make it that far into the message anyway.

You drink nine cups of coffee in fifteen minutes just for a nice caffeine eruption. You slip into the bathroom and read the diaries of Sylvia Plath for twenty minutes and come back to the same desk, but at least filled with something—with something like a recharged sense of there being meaning in existence.

In the morning you look forward to Cornelius. In the afternoon you look forward to Samantha.

It's how you get through the day.

And this happens over and over, in a continuous loop. It works in circles, like a merry-go-round. There are high and low points but always a set track. Wake up, shower, go to work, look at a naked dance team at lunch, beat off, go back to work, go home, eat, call Samantha to go out with her, meet up with Barron, destroy a part of your body, shock each other with a Taser he swiped from an electronics store, come home, go to sleep.

You can see the obvious high and low points. But that also depends where you're looking from. Much like so many other things in life, where you start is where you end. From far enough away, there is no up or down. It's all everything everywhere. It's where you go between that counts.

The only between I care about is between the legs. You get this excited, nervous feeling in your crotch as you drive to the next place you are to see Samantha or masochate yourself.

You get butterflies of the balls as you drive out to Barron's rich-ass grandma's place to house-sit her dog. But it's winter and you decide that there's enough snow covering her bushes to do some leaps. And by that you mean you get a ladder and climb to her roof to jump back-first into the snow-covered bushes surrounding her house.

You both have a lot of scars.

And then when you're done with the rooftops you rub your wounds with snow and savor the pain for about half an hour and then help yourself to a few painkillers from the medicine cabinet. You send Pookie outside to piss, feed the little guy when he gets back, sit down, and let the painkillers run their fun course. Possibly nod out for a bit and wake up and go home bleeding through your shirt, full of poetry and pain.

Your mom asks why you're bleeding and it's easy to think of

an excuse because she's one of those devout believers who's convinced her kids are just angels. Barron's mom doesn't care either way, as long as he's alive and not asking for her attention.

Sometimes when you're in the middle of a pain spree, possibly spraying each other with mace, you have some of the most normal thoughts in the world. It's at work, staring at a computer screen, that you have freaky thoughts.

You'll be crying, holding your hands to your eyes, forcing tears to clear out the pepper spray, and you'll think, *Oh man, I'm wearing two different socks*, or, *Wow, Barron's grandma has a really clean house*.

You wonder why you think like that but the only time you think about it you're fucked up at work tying a string around your finger and seeing how deep of a blue you can make it turn. After a few blue minutes you give up and try to place a call but get directed to somebody's voice mail.

TFS—this fucking sucks.

Holding the scalding-hot tip of a lighter on your skin, you wonder how Samantha is doing right now.

Dialing some corporate office in New Orleans you wonder what a scab the size of a steak would taste like.

And this is how it goes. You think about what Cornelius's new project might be, and how you can't wait to get out of this cubicle and smoke with him in an hour and thirteen minutes. You want to be kissing Samantha. You wonder about her as-yet-unseen, presumably petite vagina.

You are encapsulated by your base desires. Your parents and church leaders consider this a sin. Mortal desires are tools of the devil. But they practice peace and pray for you and compliment you for volunteering to help the elderly with their chores, or just talking to them, and you laugh and smile while fingering three Demerols you stole from Mrs. Jones after taking some old blankets up to the attic for her.

While up there the air is cold and you can hear every sound in the house. The dust dances in the waves of light pouring through the shafted vent in the back wall. And you're looking through the boxes and trunks. Reading yellow old books, looking at black and white framed pictures turned dusty and lovely. You eye a picture of a three-year-old Mrs. Jones standing next to a tall woman, most likely her dear departed mom, and it's overwhelmingly touching. Such innocence, of time and person. On the back is an excerpt from a poem you know well. "If I should meet thee, after long years, how should I greet thee? With silence and tears." And you get all choked up for poor old lonely Mrs. Jones, whose husband died last year. More silence, more tears.

And you think of those pictures and poems and people while you're suspended in midair over a mountain of snow you're falling into after you jumped off the roof or rocketed up and off a big slick white kicker.

You put most of the Demerols back before you leave.

Mrs. Jones just gave you something better.

* * * * *

BARRON STOPPED by my house on a fall Saturday afternoon when we were in high school. He was carrying two grocery bags, both with a gallon of milk inside. "Tonight," he said setting the bags on our kitchen table, "we puke!"

And he explained to me that the human body is incapable of holding a gallon of milk inside the stomach. Kind of why babies puke. Maybe.

"You mean like that old summer-camp dare?"

"Yeah, but this is different."

"How?"

"First," he said pulling a pot out of the cupboard, "we eat spaghetti."

I loved where this was going.

"Next, we color the milk with food coloring," he said filling the pot with water. "Then we drink every last drop of the milk or until we can't anymore. But we do this in the food court at the mall." Once again, I loved where this was going.

"And finally we drive different cars, like we don't know each other, and sprint to the bathroom when we're about to puke," he said and took a dramatic pause. "But do you fuckin' think we're going to make it?"

"Let's do this."

* * * * *

You DRINK the milk slowly, to get as much in as possible, which is pretty hard when your stomach is already full of rigatoni and marinara.

Barron is a great cook. He taught himself because his mom is too hot to have ever needed to learn to cook. He got a spaghetti sauce recipe from one of the old Italian women we're helping. Gorging was not difficult.

You drink half of the gallon back at your house, and you already feel like puking but you hold out like a porn star because if a tree falls in the woods and nobody's there to see it then it probably never happened.

You both get in your respective cars and head to the mall with the remaining milk in resealable bottles in the cargo pockets of your pants. You chug them in a changing room and then make your run for the bathroom.

As you uncap the bottle, now that it's real, you think to yourself, *What the hell am I doing?* And that nervous groin feeling rises and that's all you need. The milk tastes thick and syrupy and really gross by now and you really want to puke but know you can handle more. Gotta pack the skyrocket with as much black powder as possible if you want it to be a good show.

Barron is at another store doing the same thing—you hope.

With the foul white mouth of the bottle pressed to your own, you start to feel so nauseous you can barely see. You feel drunk and you know it's time. You cap the last bottle, put it back in your pocket, and start to run, making a big scene as you sprint out of the changing room, attendees calling security thinking you stole something, calling for help. Inside you smile because you know what's going to happen when you can't go anymore. But it's a deep smile because mostly you just want to vomit.

And soon enough it's happening. Not sure where exactly you are in the mall, you look around but nothing registers. That change of pre-vomit pressure rises in your ears . . . and then it happens.

LO—liftoff.

You're not sure how long you were puking for. You remember it was the next-best feeling after one particularly disastrous heave of green milk and red spaghetti sauce, you catch eyes with a short, blonde, forty-something-year-old woman, and she's bringing a hand up to her mouth saying, "Oh, my God." And she blinks and you know you look vomitus and your mouth is covered in green milk and you think, *My mom has that same coat*, and then you uncork again, making this druid gurgling sound as puke unloads from your mouth like an uncapped, demented fire hydrant poltergeist.

And . . . eventually . . . you're done. And you look down at your hideous creation and say, in a daze, "When did I eat that?" as you look at part of a hot dog. People all around you are staring and you say, "Oh my God, don't eat at Salvator's." You kind of hoped to cause a giant puke fest but everyone is more in shock than nauseous. A mall security guard comes running up to you as you pick yourself up from the ground.

"I'm so so sorry, sir," you say. "I was sick but I forgot my girlfriend's birthday and I knew she'd kill me if I didn't get her something," and you remind yourself to pat yourself on the back later for that one.

"Damn, boy! What did you eat?"

"Spaghetti. And a hot dog, I think. It's all the medicines. Oh God I'm sorry."

The confused and now sorry security guard says, "Don't worry—I understand," as you look around with gushing apologies for all, eyes red and weepy, face pale and pink with embarrassment.

"Oh god I'm sorry," you say but you're really thinking *I kind of hope Samantha doesn't hear about this*.

You take one last look at your finest hour, and you want to laugh but you just told the security guard that you thought you were okay to drive home. And you are ushered out of there, not forcefully but not happily, and you get in your car and wipe a piece of noodle from your chin. And then you have that feeling—that feeling of a crime gone right.

Then you start your car and drive home. Three minutes later, another very confused security guard also escorts Barron from the building. Barron runs to his car and drives off before the security there realizes, by the sheer quantity and color of the vomit, that the two incidents must have been related.

The shower at home feels wonderful, all numb from drugs.

* * * * *

"WE ARE young, white, straight, American men. We have every sect of people in the world leaning on us to carry them into the future or looking to overtake us after our years of a holy-unholy burden, cracking the shell of their cultures with the hammer of Christianity," I said as we walked into the music store, really on my soapbox. "But now the only thing we're known for is our aptitude with computers and the grudge of all societies against us as a result of our cracker forefathers. Fuck oppression, I mean really it's my empathy they're up against now. I really don't give a fuck about any of them. They're all a bunch of fuckups for letting assholes like me hold them down in the first place."

"Easy, man. You're going to give yourself a stroke," Barron said picking up a Beatles album.

"Hey," I said, "you started it."

"Yeah, but what do my complaints about my grim future have to do with white power?"

"Barron, I still don't get why you're so down on your future."

"Fuck, Jibba, look at me—uneducated, no college degree, no diploma, a fucking GED, youth is gone, high school is gone, girlfriend is gone. What else do you want?"

"The secret of life," I said, "is possibility. You go to sleep okay because tomorrow you don't know what sort of life you're going to be given. What kind of new or old memory you'll uncover in the attic."

"Huh?"

"Nothing. Anyways, like I was saying, you go to sleep happy because tomorrow can go any of many ways. You don't go to sleep sad and depressed because today sucked."

"Well, I do."

"Well, you shouldn't."

"Just shut up, bitch. Anyway, I'll be fine. I had another dream last night."

Oh, fuck.

That's how it always starts.

Barron was stricken with a horrible depression when he

was fourteen. He said he'd thought about suicide, even had a blade to his wrist once, note written. But one night he had a "beautiful" dream in which he was riding his skateboard and hit a little kicker he'd built and shot off it, landing on his side, tearing up his left arm and leg. "My cuts didn't bleed, though; they sent rays of light towards the sky, man, like I saw colors I'd never seen before, and I heard sounds I never even knew existed, these crazy harmonies."

He said I should have seen it.

He said when he hit the ground his demons flew off.

"I woke up that day, and I remember seeing the snow on the ground and I thought *Me and Jibba are going boarding*. I wanted you to feel what I felt . . . and you did."

So our sick fascination was born from Barron's dream that delivered him from suicide. And for the longest time he and I disfigured ourselves to try to achieve true life, the ultimate rattling buzz. Shit I don't know why I liked it and I guess I did it because Barron did. But I'm not a pushover like that. I can make my own decisions. But maybe I am a product of all I surround myself with.

You'd never guess Barron as being suicidal by looking at him. He seemed happy, sometimes crazy, but never mean or harsh or even depressed. He hates his dad, but who doesn't? He fears his future, but again, who doesn't? I'm scared of the people who don't.

Some people can't be reasoned with.

Now we're back in the record store.

"Well in this dream I was walking along under this beautiful purple sky, and I immediately knew this was the same kind of dream as before. So I'm walking along and this little girl comes up to me and she's wearing this sunflower sundress and she's just really cute. It felt good seeing how innocent she was. I'm telling you, man, it was beautiful. She was holding this sign that said: 'Do not eat my ice cream cone.' And then she grabbed and tugged my arm and said, 'Do ya want thum of my ithe cweam, mithter?' And I said, 'What about that sign you're holding?' and she said, 'Do ya want thum?' and she refused to answer my question. So finally I took the ice cream cone from her hands and threw it as far as I could.

"She started crying, man. And then the dream ended."

"What do you get from that?"

"Gotta fuckin' toss the cone."

"What?"

"It's time to make things much worse."

"What?"

"You're part of it, Jibba, but it's me, man. It's me, not you. And it's not me, not you, but we. You'll see, kid."

I was actually relieved to hear him say that, and confused.

"So what now?"

* * * * *

PER CUSTOM, I am to gather with my family during the holidays. Now that I'm retired from baseball and back from school the question has changed from how's the throwing arm to how's school going.

It's sad as you look around the restaurant at your smiling family, feeling like an outsider because your clothes were not manufactured in the '80s, neither was your haircut, choice of music, vocabulary, or shoe style. Those old fashions run rampant over the modern-day looks, as you can register a memory of these same people wearing these same clothes lifetimes ago.

Drugs.

Need drugs.

Aunt Joan shows up with her poofy hair and her fake-fur coat and her blood-red-lipstick-coated lips and is just dying to know how college is going.

How is my brother.

Out of town, you say. And then you wish you were with him, that prick, as she leans in to smear your face with designer imposter lipstick and Maybelline cheeks. You hug her frail figure and realize she's fifty-nine and your fingertips can feel ribs, bones, and fat, but no muscle. You start to feel bad for her because you know that her glory days are gone. Her family has all moved out. Kids starting new families. And then you think of your mom and the struggles she must be going through as her sons keep coming and going in and out of her house from college to home to college to work to life. It must all be so bittersweet for a parent. She cries at night looking at old pictures she has hanging on the walls. You feel like you're hanging on the walls, too.

You're probably smoking up as she's crying, hundreds of miles away.

Aunt Joan says, "How old are you now?"

Don't worry about it, you creepy woman. Thinking back on it Aunt Joan has always looked too old and fragile. Blue veins shining through the backs of her legs. A hanging, saggy bag of skin drooping underneath her chin like a pelican's disgusting beak. Caked-on wrinkled makeup to hide old real wrinkles.

Aunt Joan asks, "How's baseball going?"

Baseball is over. But she's so used to asking that question it's become custom. Unwanted custom. Forced conversations forced out of gathering customs. Baseball is fucking over but you don't have anything else to talk about so you make something up.

You think about what Barron could have meant when he said you gotta toss the cone.

Aunt Joan says, "Is everything all right?"

Everything's the same because my mother's side of the family is locked in a decade in which you were known as the little baseball player—the little younger brother of the successful brother, the Student-Athlete's shadow.

You are your brother's brother.

Aunt Joan walks away with a nervous smile.

You're still sitting down at some table with some burning candle's flame dancing and glasses being cleaned spotless and forks and spoons that are that platinum shine that makes everybody look like royalty but not feel like it at all. The tablecloths are so white that it makes you think of old music videos on low-grade televisions where the contrast button didn't work and everything white made your eyes hurt. The conversations are full of inside-joke laughter and kind mild sarcasm. The pop is flat and syrupy like head-cold medicine. The discussions, you note, are as dimwitted as anything you can remember, but they are filled with love so you are comforted. Your little cousins are running around with balloons tied to their wrists and giggling with high-pitched glee.

You wish you were in a fight.

You wish you were writing another shitty, nihilistic poem.

You wish Barron were there to make things more interesting. Possibly hit on a waitress. Possibly he brought some laxatives for Aunt Joan's dessert.

You wish you knew what Barron meant when he said you gotta toss the cone. Things are going to have to get a lot worse? But how? He's suicidal already. The kid's been watching too many movies. He needs to seek help. But he's your friend. And a great friend. The kid you want on your side if you were to get in a fight. The kid you want defending you if you're in an argument at some bar down at school. The kid who mooned people at stoplights on the bus to baseball games. He's your best friend.

All the dishes go clink and people are all making little conversations about how cute the new baby is, and joke about how old Aunt Whoever is today. The food is good. And the holiday decorations bring you back. So it's not a giant loss. But basically it's a waste of a Sunday. Basically the day went by and nothing happened that made you any better or worse of a person. You were static. And that in itself is a sin against your life. So you vow to pass someone on the shoulder going ninety miles an hour on the way home just to test your will. To feel those butterflies of the balls.

To do what Barron would do.

* * * * *

TWO KIDS playing Wiffle ball hear an explosion and find out a squirrel had bitten through the hard rubber coating on a power line and had a fatal charge of electricity suddenly surge through its tiny body. Its unnamed life over so quickly.

One kid feels this cool breeze and is thinking *Maybe my friend shouldn't be so excited about this.*

One kid thinks to himself *I've never been this close to death before.*

The other kid thinks that *Maybe the squirrel did it on purpose, to see what it would be like.*

A cloud eclipses the sun as the heaviness of the day bears down and the cool breeze flows through the children's hair like

through hayfields of the plains.
 There is such a scary beauty in death, the other thinks.
 * * * * *

BARRON SHOWS up at my house around midnight of the night he told me you gotta toss the cone. He's drunk or something fucked up, wearing all black with black steel-toed Russian-military boots. My first thoughts lend themselves to some idea of burglary.

I hear keys jingle in his pockets and think *Oh fuck he drove here in his shit-condition*. And all I can find the words to say are, "Barron, you didn't drive here, did you?"

He nods, about to fall over, with that staggering wincing look on his face. He's more than drunk.

I say, "Sweet, let me see your keys."

You remember something related from last summer.

He hands them to me and I quickly pocket them.

You're high on some laced weed at a party.

So I pocket the keys and shove him into a wall. "Idiot! What the fuck are you doing? Trying to win a retard competition?"

"Don't worry, Jibba. They'll never know I did it."

"You're fuckin' lucky," I say, "that you didn't hurt anyone."

"Who says I didn't?"

You knew the weed was laced because it tasted bad. That and the song that was usually in your head was replaced by a racing heartbeat. Your body and mind disconnected like freefalling but never reconnected.

The longer he stands there the more I know he's going to be comatose any minute.

What all did you take? What was in that shit? Your every thought bounced throughout your entire body but none were never caught by the collective thought-net. Some odd nonsense words escaped your mouth without your thinking about them, like "Myum." The paranoia and black-wall vision set in.

I walk Barron downstairs so he can pass out on the old couch. "Jibba," he says, "it was awesome."

You knew you had to leave the party before you were sucked into the oblivion-sniper's scope of your mind. Must go.

"Barron," I say, grabbing a bucket, "you're going to lie on

your stomach all night. If I come down here and you're on your back I swear to god I will Taser your balls. If you puke, you will puke in this bucket."

You fingered your keys in your pocket and you longed to be in your bed, away from the addle-minded harmonies of the universe. But you couldn't drive in your condition.

"I'll see you in the morning, man. Just try to come down easy. Whatever you're on will fuck you up if you let it get on top of you. You're going to be a pair of train tracks for the next few hours. Just let it happen."

And soon you found yourself stupidly behind the wheel of a two-ton coffin-missile. But this party was only three streets over and you figured even if you were piloting this death cloud the world will not collapse around you before you got home. And before you knew it you were pulling into your driveway, feeling that naughty rush of breaking the law. But you chastised yourself because somebody's mother was out on the road with you. And you got lucky this time. You were so paranoid you walked around the car five or six times to make sure it was parked right.

"Get some rest, man. Here's some Christmas cookies my mom made. Eat up. I'm going to bed. I gotta go to my aunt's birthday party tomorrow."

Then Barron says, "Gotta toss the fuckin' cone and watch that little bitch cry."

"Fuck her!" he adds and laughs.

You walked into your house feeling all emotions knowing how dumb you were, with that heavy-conscience feeling in the back of your head, but also the feeling of spitting in normalcy's face. *Fuck them all*, you thought, but you didn't mean it.

I take one last look at Barron as I shut off the lights. He is lying on his stomach with a thumb near his mouth like an infant, and I wonder why his hands are all dirty like that.

You eventually passed out later that night after writing some groaning poetry and trying to read some book from some author but the words looked like a whirlwind and everything around you became black as you turned off the light and behind closed eyes you heard the eternal song of the universe, watching stars form and implode, casting waves of light like waves of water and you let that song fill your heart, soft tings and swirls becoming a radiant majesty. You wanted to stay there forever. But eventually the cosmic show will lull us all to sleep. And you'll probably wake up to some Jewish guy singing Christmas carols as your mom cleans the house in anticipation of bringing in the ol' Christmas tree. But you're so high it doesn't matter.

I head upstairs to the family room and glance at the Christmas tree and turn off the lights and let the whole house sleep. The silent buzz speaks volumes as I step into a dark bathroom illuminated only by a holiday nightlight and look at myself and am curiously handsome and okay for a fleeting moment.

* * * * *

DOWNSTAIRS UNDER your feet a kid who slipped in and out of consciousness the entire night is waking up and wondering how he got there and where his keys are.

For a moment he has no idea where he is. He remembers bits and pieces of what he did last night. Tossing the cone, dirtying his hands, getting rid of hope. His mission accomplished, he celebrated by taking five pills of dextromethorphan and drinking a bunch of beers and going on a tire-sliding little drive to his friend's house.

Tossing the cone, watching the little bitch cry.

He feels great this morning. More and more of the night coming back to him. A bit of malice, a bit of pranking, a bit of anger all make him happy.

He walked into a restaurant and pocketed the keys of a woman who went to the bathroom, took them outside, and launched them into the night—keys and key-ring shining chiming and glimmering in the moonlight before falling away invisibly and silently.

He drove to a strip club and removed the tire from somebody's car, put it in his trunk, and drove off.

His pleasure came from the picture of the look on people's faces when they discovered their dilemma, or the looks he pictured if he could not be there to see them.

He poured laxatives into the glass of water of some woman-friend his mom had over.

Then he left.

He still hurt himself; there's no denying that.

It would have been funny if he'd meant it to be.

"Excuse me, ladies," he said to a couple of women walking into a restaurant, and he smiled and raised the Taser to his neck, looked them square in the eye, his face turning serious, and he struck himself with the charge.

If I had been there, I would have laughed.

Two middle-aged women have a story to tell about some crazy kid who shocked himself with a Taser right in front of them. He gave people a topic of conversation and concern.

"Did I tell you I lost my keys at the restaurant the other day? No idea what happened to 'em!"

"And I walked out of the . . . supermarket . . . and my fucking tire was gone!"

He's standing up, stretching, scratching his itchy greasy scalp, his head a little wobbly like the brain is loose inside. He looks in the empty bucket and carries it over to the bathroom where it came from.

He let somebody's dog off its leash and watched it run off. He laughed to himself. He laughed at the thought of the worried owner.

He's walking upstairs, whistling your favorite song.

He ruined people's night.

He's hugging your mom, asking her what smells so good.

Some woman had to walk home alone in the cold because she could not find her keys and she couldn't reach her husband.

He's walking down the hall, eating one of your mom's Christmas cookies.

Some kid is crying today because his dog is missing.

He's saying, "What's up, dude?"

And you say, "What happened last night?"

* * * * *

THE COMPANY I work for was given another assignment, only this time the joke is on me. I'm supposed to call a long list of men who know nothing about "broadband access solutions" and run them through such a detailed list of questions that they usually actually ask if this is somehow a joke.

They'll say, "Maybe you're looking for the tech department."

My priority call list has him on top and the tech department so low it's almost laughable. It's almost as if he knows it was I who's been pissing him off the last two weeks on a completely unrelated matter. The name of the company I work for changed from Alpha Corporation to Dove Marketing. New name, same cubicle and galley of assholes.

I just have "a few, quick questions"—I'm supposed to ask about their high-speed Internet access. In reality, this fucking survey takes forty-five minutes. I've completed just one without being hung up on, and I think the dude on the other end of the phone was higher than I was.

The kid on the phone next to me just asked, "You're on a *plane*?" and then he said, "Hello?"

I started laughing.

He said, "Hello?"

I held my finger in a fresh cup of coffee for as long as I could stand it.

He said, "He hung up on me." And he added, "Or he's dead."

I laughed. The pain hurts so nice.

* * * * *

CORNELIUS SEEMED thrilled to see me.

"Jibba," he said, "only thirteen days to go!"

"That's great, man. Now are we gonna spark this shit or just look at it?"

"Don't let me hold you back, stoner," he said handing me a lighter.

"Like the wind do I smoke," I said holding my first hit from Cornelius's new black-and-yellow steamroller, which I named "The Tyger" after the great William Blake poem. And like Blake I let out a jet-cloud of drug-smoke. "Always, and perfectly."

We kicked it for the old lunch break. He told me about different places a friend had found him to stay at in New York, about shelf space and however many cubic feet. Neither of us knew what we were talking about. We goofed on what a bunch of fags we were. Him an artist and me a poet.

I told him at least he had talent.

He asked me why I never showed him anything.

I pulled some poem I found in my pocket a while ago and

threw it down on his desk. I walked over to the painting to look for a two o'clock date and said, "You look at that, and I'll look at some real art."

* * * * *

SAMANTHA CALLED while I was at work, later in the afternoon. I can't remember exactly when. I was asleep at my desk. I immediately recognized her voice and sat upright. "What's up?"

"Nothing. Just bored. What are you doing?"

"Well I was sleeping, sort of, but I guess talking on the phone makes me look busy, so . . . score."

"Great. Oh, hey, I saw Barron last night."

"Really? Where?"

"He was walking out of CVS when I drove by. He looked pissed off."

"That's kind of how he always looks. Was he carrying anything?"

"A bag."

"A bag, eh? Must have been cough syrup. He told me he was gonna do that pretty soon."

"Do what?"

"Drink a whole bottle of it."

"Ew. What's that do?"

"Fucks you all the way to Oz's underpants."

"You've done it?"

"Nah," I lied. (Hey, this is a nice girl here; they don't find obscure drug-takings attractive.)

"Good." (See?)

"I wonder where that kid gets all his money, though. Last time we hung out he couldn't even afford to buy us twenty minutes of parking."

"Maybe he's dealing cough syrup," she joked.

"Maybe," I didn't joke, which was pretty funny.

"Well, I gotta get going. I'll talk to you later."

"Okay, thanks for calling," I said, and seeing my boss walk by I added, "Good thing we got all that cleared up. Thanks for your time." My boss seemed pleased.

By that time Samantha had hung up. I put the phone on the receiver and clicked into the Internet to check my mail, which, according to company policy, was *verboten*!

* * * * *

THE STORY of Barron.

I realize I've made him sound like a devious, no-good asshole weirdo this whole time. I call him my friend, but he's really like a brother. I'd call him a brother but people would be confused.

Here's a quick Barron story:

It's our junior year and we've just played St. Jude High School in baseball, at their field. I remember I pitched that game. We won four-to-zero. So, walking towards the bus, dripping with sweat, and all excited for our victory, I got Barron to do his impression he called Rupert. That shit was too funny.

As he pretends Rupert is getting bit by his dog, I am laughing so hard that I stumble across this garden of flowers the school had set up I learned later for the death of one of their students like ten years back. Barron cusses and drops down to his knees, trying to fix the flowers I'd crushed. I feel bad immediately but it was funny looking at his face go from old-redneck-getting-bit-by-dog to oh-shit-I'd-better-fix-that.

He's on all fours trying to fix this little section that wouldn't stay up. I drop down to help him.

We hear a yell. We both look up and see a big red dot on the horizon. We shrug it off and go back to the task at hand. I feel really bad because Barron seems to have taken this pretty seriously, and I had accidentally desecrated a noble cause. Recently, Barron would have done it on purpose. But not this particular bed.

Before we know it, the red dot turns out to be this giant woman. I mean huge. She's wearing a red muumuu and appears to be having trouble breathing. Her haircut is dyke short, her fingers are chubby, and her mouth is as dirty as mine or Barron's.

"What the fuck do you think you're doing?" she wheezes, sweating profusely around her jiggling neck. "That's a dedication to Susie Kepler. How dare you little hooligans mess with that!"

I stand up slowly. I see Barron do the same. I explain, "I'm really sorry. I accidentally walked into the flower bed when I wasn't looking. We were just trying to fix the damage and get out of here."

The rest of our team is on the bus already, behind us, like ten feet away, dead silent. I hear different laughs as this woman really tears into us for being so disrespectful.

Finally, I decide I've had enough. Fat bitch was beating a dead horse. "Listen, ma'am, I'm awfully sorry for what I did. I understand that this flower bed is a serious dedication, but I'm not going to stand here and listen to you wheeze and cuss me out for something that was unintentional. I'm sorry, and we're leaving."

"Now you hold on just one damn minute," she yells as we walk away.

Barron stops. He turns around with this look on his face. It's hard to describe the look, mostly just his usual angry expression. But something more.

"Settle down, ma'am," he says and starts walking away. Suddenly it's so silent that we could hear cheering at the softball diamond on the other side of the school grounds.

"What?! Lemme talk to yer coach!"

"Our coach drove separately," Barron says. "His wife is in the hospital."

By this time I was sitting in my usual seat at the back of the bus, because I'd had enough of that woman. From there I was watching this all go down.

"If you want to speak to our bus driver, I'm sure he'd be willing to talk with you."

I'd never seen Barron so patient and kind and sincere.

"Don't you have any other damned coaches?"

That's when our third baseman, this funny dick named Greg, shouts through his window, "Settle down, Kool-Aid Bitch!"

The bus erupts in laughter. I admit even I laughed—it was mean but funny. You should have seen the look on Barron's face. It looked like he took the brunt of the insult. "I'm sorry, ma'am." And he walked on the bus. "Get me the fuck out of here, Jimbo." (Our bus driver.)

The bus was joyous with Greg's little comment and our victory and everybody whooped it up, having a grand old time. Everyone except Barron. He sat alone in the back, not talking to anyone around him, even me.

"What's wrong, man?"

"Nothing," he barely got out. His voice shaky.

"C'mon, pimp. Tell me."

He took forever to answer, staring down the back of my seat. His hair wet and messy from the catcher's mask, his hands and arms and face and everything all dirty. Everything but little lines coming from his eyes.

Barron was crying.

"Susie Kepler was my aunt."

Barron didn't talk to me or anyone again until I picked him up for school the next morning. "I'm sorry, man. It was a mistake. I'm really sorry."

"I know. It's all right, Jibba. I just miss her is all."

"Your aunt?"

"Yeah," he said quietly.

"You guys were close?"

But he didn't answer. His eyes were full of tears again.

* * * * *

THAT HAS to say something.

What's it telling me?

* * * * *

ANOTHER BARRON memory:

Every year my brother's friend throws this wicked party the weekend before school starts. Girls and music and some light drugs and some heavy drinking. It's a well-known party.

The summer before our sophomore year, Barron and I decided to walk there because we were both too young to drive. It was a decent walk, probably a little over a mile and a half. But it was a pleasant day and we didn't want our moms knowing where we were going so they couldn't drop us off. But that was no problem, we always walked everywhere in those days.

Long story short, I drank way too much and smoked on top of that. So by the time we're ready to leave I can barely see through the little slits of what's remaining of my "open" eyes. My brain is fucked and I just want to pass out right there.

I remember a girl walking up to me and hugging me but my mind was so set on making it up the stairs that I mumbled something like, "Rape ya later, baby," and continued on my way. And I don't remember what she did after that. All I knew was that I had to find Barron and get home.

Eventually, Barron found me. He saw how fucked-up I was and told me to get some bread. My mouth was so dry that I'd chew and nothing would happen. I could not produce saliva and I could barely swallow. After ten minutes of that torture, we started on our way home.

We decided to cut through the park to get to my place as the crow flies, as they say.

ASAP—as soon as possible.

GTDBH—get this drunk bastard home.

Even though I went before we left, I found myself with an overwhelming need to piss. I was so overwhelmed and so absolutely fucked that I just stopped where I was, leaned against this fence that surrounded the city pool, and I started pissing in the bushes.

"Jibba, what are you doing?"

"Pissing, man."

"No I mean . . . Dude, stop! Let's go!"

"What do you mean, stop? I can't stop."

"Excuse me, son. What in the hell are you doing?" I felt the flashlight beam hit my neck. The rest of the story gets choppy. I'll just share the fragments I can remember.

The officer says, "Why are you pissing on a fence?"

I say, "I'm sorry, officer."

The officer says, "Did you know there's a portable toilet right over there?"

I couldn't see that far. Liar. But it turns out he wasn't lying and I probably could have pissed on the big plastic box from where I was standing.

Now there are three cops surrounding me, flashlights ablaze across my face, making my already squinted eyes veritably closed tight. I must have looked funny.

"Looks like we gotta take 'im in," the cop says.

I still have to piss. I wonder where Barron is.

"Get out of here, son. We'll look the other way. We know you've been drinking so don't press your luck."

Barron was standing next to me.

The flashlights leave my face and slash his.

"Sir, this is my best friend, and I'm not leaving him drunk like this with you guys. I don't know who you are."

"We're cops, idiot."

"Great. You're cops. Good for you. He's my friend. I'm staying."

Now that's as good a friend as they come.

Now we're both in the back of the squad car, riding along, lights on. I remember the shame of the situation and how great a friend Barron was.

"Well, at least we got a ride home," Barron joked.

* * * * *

THAT'S BARRON. A great friend, loyal like a dog, caring like a brother. There's nothing I wouldn't do for him. It's for that reason that hurting myself is justifiable in my eyes. If Barron did it, I had to do it.

We spent every day we'd known each other looking for a good time. It was like we really understood the power of our youth. We were just looking for some laughs, later some drugs, some girls, and always a good time.

Us and everyone else.

* * * * *

TWO NIGHTS ago Samantha was talking all this good about me. How hot I am, how cool I am, how nice I am, how she'd never get someone as cool or great as me.

I figured she was telling the truth. What a fool I was. First off, I should have known she was lying when she said I was good-looking. But I guess my own sense of logic took a break, especially because I truly wanted to believe the lies.

And now the last two times I've talked to her it's been just the opposite. Cold, distant, at best indifferent. Clinical.

It turns out she really wants my baseball friend—that she's "totally in love" with him.

Now I don't fault him a bit. He gets girl after girl, all looking to make him theirs. They think he's hot, and he's confident, and if I were him I'd be doing the exact same thing as he does. Hell, I'm even jealous of him. He's smart, lucky, and good-looking. I'm still trying to figure out what I am.

So she's fallen under that every-other-girl-I've-ever-known spell where she thinks she can tame him. She's looking for a fulfilling relationship with a bad boy. He's looking for a blow job. It's really a simple equation. Cute curious girl + hot older experienced guy = drunken blow job = a booty call on the guy's part and a mindfuck for the little girl.

My word of advice for girls: if you hate him so much, stop sucking his dick. He's not going to change and treat you better with the more blowjobs you give him. In fact, he's going to stay exactly the same because you're paying him the ultimate compliment! (A blowjob.)

If in order for me to get cute girls to blow me all I had to do was treat them like shit, I'd be all over that. But the other half of the formula is looks. Those never really came about in me. I'm a rather ugly kid.

Okay, fuck me, I'm being a bitch.

Long story short, it's goodbye to Samantha. I pride myself on not playing games when it comes to getting girls, relationships, and matters of the heart-parts. I'm as straightforward as can be.

Which is why girls like Samantha like to be my friend, but they'd much rather suck the dick of a mindfucker.

* * * * *

IT'S THAT feeling you get as you release that first pitch of a ballgame. Or when you kiss someone for the first time. And it's been so long you wonder if good buzzes still exist, because even self-induced orgasms carry the same shame as taking drugs. It's that feeling just before the moment of impact on the football field, where every single idea in the world falls away and all that matters is that particular moment in time. And it had been so long since it happened.

* * * * *

"THE FIRST time is always the best," Barron tells me as he pulls open the sliding glass doors of the fifth-story balcony of the hotel room we're in. Directly beneath us is a swimming pool twice as big as an Olympic one. At its deepest it reaches fourteen feet. It's nighttime and the pool is closed. We're seniors in high school and we were the two who held this little hotel party. It was only like fifteen people deep but it was definitely a good time. This wasn't our hotel. It was Barron's grandma's. Her husband rented it out for when they just wanted to get away from the house. (Yeah, they were that rich.) The lease hadn't run up yet after his grandpa died and his grandma said we could go there whenever we wanted to relax.

This thing was a castle of a hotel room, pretty much as big as my family's house.

It's best the first time because you don't know what to expect, or how to prepare—it's dynamic.

Elegantly furnished, no expenses spared, leather furniture floating atop thick carpet all running all which ways like a sea so tranquil and all us little Jesuses walking across the top, holding beers, bongs, bitches, and all that shit.

The unknown free fall scares us all.

Along with pleasure comes a bit of pain, a little challenge, or more than that, a buzz for your buzz.

Five stories above a pool and you think of the first time you went cliff jumping with Barron on vacation in Utah.

"We gotta do it, man." But I already know this. I was just scared. It was that simple. No butterflies. This was a balcony dive free fall more than sixty feet into a pool that looked like a glowing green pane of glass. The fear sobered and intoxicated me.

"Ready, bitch?"
"Let's do it."
Jump.
You're falling
forever,
but it's
more like
the pool
is rushing
at you and
you're
floating
in space.

Barron calls what you do with your arms "rolling up the windows." On the way down you think *Damn, what the hell was I thinking, I'm drunk and high and I have a piece in my pocket. I'm falling from a fifth-story hotel room and here comes a glowing green pane of glass, a world of hurt.*

Splash!

Then you're at the bottom of the pool, almost crying because that was so worth the fear. You're more alive than ever before and you come to the surface with a scratch on your hand you don't know where you got it and you sound your barbaric yawp through the pool-facing windows of this elegant hotel.

Who has time for normal worries when you do shit like this?

* * * * *

"So Samantha's gone, man," I told Cornelius, fingering my dangling necklace. This type of shit always happens to me. I stretched in the chair and saw Cornelius looking at me sideways. "What's up?"

"Do you know what kind of ass-kicking you need right now? Listen to me, man. You're a great person, a real cool dude, you take stupid-ass chances, do stupid-ass shit, but you have a real head on your shoulders, when it's not up your ass. You just need to stop being a little bitch and take the pussy off the pedestal. Get *in there*, man!"

Cornelius walked around the desk and sat in his chair, which made the usual squeak.

"I know, man. It's not as easy as it sounds. Our brains have their own fingerprint, you know? Hell, why aren't you married?" I adjusted myself in the chair in the corner, lifting my ankle onto my knee.

"'Cause I got the same fuckin' problems," he said. "Look at me. I'm an unhealthy loser. I own a fucking *art* store. I have about as much self-confidence as a penguin with herpes."

"Dude you're talented as fuck. You got lots of potential as a mate, mate. Okay, that sounded gay, but you know what I mean."

"Brain's fingerprint, as you said."

"Ah, fuck. Indeed," I said.

"Jibba, how much do you know about girls?"

"Not a damn thing."

"Exactly. Neither do I. All I can do is guess, and I usually guess wrong."

"Good way to put it."

"Thanks."

"Well, anyway, maybe you'll get your girl in New York. Bitches 'round here is ugly as shit anyway. Fuck 'em all."

"I'd like to."

"Me too," I laughed.

"I'm pretty excited, Jibba. I pulled every string I have to get some interviews and shows at some different places."

"Atta pimp."

"Yeah, I really need it to go well. Oh, and by the way, do you have a collection of poems saved anywhere?"

"Yeah, I always have my disk on me. Here. Copy away."

"I liked that poem you showed me. I'm always reading, so I might as well lend an eye to ol' Jibba's roaringly disturbing poetry, eh?"

"Indeed. Thanks, man. What did you mean when you said you know someone in the word biz?"

"Well that is to say I knew someone. See, I went to a reading by Allen Ginsberg when I was about your age. It ended up I was standing behind him in line to get some food from a vendor afterwards. I remember he gets a hot dog and some peanuts. I had to laugh at the fittingness of his purchasing foods that looked like a cock and balls. Anyway, he takes a bite into the hot dog and says, get this, 'This fucking shit takes like shit.'

"Again I had to laugh because here was one of America's most celebrated poets, one of the brightest and most well-versed minds in America, and the way he described the food was, 'This fucking shit tastes like shit.' I loved it. So we ended up talking for like ten minutes, neither of us really identifying that he was Allen Ginsberg, the man who wrote "Howl," the man who wrote "Kaddish" and "Mind Breaths," and we sat there and talked about the Boston Red Sox and hot dogs."

"That's dope as hell, man."

"So yeah, it's my little joke to say I know somebody in the poetry biz."

"Shit, what biz? Nobody reads poetry. But enough about

that. What do you think I should do about Samantha?"

"Don't give up on her—she's just a dumb kid. She really seemed to like you, despite the fact that you're ugly and ain't getting any prettier."

"Yeah?"

"Yeah. I told you—you're a catch. Let this little thing mature, maybe realize what an idiot she is, and let her come back to you. On her hands and knees." He winked. I laughed.

"Thanks, Cornelius. You're the bees' meow. All right, I'd better get going. My whore boss must be worried."

"Hey, Jibba, before you go . . . I have another favor to ask."

* * * * *

"What's up, Jibba? Where have you been, kid?"

"Working, man."

"Sweet. Actually that sucks," he said and laughed.

"So what are you doing?" I asked.

"Not much. I was just reading some dumb book. Hey, you wanna go to my grandma's with me?"

I'd been wary of Barron since his latest dream. I just didn't agree totally with his actions. But I missed my friend and it had been a week since I saw him last—the morning after I'd found him at my doorstep drunk, dexed, and dirty.

"Sure, man. When?"

"Now."

"Okay."

"I've got a story for you. And grandma needs us to shovel her driveway."

"A'ight."

"Cool. See ya."

Just as I hung up the phone, Samantha called. I saw her name flash on the ol' caller ID and I just let it ring. I didn't have the time or inclination to talk to her to tell her why I didn't want to talk at the time. Clever, huh?

The answering machine does its thing as I open the closet to get my jacket.

"James? Anyone there? I'll wait a little bit to see if you're there 'cause I really need to talk to you. It's been so long since I heard from you. Are you mad or something? Well you're obvioously not picking up so I guess I hope I talk to you later. Take care."

Sometimes you just can't be the man you want to be.

* * * * *

BARRON SHOWS up at my house a couple minutes later, just as I find my wool gloves, ready to go shoveling.

I hop in his mom's truck and say, "So what's this story, man?"

"Just wait. You'll see," he says grinning like a bastard.

Barron was also wearing gloves, which looked odd because he never wore them. Ever. He had long sleeves tucked into the gloves, which just looked foolish. Was he losing it?

"Sup with the gloves?"

"Hey! You'll see. Take your time, my friend. It'll come to you."

So he drove out to wherever his grandma lived—who knows, Mansionville—and she fed us like crazy and gave us both twenty dollars for our labor. I saw her shaking, melting-wax grandma hands hand over the money to us. She clenched our young hands firmly and said, "Oh, you boys have been the best of friends."

I tried to hide my discomfort and I saw Barron was beaming with that big goofy grin of his.

Then we went to the garage and got the shovels and started on her driveway.

* * * * *

WE'D BEEN shoveling for nearly ten minutes and he still hadn't really said anything. I was growing impatient but only because I knew that his story was big. So big he was having trouble starting it off.

I tried to wait my friend out, to let it come to me, but the ignored intrigue was starting to piss me off.

"So what the *hell* is this story?" I asked, heaving a shovelful of snow during the word hell.

"Okay, man, here it is. But let me tell it all the way through before you ask any questions. It's kind of long."

"Yeah, yeah, let's hear it already."

He rested his arm on the shovel like a hillbilly fence post. "It actually started that night when I did all that shit and ate all that dex. I woke up that next day feeling great, and I got my keys from you and I left and went home to get some actual sleep. I was looking forward to another night of tossin' the cone and was just as excited when my mom woke me for dinner. It was like six, or maybe six-thirty. Yeah like six-thirty but I don't know. Anyway, it was dark already. I'd planned to go out and just do whatever came to me. I was really thinking about cutting the wires on houses with Christmas lights like we always talked about. I figured that'd be pretty funny.

"And so I did it. I was running from house to house, cutting wires, kicking over lawn ornaments and shit, you know, like when we were fifteen. Anyway, I'd been doing that for like two hours when one of the house's lights came on and it scared me so much I didn't know whether to shit or go blind. So the lights come on and I'm taking off through the backyard and there's a guy yelling like shit but I realize halfway across the yard he wasn't yelling at me. I heard like these muffled sounds below the guy's yells. They had a sick, like a sadness to them. So I cut across the yard and back up the house unseen and sneak up to the window where all the sound is coming from, and man, you'll never believe this."

"What?"

"Well, I walk up to the window, crouched real low, and I peek in and it's this big swarthy guy. He's all sweaty and his hair is greased back and man, he was plugging away at this girl. She had to have been younger than us. Fourteen at most."

"Oh, shit."

"Jibba, the girl was tied up, gag in her mouth, crying. It looked like she was long past trying to yell for help. No shit."

"No fucking way."

"Yeah. I couldn't just sit there and watch, man. You know? The girl was so young and scared and crying and dammit, Jibba, you should have heard the sound of her voice, all feeble and . . . .

"I swear I felt just as bad as she did, man.

"So after I turn around, sit down, and kind of start crying over this little girl . . . this rage boiled up in me. You should have seen it. And out of nowhere I have this plan. I go to my car and pop the trunk and get out my old bat that I had in high school.

Jibba, you've never seen hate and worry like this. You've never seen anything like this."

"Damn."

"Yeah. So I fuckin' chuck a big icicle right through his front window and run up his porch out of sight in a dark corner. I'm scared because I figure any guy that binds, gags, and rapes young girls has got to have a gun, right? But fuck it.

"Now I'm standing there, blood ablaze with hate, temples laced with alkaline, scared and excited and enraged and all these emotions and I'm almost overstimulated to the point of paralysis. I want to kill this kidfucker.

"For a while, I hear nothing. Nobody comes to the door, but then finally the door squeaks open very slowly and I'm about to murder whatever is moving it, but I hear sniffling and see a small, feminine hand.

"Jibba, he sent the fucking girl out, man. He sent the girl out to find out who hurled an ice spear through his window.

"Anyway, she sees me in the corner after a while and she's not scared. She just stares. I'm telling you this was a defeated girl. Nothing in there. I did the keep-quiet thing with my finger to my lips and she nodded, tears falling from her face. I motioned for her to walk over by me, and she did. And then I waited while she shivered behind me.

"After a while, the guy yells something out. He's like, 'Whoever the fuck is out there is about to get a serious ass-kicking!' A minute later I saw what I was hoping to see. The door flew open and the big motherfucker came out ready to take on all comers. And here I fuckin' came.

"I stepped out of the shadows and we caught eyes for a split second but during this moment I was already bringing the bat back. He had this look on his face like *Oh, that's it?* But I guess he didn't see the bat. Anyway, Jibba, I hit his knee so hard that I guarantee he'll never walk again without a cane. It was disgusting and awesome. I felt the ligaments pop. But the rage was burning. I kept going. He fell to his hands and knees and I golf-clubbed him in the ribs as hard as I could and realized that if I hit him with the bat again I'd probably puke. So I dropped the bat, straddled his chest, and started punching, and I mean punching his face to red jelly. I couldn't stop."

Barron pulled off his gloves and I could see that his hands were covered in welts, bruises, swelling, and blood.

"The only reason I did stop was because I was afraid I was about to kill him. Jibba, rising off that bloody mess was the greatest feeling in the world.

"Now you know I would never hurt anything but myself on purpose—"

"Uh—"

"Trust me, not physically. But when I saw that girl wincing all pathetic like that, I snapped, man. But the thing was, I looked over at the girl and it looked like she had no idea that anything had happened in the last ten minutes. She looked the same as when she opened the door, kinda sad and swoopy-eyed.

"I went inside and picked up the phone and dialed 911. I said, 'I'm a pedophile and I like to rape little girls. I got what I deserved.' And I set the phone on the table so they could trace the call and find the fucker. It felt just like a movie. I wiped the phone off with my shirt, picked up my bat off the porch, and looked over at the girl. But I still couldn't say anything to her.

"Then I left.

"Man, you have no idea what a euphoric drive home that was. And I was thinking . . . That was one of the greatest and most fulfilling cone-tosses possible. It was everything I've been talking about!

"And it felt like I was walking on falling raindrops when I got home—I felt fuckin' *magical*, man.

"In fact, the whole experience gave me a plan.

"Jibba, my friend, I finally figured out what I'm supposed to do."

"Hold up, man," I said. "Are you being serious with me about all this?"

"Every word, dude. I swear."

"Whatever your plan is . . . I'm in."

* * * * *

Sender: Jibbawocky@aol.com
Recipient: tsquir@us.navy.etau.mil

Frue,

Sup pimp? How ya been and alladat?
You never got back to me. Too busy blowing a bunch of dudes? Check your email you fucker!
Hey I heard you're gonna get to fly in for Christmas. Your mom said that might happen. That would be too sweet. We'd have to get ripped together. I don't care if it's at the family party if that's all the time you're home. We's gonna drink and make fun of our '80s family and shit. It'll be straight out of Less Than Zero. *Thanks for recommending that book. It was sweet. You should see how many books I've read since I got home. I'm a sick bastard. Actually I just read all day at work. I honestly do about fifteen minutes of actual work per day. These muthafuckas think I'm calling people nonstop but all I do is dial this number I know never answers and tuck my book beneath my desk where I can see it and pretend I'm on hold. It's too sweet.*

Hey, I have a story to tell you about Barron. Some crazy shit. Aight, gotta go. Hopefully I'll see you soon. See ya, playa.
  ~~ Jibba Jaws ~~

* * * * *

IT WAS last summer, the last season of summer baseball I'd ever play. I did not receive an athletic scholarship to any schools, despite all my successes. I knew in my heart I was good enough, but I just didn't have what college coaches wanted, apparently. (I don't take performance-enhancing drugs—I take the other kind of drugs.)

All my life summer baseball was the pinnacle of the year. The days would start off with Barron riding to my house. We'd eat some breakfast and we'd honest-to-God play pick-up baseball from like ten a.m. to four p.m. Our baseball-energy was boundless. We'd play home-run derby in old shorts and tennis shoes all day, every day. The sun would beat down on our capped heads. We'd sweat through our clothes in the shimmying, scalding heat that we'd barely notice. We were kids playing a game.

A gaggle of various types of freestyle bikes would gather like fans outside our make-believe Major League Baseball exhibitions.

Nobody liked first base or right field so we played "pitcher's poison" and anybody who wasn't cool enough to pull the ball was out. (Six years later, our summer coach was begging us to hit to the right side, to drive the ball where it's pitched.)

We played because it was the greatest thing in the world. There was nothing but enjoyment and happiness in our little games. And then we'd go home, eat dinner, and come back up to the same field, only this time in full uniform, ready for battle when it really counted.

Our summer boys' baseball league had an all-star team in each level, and Barron and I were always on whatever all-star team we were eligible for. Barron was the most feared hitter, and I was the most feared pitcher, at least around our age then. In-house games were for bragging rights. "You play for Intro-tech—you suck!" or "Wow, you're on Valiant Towing? You guys are amazing, dude." It's how it was.

It was its own society where all-star team members were thoroughly respected by fans, coaches, and other players. In that society, Barron and I were heads of state. In that society, life and class were dictated by talent. Everything had its order.

The weekends were spent "traveling" to nearby cities for all-star tournaments. This was as good as it got. I'd pitch, Barron would catch, and everyone had a good time. We were successful, feared, respected, and fun-loving. Never cocky. Never showy. We were just ridiculously talented kids.

Between games we'd gather in gazebos and eat scads of McDonald's and other vast quantities of anything. Barron would make fart jokes and talk about all sorts of crazy stuff, with hot dogs and pop shooting from our mouths as little Barron silenced us all and then ripped what he called "a long, wet one," and he'd yell, "Oh shit, I think I just shit my pants!"

Barron taught us all how to swear.

In that sweltering summer weekend heat, I'd sweat and stink and not care. Because we won, and it was fun.

Our parents grew closer as friends, reuniting every summer to watch their boys play together on the weekends and against each other on weekdays.

There was that feeling when our coach would open a box of

of brand-new uniforms. New bats. New gloves. New hats. The same great feeling.

I was a terrible worrier before every game, afraid I wouldn't have my stuff—that I'd get hit around and all the bad things I thought about myself would be true. I feared failure. I feared loss. I feared the unknown.

I'd get up there, right on top of the mound, all eyes on me. I'm about to start the game. The anticipation. The fear. The excitement. It was this literal *rush* when the ball left my hand. All my nerves and timidity turned into a burning inferno of desire for veloci-victory. I had a sick desperation to win.

In-house league paved the way to high school, where again Barron and I played together as the same old tandem since we were seven. He never outgrew the farting humor in high school and was the pride of the team—setting the formidable school record for home runs (both single-season and career) and hilarity. But behind his towel snappings and naked locker room talks there was this misunderstood genius that never really peeked out unless he had every reason to be serious.

Practices were long and conditioning was arduous but it made us better players and unite more as a team. Saturday mornings, after practice, we'd drive out to this greasy spoon restaurant and basically take over the place. All fourteen of us. We'd drink together on weekends and hook each other up with random girls we'd know who'd blow, you know?

Games would be great, that buzz of being the best. That punch-drunk feeling of victory. It never got old, until it did, at the very end of my playing days.

High school summer baseball was the same but on a different level altogether. The same in that weekends were for tournaments, but now out of the state. And weekdays were for leagues, but our summer league teams were made up of the best players from every community in the state.

The competition was tough, the coaches were smarter, and the players were better. But so were the friendships. We'd party in hotels, getting high and drinking and just totally dicking around with each other. It was a brotherhood. And it was beautiful.

So it's the last summer I'd ever play this amazing, beautiful game competitively. I'm cherishing every second, knowing this is the end. Knowing that I was in a car slamming on the brakes but I couldn't stop the unavoidable. The end of summer baseball. The end of my youth.

Every year since I was seven, every summer, the final tournament of the year was played in this industrial city upstate. It was a gathering of all the best teams in the state. The best of the best.

So it's my final summer of playing baseball competitively and I'm standing on the mound, holding the game ball, waiting for the umpire to give me the signal to begin the game. I'm wracked with nerves because this, right here, is the American Boys' Baseball State Championship Game.

Barron settles into his crouch behind the plate. I think, *Wow, this might be the last game he and I ever play together.* The winner of this game moves on to the Regional Tournament. The loser goes home for the summer, forever.

I hear my mother yell, "Let's go, James!" and my brother is there and so's my dad and for whatever reason, I don't know why she came, the only girl I ever loved. But that's another story for another time.

The pressure is almost unbearable. I'm beginning to get depression on top of my nerves and excitement.

I have full confidence in the competence of the players behind me. I know them like brothers. Because after all, you saw your summer team more than you saw your girlfriend or family. We were the best team in the state, and it was time to prove it.

The umpire gives me the signal. He points, I nod, Barron flicks me off like he always does before my first pitch of the game. Fastball—as hard as you goddam can.

It's almost like an orgasm flowing through my arm as I grunt an eighty-eight mile per hour strike for the first pitch of the game. Strike one. The game has begun.

To say it was the best game of my life would be an understatement. The end score was five-to-nothing. I threw a one-hitter, had two home runs, and also what my coach called "the hardest hit ball I've ever seen."

I remember that hit. I actually grunted, loud, as I turned on it—this laser line drive that landed near the left fielder's feet and skipped past him and cracked into the fence. Stand-up double. My last at-bat ever in the state tournament. My coach yells to me, "What are you going to do next, drive the team bus?" and all I could do was smile and pant.

After the game ended, after our coach told us how proud he was, after my mom and dad hugged me, after Barron and I celebrated as state champions, we were awarded our medals, had our picture taken, and were treated to a fireworks display in memory of the industrialist who built this beautiful park and worked his whole life towards making baseball available to all.

I remember looking up at those fireworks and hearing Frank Sinatra sing "My Way" through the stadium's speakers, my face and the faces of my teammates bathed in shimmering colorful explosions of light, covered in sweat and dirt, with baseball pains all over my body, and I realized that I was conscious, sober, and not freefalling my way to pain, and I'd never felt so good in my life. I desperately wanted to be locked in that feeling forever, to know it without end. And though time has sobered the euphoria of that day, it still glows with warmth in my heart.

Unfortunately as I get older and further from the moment, I'm finding that it glows a little less every day.

* * * * *

"It's BETTER than winning the state championship, man," Barron tells me.

Never.

But anything close is worth trying.

* * * * *

WE WATCH too many movies.

Entertainment, besides freaky highs, is how we spent a lot of our time. Barron and I quickly became connoisseurs of movies just after our freshman year in high school. But here's the major difference between me and Barron. I was the kid who read the book before he watched the movie, and he was the kid who maybe read it afterwards, but probably not.

It was a working relationship. I told him what to read, and he told me what to watch. "Symbiosis, man," he once told me. "We both work off each other." And it went deeper than that. We both had the qualities we wished for ourselves. We saw them in each other. Barron had that likeability and charisma that I always wanted. I had a level of kindness that was just not present in his family. He was an extroverted nutball, and I was an introverted neuroball.

A favorite pastime of ours involved getting ripped and going to the been-in-the-major-theaters-once-before-but-now-costs-a-lot-less movie theater. Since it only cost a buck, we'd sometimes pick the worst movie possible and be like the only people in there and we'd perform our own *Mystery Science Theater 3000*, just totally ripping on the movie. Feet sticking to popcorn floors, crimson carpet in the aisles with those clear rubber strips of lights along the sides. The theater predated cup holders and adjustable seats and there was that cola-and-butter-and-sugar smell baked into the walls.

When you're drunk enough, lighter burns don't hurt that much. So the key is to burn the burns. That hurts like you'd never believe. We'd play this game in the empty theaters where you'd each throw up a certain number of fingers and guess the sum of the two people's fingers when added up. Whoever got the number right, or whoever was closest, got to burn the other kid with the lighter.

It hurt so bad but was all for a good time. I never had any of those dreams like Barron and I had my own reasons for suicide but I took part in his masochism because it made me happy. I was a better person. My pain was my cure. The irony of it all leaves me unnerved.

We probably watched too many movies and TV shows. Violence and pain onscreen were just so phony and flat. Explosions and blood and guns just got more and more unremarkable. Jerry Fuckheimer and the rest of those action-explosion directors are all so predictable. Barron and I almost see it as if they're trying to do a parody of themselves. Like if they gild the fuck out of the lily it might swing back to being beautiful. They never show the real pain, and in reality they can't. So why bother? We know pain. Everybody knows pain. Mental and physical, real scars, hidden scars, all that mess. You can't put that on a screen.

You can try, and we'll watch, but that ain't it.

We watch too many movies? That can't be it. That's an easy blame.

It's like I don't want to know the real reason.

* * * * *

AFTER CORNELIUS and I had smoked too much weed, we felt like listening to some music and letting it become our conversation. He threw on "The Dark Side of the Moon," and let me tell you, that shit was talking to me. ("I'm not frightened of dying. Any time will do. I don't mind. Why should I be frightened of dying? There's no reason for it—you've got to go sometime.") It's all nonsense if you really think about it, maybe. Or not. Maybe it's all perfect. I tried not to think about it. I'll just say that it all seeped into my bones and I closed my eyes and felt it filling me with light. My gone mind and those grand tunes were so glorious that I lost myself for a minute. I felt I had tapped into something greater than the conscious and the subconscious, like I was seeing the universe in the burst of its ongoing development rather than that moment later when the brain interprets what's happening, and I got this tranquil feeling, like I was sedated, and when I woke up, the world was much more sharp, clear, and meaningful.

By the time I was fully awake, I had lost all that again.

* * * * *

IT IS my final day at this job calling corporate executive assholes and informing them about the vast opportunities my company can provide, listening to unoriginal voice messages, playing solitaire on the computer while pretending to be on hold, full of sorrow and loathing, reading poetry and thinking about little dancer girls.

I am happy because this job is over and I get the next week off to just dick around before I have to go back to school, but I am sorry because I hate when anything ends. Even if it's a job I didn't like from the beginning. I feel some manner of sadness and wistfulness wash over me as I look at my pathetic "cubicle" and old black phone and ancient computer. I always get this way, when anything ends.

Some lady comes by and thanks me for all my "hard work"

and gives me a gift certificate and informs me that the "project time" (PT) has "run up." In other words, I've been laid off, and I have to go back to my glorified unemployment office and let the head lady know. I feel sorry and sad as I pocket the envelope and look around at the defeated kid and the orca woman next to me.

GFNCNW—goodbye for now, corporate nightmare world.

I hated this job.

There is a pit inside of me that is both swollen and hollow, and it is being held open by the knowledge that I will probably have to return to some horrid place like this again, after I graduate from shitty college.

I need the assholes here to know that I hated this job, but I can't tell my boss because she's the one who sends my pay-activation slips to the temp place, so I decide to do something else before I go, to leave an unsigned artistic message.

I steal one of the big ugly marketing telephones from an empty desk, bring it downstairs outside, get a bungee cord from my car, and lynch the phone in a tree right outside the front door of the building.

This feels really good.

But the phone is black, and as I look at it I realize that my "fuck you" appears to be directed at black people, so I bring the phone system over to the concrete and curb-stomp it, leaving behind a more universal message: "Fuck this job, and we're all wires and circuits on the inside."

Yeah, man.

But even still, as I drive away from that wretched place, the dark office building lingers in the rearview mirror, and it feels like a living death over my shoulder, in my peripheral vision—my pointless past and my untold future right there in the golden-glowing mirror, in that blank-gazing building.

I don't know; it's fucked up. Like I said, I get weird when things end.

* * * * *

By the time I'm home, though, I am overrun with thoughts of young Samantha, who finally cleared things up for me last night. I never thought being a nice kid would actually come back to hurt me, but in this case it did. You see Samantha informed me last night, as I sat in my dark room talking to her on the phone wondering why she keeps calling me and wanting to just talk and shit like that, she said:

"'Cause you're a really nice, funny, interesting person."

"Oh."

"That's why nothing could ever happen with us. I mean like three weeks ago you would have been some random encounter, but now that I know you so well it could just never happen."

What a load of bullshit, I thought to myself, feeling down because the nice kid never gets the action. And it's about time I put a stop to that. That chapter is over.

"What a load of bullshit," I told her, with as much strength in my voice as I can remember.

"What?" she said, startled.

"This is such a load of shit. You have no idea what you want or what you're even thinking. And the way you justify yourself is such a pile of shit that I would laugh if I wasn't so goddam depressed. Jesus, I thought *I* was a mess."

Come on, I know I could have been better than that. Why do I suck when it counts? I guess I'm just too down to care anymore.

"Um—"

"Goodbye, Samantha."

"James, wait—"

Yeah, right. She's gonna tell me something about how cool of a kid I am. I've heard it all before. Whatever.

"No."

I hung up.

You see it's not like I was just in it to get some. My most recent actions would prove that to be true, but in my heart I cared about her. And the matter of getting some would mean more because of that, even though I was leaving soon. I cared about her. And that's what hurts. Because I don't need another friend, which is all this would've amounted to.

So I'm sitting here at my old, pathetic desk, in my room, biding my time till five-fifteen when my brother gets back and I can leave, go to the high school, go for a run, come back to my house, and get totally loaded with Barron and some girl he met the other night.

Right now, I don't care about much. So I step into the bathroom and masturbate out of spite and anger. Those are always the best. Then I step back to my desk in my room, pick up my little pocket stapler, and drive a stable into my thigh. And the pain is wonderful.

But I just don't care about much right now.

* * * * *

LATER, I was standing in the middle of my room, completely naked, listening to some mellow music, thinking about writing a poem, when the phone rang. Barron told me he was coming to pick me up, to take us all to one of those trendy restaurants with the crazy shit on the walls. It was going to be me, him, his girl, and one of her friends. Nice.

I asked him what he meant about his plan, from before. He told me to just chill and get dressed and enjoy the evening. I guess his plan could wait.

I couldn't.

I got dressed and spritzed on some cologne and waited impatiently for Barron, eager to see what this "double date" was all about.

* * * * *

I REMEMBER at one particular tournament down in Indianapolis, our summer team was staying at this really cheap hotel that was next to a strip mall that had a pizza place, a gun shop, a dance club, a liquor store, and a porn shop in it. We were stationed in the height of the slums, but we got by. It could have been a lot worse.

Barron and I were rooming together, along with our shortstop, Cody, and third-baseman, Greg. We had a late game the next day, and we'd won that day, so we were feeling up to a bit of the old ultrafun. We had Barron use his fake ID to get us some alcohol. Then we got totally fucked and shot over to the dance club to dance with all the practically nude, fellow drunk, trashy-ass girls. Get our groove on, so to speak, you know.

Inside those places, it smells like damp clothes, smoke, alcohol, sweat, and liters of cologne. The music is so loud you feel it in your bones, but it's never quite comfortable. I can never lose myself in it. Just not my style, I guess.

It was definitely Barron's style. The kid's got mad moves on the dance floor. I pretty much move off the dance floor. I know my niche.

So me, Greg, Cody, and Barron are all at this club, way past curfew, drunk like crazy, I'm stoned as well (because I pitched that day, and our coaches never let me play the day after I pitched), and we just have this crazy night. Cody eventually puked in the bathroom, Greg almost got into a fight, but it pretty much ended when Barron came over to see "what the problem" was. It's always great having a big, sick-ass kid who you know could whup some ass in a fight around when you're at a dance club.

"Hey, do you have a lighter?" the girl in the pink half-shirt deal with tight black pants said to me, holding a cigarette to her lips.

"No, I'm sorry. I don't," I mumble, so drunk I'm surprised I haven't passed out yet.

"You idiot," she says.

"Wha'?" I slur. I've got mad game.

"I was trying to pick you up. You failed. Always have a lighter on you," and she walked away.

"Aw hell, I'm sorry," I said, not quite feeling the regret yet, but knowing I would when I woke up tomorrow. I turn back to the spinning lights and throbbing bass and the smoke and the sweat and it's all overstimulating and nauseating.

Barron ends up bringing this bomb-ass girl back to the hotel with us. Blonde, sexy, you know in that whore way. Anyway, it pretty much comes down to Cody, Greg, and myself having to wait outside the room, smoking up, and just talking for like half an hour while Barron put it to this girl. I mean I know it's not my business but I could hear the girl screaming, she was a screamer, and the door was closed.

"Dude, put your hand on the window. It's shaking."

"Holy shit, man—it is!"

So Barron keeps drilling this girl for what seems like forever and then it finally quiets down. There is silence for like ten minutes as me and the boys eagerly awaited getting some sleep. Eventually, the girl walks out, no shoes on, kind of smiles at us, and we kind of smile back, and she does that wipe-the-corner-of-her-mouth-with-the-back-of-her-hand thing that so many whores do. I sorta laughed and walked into the room. And once she was out of sight, we started clowning Barron about it. He clowned back by reminding us that he's the one who got laid.

Thirty minutes later we were all passed out and a policeman was knocking at our door.

* * * * *

So WHEN Barron told me he met this girl we're partying with tonight at a dance club, my immediate mental image was of the bomb blonde whore. It's just this picture I have of girls from dance clubs. So I was kind of excited, hoping she'd bring one of her beautiful slutty friends so I could maybe get some action. The whole Samantha thing has surprisingly pretty much left me heartless. You can call me a jerk, or worse, probably. You can call me an asshole, but hey, I really don't give a fuck, because the nice smiling friendly guy routine got me a really good-looking junior girl who's just a friend. And that's just what I was hoping would happen during my return home from school.

"Hallelujah. Holy shit. Where's the Tylenol?"

* * * * *

THREE LOUD bangs at the door awoke me from sweet sleep. I saw a flashlight's glow dance across the bottom of the door. "Wake up!" the cop says.

"Jesus, Barron, she wasn't a prostitute or a statutory, was she?!" I ask him, still drunk and hideously tired. Cody and Greg sit up, rubbing tired eyes with drunk hands. "Hmanhan," Greg says.

More pounding on the door. *We're fucked*, I think to myself. I jump up and put the bowl, weed, and liquor bottles into my bat bag and bury it beneath the other bags in the room.

"Get the fucking door, Jibba!"

"There's someone at the door, you say, Greg?" I ask sarcastically.

I stumble across the room, kick a Corona bottle under the bed, and fall against the door. I rest there for a second, my last moments as a free man, feeling like I'm about to step into the spinning blue and red lights. I think about Raoul Duke saying,

"Many fine books were written in prison," and I open the door.

The man was extremely tall, with a thick mustache on his cop mug. His flashlight flashed across my face and I'm reminded of pissing under the influence in a public park. I try to stay cool.

"Hello?"

The man shrugs. He must have seen how red and baked my eyes were. I wish I had some damn eye drops.

"Yeah, uh, we need you fellas to pack it up. One of the electric transistors blew over yah and it's a fire hazard for you to stay yah. We already talked to your coach, and if you have any questions, ask him."

"Thanks, officer," I say and close the door. "Yah fuck."

I scratch my eyes and cringe as Greg throws on one of the bedside lamps. We'd been asleep for less than an hour, and as it was, according to a late schedule change, we had a game in four hours.

So we gathered our belongings and stole some blankets and pillows. Our first and third basemen ended up throwing a mattress from the second floor down to the parking lot, where we spent the next few hours trying to sleep out in the elements with stolen supplies under the open mouth of the summer sky. So many stars out that night, and better them than rainclouds. Barron spent most of the time with his headphones on, singing way off key, and making everyone laugh even though they wanted to sleep. I wanted to puke. I also wanted to sleep. I wanted to be in a nice warm bed in the hotel that was a hundred feet from us. But no, not happening. I'm lying under a blanket of stars listening to my best friend butcher some of my favorite songs.

DE—damn electricity.

Killing squirrels, my immortal delusions, and now my coveted, well-earned sleep.

* * * * *

THE HEADLIGHTS dance across my living room wall as I'm splayed out on my couch waiting for Barron and the hoes to stop by and pick me up. I put on my "lucky" boxers for the evening (even though I'm not the type of kid who gets lucky all that often) and my "lucky" undershirt. It's the shirt I wore under my uniform my entire senior year of baseball. I really believe there is some sort of mystic energy in it because every time I wear it good things happen, and I am filled with these reassuring feelings of excellence and tranquility. That or I'm full of shit.

I get up and throw on some shoes and step out into the cold, snowy, winter night. I see Barron is again using his mother's SUV for the evening, treating these ladies to the old classy ride. That pimp.

I fight a smile as I walk past the front of the car and head towards the back passenger-side seat, having seen that Barron had his girl riding shotgun. Fine by me. I think to myself *Damn I hope she's sexy and slutty* as I pull the door open.

I open the door and this incredibly cute, incredibly nonslutty-looking girl is smiling at me. We catch eyes and I don't let up. I keep in with the look. I tear into her mind, and some connection is made. Eventually the girl lets up as I finally get into the car.

She had long brown hair. Wearing those tight black pants with these slim legs and just this girl was fucking scorching. My dick was drawn to her like a divining rod. That's all I can really say.

Introductions are made. I am James, but most people call me Jibba. She is Nicole, but most people call her Nikki. Barron was Barron. His date was Jenna. Now that bitch was one hot-ass-looking slut. And you could tell she was a slut. She had that same look as the blonde girl from Indianapolis, almost down to the last detail. I was so captivated by the girl sitting next to me that I was praying she wasn't slutty. That she'd never been slutty. That she was a virgin. That she'd never done anything before. I don't know where it came from but this girl had me in a bad way. I looked over to her and we reconnected. It felt so nice, like what I needed.

I must interrupt myself here and say that I never look people in the eyes. It just makes me feel uncomfortable. I really can't explain it.

But this girl . . . I could look into her eyes all day, and especially all night. And I wanted to. And I did. And it was great.

"Barron, where we going?" I say, still loving my lovely Nikki.

"Change of plan. Fratelli's," he says looking at me through the rearview mirror.

"Damn, kid. I didn't bring the mortgage. But I guess these girls do deserve something nice, right? Just not sure how I'm—"

"I got plans, Jibba—all kinds. I told you; I got it covered," he said and looked at me again in the mirror and winked. I had to laugh. "Hope you girls brought your running shoes."

Nikki looked around nervously until Jenna laughed when she realized Barron was joking.

So me and Nikki had a little conversation, just clicking all over. Casual contact. Loving every inch I could see of her smooth skin. My chest hurt I wanted her so bad. I wanted to love her. I needed her.

Things went just as smooth in the restaurant and I learned that Nikki was a senior at our rival high school and Barron met them at a dance club but Nikki rarely goes and Jenna goes all the time and it was the only time Nikki had ever gone to that one. I was so relieved. I was so happy. This was too good to be true.

Afterwards we went over to Barron's house because his mom was staying at his grandma's house that night and we obviously decided to drink where there were no parents. I slept there so much as a kid that they actually had a "Jibba Room" for me, which was pretty much my room so I had no problem staying there with those two girls the way I was feeling.

We all got real drunk and I was so happy Nikki turned down Barron's offer of weed because any girl who smokes weed is a whore. It's a fact. At least according to my first quarter at college. Might not be true.

So I was forced not to smoke but it was a more than even trade. I'd take this cute brunette girl named Nikki over weed any day anytime (and if I could sneak a mix of both—so much the better, eh?).

So I'm sitting on Barron's couch and we're watching some movie or something. I wasn't even paying attention. Nikki is lying on the ground facing me with her feet right by mine.

Now I'm not the most experienced kid in the world, but common sense explains the whole contact step of the ordeal. So I rest my foot against hers, very lightly, but contact was made. She did not move. That was the best part. If the girl does not like the contact, she will move. Again, common sense. Not only does she not move away, but she ups the pressure and all of a sudden we're playing footsie and making that powerful eye contact again and before I know it she is snuggled up in the cove of my arm and chest. I had my arm up on the back of the couch and she made herself so comfortable in that little nook. Her left arm was draped across her beautiful stomach and her hand was playing with my hand. Then she was tracing the contour line of my boxers with her fingers and I was thinking about how perfect this girl is. Every aspect of this girl . . . so perfect.

We finally adjourned to "my" room where we didn't have sex. That part of the night was actually okay. She wasn't the type of girl who just gives it up when she's drunk. She was a good girl, with a naughty mouth. And it was so perfect.

And I was so happy.

And I started to finally give a fuck.

* * * * *

So AFTER he drops off the girls Barron tells me that his plan involves that pedophile bastard that he'd beaten. And then I close the door and he drives away and all I know is that I have more to look forward to than ever before.

All I can really do is think about how tired and excited I am and how long it's been since I hurt myself. I feel so good that I need to hurt myself. So I do.

I call Samantha.

* * * * *

So I'M sitting there in my room with some old song playing from the tape she made me when we used to talk (I act like it was so long ago, and after last night it kind of feels that way), and the phone's resting against my ear and ringing on the other end.

Then Samantha picks up.

"Hey, you called?" I ask, sounding indifferent.

"Yeah, I wanted to talk to you. It's been like a week since I heard from you. Where have you been?"

"Working. Chilling with Barron. You know."

"So how have you been?" she asks.

"All right, I guess. Pretty good."

"What's wrong? You're not your usual self. It seems like

you're holding something back."

She's quick.

"Case closed, Sherlock."

"Okay, you don't have to be rude."

"Yeah well I figure I can tell you since we're such good friends and all—"

"Tell me what?"

"I met this girl. She's fucking amazing," I tell her, finally letting the smile into my voice.

"Oh," she says. "Who is it?"

"I don't think you know her," I say. "She goes to a different school."

"That's . . . good," again she trails off. Then I hear a sniffling on her side of the phone.

"What was that?" I ask.

Another sniffle.

"Nothing," my "friend" says, crying.

"No, seriously. What's wrong?"

My "friend" can't feel happy for me?

"Nothing!" she grunts back. "Nothing is wrong. I hope you're happy!"

I'm slackjawed in confusion. What the fuck was that? I just wanted to torture myself by calling the girl who just wanted to be friends with me.

But then I thought to myself, *How was that supposed to hurt me? All it did was hurt her.*

Maybe Barron was rubbing off on me.

* * * * *

YOU SEE the reason Nikki is so amazing to me traces back to a predecessor, to my junior year in high school.

Her name was Belle. Well actually it was Isabelle but she hated that name. She was this cute girl who had transferred to our school from down in Georgia. She had this beautiful Southern twang to her voice, and this girl was just glidingly pretty. She was a year younger.

The more I think about it, the more she reminds me of Nikki.

She used to laugh when I would jokingly call her a hillbilly if she got something wrong in class.

L?—love?

I really never knew. It was close . . . whatever it was. It was such a short stint of time, though. We only "went out" for like five months. And even then I barely ever got to see her because I had baseball on the weekends and she worked at night during the week. I looked forward to seeing her after tournaments, but I knew baseball a lot better than I knew women. And I always worried about her. I really thought she was the girl I was going to marry. (Kids!)

I don't know what exactly happened.

I do know that was the best summer of my life.

Just holding her hand in the park at night if and whenever else we got to meet. Swinging on swings. Lying on our backs on the little-league outfield looking at limited stars on suburban skies. Watching the simple pops of small-town fireworks out near the area where Barron and I shot each other with paintballs.

Something happened one night. But it wasn't exactly a particular night, just some night. It was over.

I guess you could say she dumped me. Is that what the kids are calling it these days? Getting dumped? I don't know. I'm out of touch. She broke up with me. She ended it. She pulled me aside one night at a school football game, in front of everyone in the school. She pulled me down to the front of the stands and broke up with me. Evidently the "other night" (some night) she realized "this" really wasn't going to "work out" and that it would be best if we would just take "it" easy.

I tried to smile. I tried to nod. She walked back up to the stands. I looked up and saw all these fucking pitiful faces pitying me, so I walked home, right then. I hopped a fence and walked and cried and chucked rocks ninety miles per hour at the trunks of quiet trees.

Basically I was literally nauseous. I really wanted to puke. I felt so dejected, rejected, embarrassed, destroyed.

I read somewhere that emotions are like a sock. When they are fresh you can stretch them with relative ease and they'll always come back to their original form, but the more you stretch them the more worn and loose they get, until finally they don't pull back into their original shape. They just sag around your ankles and they're useless.

The sock of my emotions was irreparable after that night. It seemingly lost all snap.

A week later Belle was deepthroating the quarterback.

A month later the quarterback was done with her and they broke up.

I really lost all emotion after that. I remember I was sitting on Barron's deck in his backyard and I was on the verge of tears.

"Fuck it, man," he said. "Nobody is worth your emotion besides yourself and your family."

"It hurts."

Then he shot me in the shoulder blade with a paintball gun and in that instant I was all sorts of Zen because Belle was a million miles away.

After her I tried not to care what anyone thought.

After her I decided to just fuck 'em and chuck 'em. But that never really got me far with girls. They didn't like that attitude. I wasn't attractive enough to pull it off, I guess. I try to make decisions, but decisions usually make me.

I was never the same.

I still got play every now and then.

But I was Kurt Cobain: "I'm so horny—that's okay, my will is good."

Even when Samantha told me all that shit about how she just wanted to be friends . . . I'd only let the pain go down so far, like Roark.

I am a product of my influences.

And nothing ever really got me. The only shit in life I lived for was the purity of it all. And purity doesn't reside in the mind like emotion. Your emotions are your reaction to the world, which cannot help but be pure, even at its ugliest. And, in turn, pain is pure. Pleasure is pure. An orgasm is itself pure. The sky is pure. Sunshine is pure. All things physical have the ability to be pure. And in turn nothing mental can ever be pure. It's too unknown, the brain's wicked ways and vile wattage. What are we dealing with?

So all I had was love and nobody to love. Except Barron, I guess, in a way. Which is troubling, I admit.

I tried to leave emotions at the beginning of my senior year. I no longer cared about anything except to strive for pleasure and pain.

I was Jim Carroll. "I just want to be pure."

So now I feel something besides a physical want to be inside the girl I'm looking at. I want to be with Nikki because I feel better about life around her.

All this bullshit and I'm leaving in less than two weeks.

All this bullshit and Christmas is in two days.

And I still can't get her out of my mind. I can't get excited for Christmas morning because she won't be there with me. I can't croon along with Nat King Cole singing Christmas carols because she won't be there to laugh at my horrible voice.

L?—love? I really don't know, but this is new.

I wonder what is this wondrous air upon which I walk.

Whatever it is, it's marvelous.

I'm almost always goddam wrong.

* * * * *

I IMAGINE at this point I am a total hypocrite. I say a girl named Belle broke my heart and made me not really give a damn about anything, but then I'm hurt when a girl named Samantha just wants to be friends.

I have this façade of indifference atop a layer of indelibly deep emotion, but really in the end I want to be Roark. I'm an individualist, an egoist. I care only for myself, as does pretty much everyone else, whether they want to believe it or not. Sometimes we just can't let ourselves face the unromantic truth.

Call me an asshole but I was hurt by Samantha not because I really cared about her but the fact that I wanted her and couldn't have her the way I wanted, or I could have but I blew it at some point. But even that is bullshit because I liked her smile. And when she smiled I cared for her.

I wanted to kiss her and explore her body.

I didn't really want to love or care for her, though. She wasn't that smart or witty or anything.

But then again I've always been a hypocrite. Now I just don't give a damn who knows, because I am all that matters. In that matter I truly am the egoist. Aren't I?

I really should stop reading and watching movies and listening to music and hanging out with anyone and pretty much listening to anything that is talking. Because I've said it before and I'll say it again: "I am a product of all I surround myself with."

I'm not the egoist.

I am Barron.

I am Nikki.

As I read *The Bible* I become the converted. As I read science fiction I become supernatural.

I really have no control over my life anymore.

Maybe I hurt myself because it's an act of defiance against what I'm supposed to do. But then again it was Barron's idea, so what am I defying? There's no me to defy.

* * * * *

"AND SO this is Christmas . . . I hope you had fun . . . Another year over . . . A new one just begun . . . ."

So Jesus was born on this date like two-thousand-something years ago. And two-thousand-something years later I wake up with cottonmouth and all sweaty even though the house is freezing. So cold that I put on this old gray sweatshirt and these old running pants.

I think about Nikki as I brush my teeth in my dimly lit bathroom and wish she were here with me so I could hold her and all that.

I walk out into our living room and mom is sitting in her chair sipping coffee looking at the Christmas tree with these thousand twinkles of multicolored light in her eyes.

My dad horks morning smoker's mucus and joins us and I say, "Merry Christmas," with this tired half-smile and hug them both and everything is so quiet and beautiful. The old Christmas knickknacks all seemingly floating on mundane old end tables, a real Christmas tree stands in majestic attention in the corner of the room. We have no fireplace and therefore no stockings. Soft Christmas carols soothe overstressed ears and minds and somehow, just as my brother comes into the room, I am five, six, seven, eight years old again with my high voice and chubby cheeks. Nikki still lingers in my mind but it seems like there is some force surrounding this morning that blocks out all non-Christmas-related thoughts. And this safeguard won't let anything in besides remembered happiness.

So then we all gather around in our little family circle and open presents.

I get some new pants and all sorts of books and movies and music. Apparently my parents don't want me going anywhere when I'm at college. They just want me to stay in my room and be influenced even more so by this onslaught of worldviews.

And to think I should have seen everything coming by what I got. Because in the end, the end is always the same. The story always ends. You get that feeling of accomplishment or inspiration, and you know you could make a better movie, or you could write a better book, or you really know what they were trying to say, and you have that feeling of euphoria wash over you and then retreat like the tide as the normalcy of everything sobers you back up. And you know that you're back to where you were. Where the end is always the same.

Just like *Brave New World*. That rotten warning.

I should have seen it coming.

* * * * *

LATER THAT day, we go to church. The Catholic priest, with his dead smile, reminds us all that mass is said every Sunday, not just twice a year (Easter and Christmas). This provokes a warm chuckle from the regulars and nonregulars alike.

I just sit in the corner and stare at my feet. I've heard all these words a million times before, about the birth and the glory and the promise, and I mouth them emptily as I turn a patch of carpet into a distant wasteland, where the stale air sweeps over dry nothing, where emptiness grows, where the shadow of my foot twitches restlessly, where the pool of my loathing collects and sits invisibly and heavily.

We are saved, but still we must beg for forgiveness, and we must never stop begging, because we are never saved.

Joy to the world.

* * * * *

SO NOW I have exactly nine days until my dreaded return to college. This vacation has proven to be so interesting and fulfilling that I honestly loathe the thought of going back to school. I don't want to leave Nikki and she assured me last night that she doesn't want me to go either. I'm going out with her and Barron and Jenna again tonight.

And then the whole Barron thing has got me wanting to stay here too. I know he's going to tell me what this plan is before I head back to school, but he's got me so interested in it by not telling me about it that I'm pretty much desperate to know. He also said he had a good idea for some shit we could do. He came up with huffing noxious cleaning fluid and jumping off his roof onto the giant trampoline (a birthday present) in his backyard. I'm really excited to try that. He calls it "Huff, Huff, and Away!"

And then Cornelius keeps sending me emails asking me when I'm going to stop by his shop so we can smoke and look at naked girls and shit again. He also tells me he's really excited to head to New York. He's got a little countdown going and he's already decided on an apartment somewhere in the Lower East Side, wherever that is. He says it's like art central somewhere around there. I really don't think he knows anything about the art world but his talent is undeniable. If I had any money I'd buy some of his work. He's got the potential to be amazing. Hell, he's amazing already. So much detail. Truly the work of a madman. I tell him since my mom isn't making me work until I get back to school I'll stop by real soon.

Frue still hasn't gotten back to me. That bastard. But then again I know nothing about the armed services and I can't imagine they just let anyone go on the computer whenever they want. But I want him to get back here so I can tell him about all this stuff. About work, Samantha, Barron, the pedophile guy, Cornelius, Nikki, school, drugs, and more stories of what he called "stupid shit." As in, "Are you guys still into that stupid shit?" referring to our destructive-enlightening activities.

I really don't want to go back to some boring school where everybody is drunk or baked all the time talking about how drunk and baked they are and how cool they are and it's all just so phony compared to this. I've got all that I need right here. They are amateurs.

My best friend beat a rapist with a baseball bat. I can't even believe it myself.

I met the girl of my dreams not long after that.

I made a girl cry just by telling her I met someone else.

I am the man.

I am because I'm afraid not to be.

* * * * *

BARRON SWINGS by later on just to chill and play some table tennis. His unemployed ass never has anything to do.

"So are you ready or what?"

"For what?"

"Tonight, man! That girl is all over you. Jenna was telling me about it."

"Really?" I tried to hide my red-faced excitement by turning away to pick up the ball.

"Yeah. She said you were the coolest person she knew and that you were 'hot.' Ha, you pimp."

"Oh, man, that is a good to hear," I said. "Fuck yeah."

"Good. Tonight we're just gonna meet at my house and get some Chinese or something. Get ripped, get fed, get it on."

"Nice."

And then this silence came over both us as and we just volleyed the ball over the net back and forth while some old song played in the background. It was like ten minutes until Barron interrupted our silence and said, "So go ahead and ask."

"What?"

"Oh man you want that girl so bad."

"What do you mean?" I smiled.

"You haven't asked me about the plan."

"Oh yeah," I said. I really hadn't thought about it, but I got excited because it seemed like he wanted to talk about it.

"Well?"

"So, Barron," I said, deliberately taking my time, "what's, uh, what's this, uh, this plan all about?"

He laughed. "Atta boy. All right . . . like I said, it has to do with that fuck who was fucking that kid. Did you know they didn't arrest him or anything? Girl was gone by the time the cops arrived. They're still looking for me, but they don't know who I am."

"So what about the guy?"

"Well first off I found out who the girl was."

"Who?"

"It was Jenna's cousin's neighbor."

"Um, how—?"

"I actually talk to girls, Jibba. I don't just stare at their mouths and go paralyzed like you. I *care*," he said and laughed.

"So how did you really find out?" I asked.

"I was talking to her about the thirteen-year-old girl who made a porno with her boyfriend. Remember that shit? They were from—"

"Yeah, yeah! I remember that! We watched that movie over here one day after practice."

"Girl in that video was sisters with the one I found getting raped, man."

I was taken aback. I knew both her and her sister. The porn-sister used to go out with Greg; she once said I was a sweetheart and that my poems were "weird, but really good." Her younger sister, the raped, had always been a really quiet-but-kind tagalong.

I couldn't believe it. I wanted to get some revenge on that fucker even more now.

I must have gotten a pissed-off look on my face because Barron said, "Yeah, man. I thought so."

"So what do we do?"

"Well it's really quite simple." He paused. "We offer him something he wants and then we give him what he needs."

"We're gonna ruin his day, huh. Throw away his ice cream."

"Gotta make the little bitch cry, man."

I laughed.

* * * * *

So BARRON and I finished our volley of table tennis and smoked a joint in my cold garage. We decided to do some "shit" and Barron took off his belt and snapped it like an abusive father.

"Where d'you wan' it?" he asked me real slow, creepy-like. Or at least it seemed slow because I was high real bad. I turned around and pulled up my pant leg and flexed my calf.

87

"Good call," he said, pulling both ends of the belt into one hand. I started flinching.

Then I heard him pull it back and whip the broad leather belt across my flexed calf.

SNAP—situation normal, absolute pain.

The smarting jolt flashed through my eyes like white light and my endorphins released this surge of euphoria in the back of my head. I promised myself I wouldn't yell, but I grunted still pretty bad.

I looked back at the welt on my leg and I had to laugh. Luckily it was winter so I could wear pants to cover that up. The damn thing was bleeding. The pain hurt so great. A sunrise right under my skin. Pain and color radiating. A percentage, a small, humble percentage, of that moment when the squirrel ate all that electricity.

"Your turn," I said as I leaned against my bike, trying to keep my weight off that throbbing leg, every now and then leaning on it for another rush.

Barron laughed at the way I was standing and turned around and pulled off his hooded sweatshirt and T-shirt and I saw these ten cuts, five on each side, near his shoulder blades, that looked pretty fresh.

"Oh, man, you were really putting it to her, eh?"

He laughed. "Oh, yeah. You should hear that girl moan. She had to put a pillow over her mouth because the astronauts were complaining."

"Lucky bastard," I said and trailed off, looked at the belt in my hands, and said, "Are you sure you want your back?" I said and laughed at my cannabis sentence.

Barron laughed. "Yeah, man."

"All right. Your life," I said and started pulling my arm back.

"Exactly," he interrupted me mid-arm-pull.

"What?"

"It's my life. I'm glad you understand that."

"Okay, smartass."

"No, Jibba. You don't understand. Before you got back I remember talking to you on the phone that one time and you sounded like such a controlled bastard. Talking about those phony-ass friends you were making down at the so-called palace of refinement. Everybody getting drunk and smoking up to be cool or something. Or because everyone else was doing it. I know you better than that, but you were catching on to their false shit. And it was pissing me off. But I really couldn't do anything about it.

"Now what I need most out of you is to understand that you control your life, because it is yours. You are the master of your universe. Do you get that yet? Don't answer that. What I'm saying is I know you're not happy at that school. And that you need to be somewhere where you'll be happy. I know you want to be with Nikki on some secluded beach with an everlasting sunset and a billion stars streaking across the sky as she slobs your knob and shit. I've read your stuff. And I want you to know that all that shit you learned at school will never compare to the shit you're learning here. Or even there in your dorm. Or to the shit we've already learned. That feeling you have when you're sitting there all alone because the kids in your hall are the kids you didn't like in high school and now you have to live with them. You gotta know that that is a learning step for you. Eat that shit.

"The good will always equal the bad. All this pain we're putting ourselves through is so we can feel the pleasure later . . . when we pop pills or smoke dope or even when we're retired from all this. When we look back we can say we lived our fucking life to the fullest extent. *Ours*. Your life, and mine.

"Do you know that yet?"

I really didn't know what to say. I just tried to let it all sink in.

"Quit stalling," I said.

He smiled knowingly. Barron was my best friend.

He turned. There were the cuts again.

Then I pulled my all-state arm back and veloci-slapped the belt as hard as I could across his back. He shuddered and flexed his back and walked forward like a chicken, in pain, the blood already seeping out.

"I'm doing this for your future happiness."

He laughed between grimaces.

* * * * *

So WHAT you never wrote in your little thing here is that you met

met up with Belle that second night you were back for break. You were out looking for jobs and you stopped by Belle's house because she kept writing to you while you were down at school talking about how bad she wanted to see you when you got back.

You were bored. *And besides*, you thought to yourself, *who gives a damn anymore?*

So you pull into her driveway and get out of the car thinking *Am I really doing this?* as you knock on her door. She answers in her pajamas because it's late and she's still in high school. She screams, "Jibba's here!" and gives you a big hug, much deeper and warmer than you were expecting.

And reintroductions are made. How-are-yous are exchanged. Eyes are looked into. You remember something like love. And you try to forget about it and be in the moment.

"So how's school?" she says. But all you remember is seeing her hugging the quarterback of the football team and then looking into his eyes and kissing him.

NFPTW—nice fucking party that was.

She looked over and tried to smile at you . . . attempting that edge of friendship. You avoided eye contact and shook your head and walked away, muttering something.

"Oh, really? How's baseball going?"

Like us, it is over, and you are fucking depressed. You can see her at your summer games, cheering you on. She looks so beautiful the way the sun sets behind her in the bleachers and her brown hair is golden around the edges and her smile is right at you as you stand in the on-deck circle.

"So why didn't you try out?"

Yeah, Jibba, why didn't you try out? You were *so good*. And it all traces back to the best game of your life. The one she went to. You were standing on the pitcher's mound and you saw her car drive by. You knew it was her. She was alone. She drove an hour just to watch you play baseball. But what was she doing there? She'd already moved on from the quarterback and she was going out with some kid in her grade who was a pretty nice kid, you guessed. But she stayed the whole time, even when it got late and cold outside in the far fringe of summer.

"Oh, I see, I guess. Well, it's good to see you!"

There was a scout in the stands from the state school you planned on attending. He was there exclusively to watch you. And then you played the best game of your life, overcoming the nerves of having that scout and the only girl you've ever loved in the stands. And you hit two home runs. And you looked at her as you rounded third on your trot . . . she was clapping. You caught eyes. Isn't that enough?

"Oh, I've been pretty good. Yeah, Mike's great. He's actually stopping by later."

The scout saw you play your best game and never contacted you afterwards. Apparently you weren't enough of a man for anyone to believe in you. But you really didn't know. You really didn't care except you knew in your heart you should be playing. And it all sank in . . . This was what Barron called a more important learning experience than any high school or college bullshit rhetoric. He called it the freedom from desire. You've never gotten anything you wanted, except a few things, and they weren't enough.

"Yeah. So did you hear?"

He basically stated that the things you desire will always end up hurting you in the end. Scarring you needlessly. Baseball and Belle were just the perfect examples. Barron was living the Socratic life. "I being with the fewest wants am closest to the Gods." He said that what you don't want can't fuck up your life.

"No, silly—I got a puppy!"

And it all sank in later. It just hurt at the time, like learning always does. Getting home, the euphoria of the evening gone. Checking your email. Finding nothing from Belle. So you stand up, turn off the computer, and reluctantly peel off your jersey and get into bed. Looking through the window with your hands behind your head and thinking about the first time you ever kissed her. Remembering she said nothing to you after the game. She just left . . . just as wordlessly as she arrived. She was more than just gone after the game. She was gone, gone, gone.

"Yeah. Don't you love him? His name is Skip."

So you snap out of stupid memories to find a dog sniffing your legs. So this was Skip.

"Mike got him for me."

Okay, that's enough. You didn't realize that you still cared for her that much. You didn't realize she meant so much to you. You hear the name Mike or Rock or Cody and you want to leave.

So you do.

"Aw, already?"

You nod, give some dumb hug goodbye, and feel much better as you get into your car. That's what you needed. It had been so long since you hurt yourself emotionally. You're in town now and it's time to start getting Barronated.

You had that kind of pain in mind when you called Samantha to tell her about Nikki. But sometimes things turn out differently than you wanted.

That's usually how it works.

So on the way home you hope you meet someone who will get Belle out of your head.

And then one day you meet someone who does not only that, but changes your life.

Forever.

Because now things get weird with Samantha.

And Cornelius.

And Barron.

* * * * *

I GOT my brother to drop me off at Barron's and I told him to tell our parents that I'd be spending the night there. He pulled into the driveway and said, "Oh yeah, when I was on the phone earlier that Samantha girl called. I thought you said you were done with her."

"I am."

"What should I tell her next time she calls then?"

"I don't know . . . I'll take care of it."

And then I got out of the car and headed for the house.

I could hear the music playing as soon as I stepped out of the car, and then I noticed a little red car on the street and I figured that the girls were already there.

The music was loud, which was uncharacteristic of Barron because the kid usually didn't even listen to music, and immediately I felt like something went or was going to go horribly wrong or horribly right tonight.

As I stepped through the door I could feel in my feet that the music was coming from downstairs. I broke the threshold of the kitchen and saw Nikki standing by the table.

She hadn't seen me yet, as her back was to me. But she looked kinda slumped down and bored. I had to smile at how pretty she was in the low light, even though I couldn't even see her face. The anticipation was enough to drive me crazy.

I cleared my throat to get her attention and she turned around and smiled wide. "Hi, James!" She got up and came over and gave me a hug.

I talked to her for a minute but I don't even remember what we said. I was just looking at her. She never ceased to amaze me. Then I asked her who all was downstairs and what the music was all about and why she was up here instead of down there.

"Um . . . I guess you'll have to just go look for yourself. I don't really want to talk about it."

So I kissed her on the forehead and made my way downstairs. She said she'd stay right there until I got back.

As I made my way downstairs the music got predictably progressively louder. The bass, deeper. The treble, sharper. The music becoming the vibrating air I breathed.

A thin band of red light beamed under the seam of the door at the bottom of the stairs. I put a hand on the door and felt the pulse of the room.

Then I heard laughter.

I opened the door slowly, taking in the whole scene a bit at a time. First I saw Barron's red lights shining right into my eyes. It was this light thing he bought at a flea market for like five bucks. It was a steal. It made his basement look like an opium den, all swanky and weird.

Then I saw Barron sitting on the back of his couch. He hadn't noticed me. He was drunk as all hell. I could tell just by the way he was sitting.

Then I saw two girls, both completely naked, dancing with each other. By dancing I mean they were moving to the music, by with each other I mean they had their hands all over each other. I could make out Jenna in the poor lighting and there was another girl of equal beauty in her arms, her hands, her fingertips.

Two girls dancing together in the middle of Barron's basement, naked, feeling each other's body, and Barron sitting on the back of his couch, drunk, listening to music he'd never listen to, telling the girls what to do.

"More of that," he told them.

The next afternoon he tells me that the only way something like that could happen is because he had the freedom from desire for something like that to happen. He played it off as not that big a deal and everything else fell into place.

That night he said, "Jibba," and motioned me over. "Take a seat."

So I sat down and watched two bomb-ass bitches kiss and dance and open a gyrating lesbian mutual petting zoo.

Barron's head moving back and forth to the bass line. My hands at my sides, feeling like a voyeur in some immoral game of "I Spy." The girls before us, their smooth skin pink in the red light, filled with lust and rhythm.

Everything was so wonderfully dirty.

Nikki was upstairs sitting at a kitchen table, waiting for me to come back.

The dancing girls became dancing-and-kissing girls.

I was lost. I needed a drink. So I clapped Barron's knee and said "Have fun" and went upstairs.

I looked over at the girls as I made my way back across the basement and one saw me and pursed her lips. I couldn't tell which one she was. I think it was Jenna's friend. She made the kiss face to me. And there was something oddly familiar about her.

Nikki.

Get back to Nikki.

"Jibba!"

I turned around. "What?"

"Why don't you stay around for a while?"

"I am," I said. "I'm just going upstairs, to check on Nikki."

"No. I mean stick around down here. Have some fun."

Jenna was licking her friend's neck. Her friend had a pre-orgasmic face going.

I should stick around for a while.

Nikki.

It's all about Nikki.

"Sorry, man."

Then I went upstairs as Barron said something low enough for me not to hear it. He shook his head.

*****

"WHAT THE hell is going on down there?" I asked Nikki as I broke the threshold between the basement stairs and the kitchen.

"I don't know. I don't even want to know," Nikki said, obviously uncomfortable.

But Nikki knew what was going on.

"Why do you hang around with that girl? You seem so much different than her."

"I could ask you the same thing."

"What do you mean?"

But I knew what she meant.

"You and Barron are so different."

"Not really. Well, yeah, I guess we are."

But we aren't.

Are we?

"But he's my best friend."

"Well, so is Jenna."

I suppose it's only fair that I not judge in this situation.

Nikki says, "Do you know what he did before we got here?"

"Um, he said he had some errands to run and that I should call before I came over to make sure he was here. Why?"

"Well I don't know. But he said 'the first stage of the plan' was ready. He said something about how 'a few days from now it's all going down.'"

"Cryptic as ever. Yeah, I figured whatever this plan was would happen before I left. But he didn't give you any details?"

"No. After he said that he took Jenna and Samantha downstairs."

And I go deaf.

And I have to sit down.

And I can't talk.
"Samantha?"
"Yeah. She goes to your old school. A junior."
"Yeah," I mumble, "she does." I stare at the ground.
"What's wrong, James?"

* * * * *

So SAMANTHA somehow knew Barron and Jenna. And not only that, but she was apparently a part-time lesbian with Jenna and a stripper for Barron. And to think that all this time I was too nice to do anything with.

Girls never give it up to nice guys. It's a scientific fact.

Nice boy meets a pretty girl. It takes him a lot of wit and three or four months to fuck her.

Asshole boy meets a pretty girl and if he looks good enough and acts like he doesn't care (or no acting is needed), he's introducing anal sex within a week.

NMFGS—nothing makes fucking goddam sense.

But it's not really that I care all that much. I mean what am I really going to do about the fact that the girl I was lusting over this whole time is downstairs making out with my best friend's fuck-buddy? Sometimes shit like this happens, you know?

Right?

Too much thought.

I look good tonight. I notice looking in a makeshift mirror in the kitchen, the large reflective darkened window above the sink. But Nikki looks much better.

It's all a choice. Barron told me to stick around downstairs, have some fun, as it were, and I really have the choice now. I mean I know that Samantha likes me in more than just the friendship way. She even made the kiss face downstairs when I didn't recognize her.

I remember now that I could smell the alcohol in the air. No wonder she didn't overreact or anything like that. She was wasted and making standing love to Jenna.

But why didn't I recognize her? Well that's because it's not that often that you see the girl you want in a lesbian fuck fantasy, greased up and naked in your best friend's basement.

The other side of the choice is just to sit here and forget

about the fantasy downstairs and hold hands and laugh with Nikki, maybe make love, but make love, not fuck. The girl that is lovable and what you always wanted.

I looked over to the clock on the wall and the numbers seemed to be sliding by minute after minute after minute. But what to do now but take action and be accountable for my decision? Stay upstairs with Nikki and smile. Go downstairs with Barron, Jenna, and Samantha and make some funny faces all night, inevitably hurting a beautiful, wonderful girl. You want her, but didn't Barron warn you about that?

What good is love when I'm leaving in a few days anyway? Just to think that it's not even New Year's and this type of shit is going on. All the possibilities for a millennial night like that. Because every new year is special. All our footprints from the past year rise to the sky and all the chemicals we injected into our bodies and then pissed out rise into the sky in the form of rain and trickle down onto old farm fields to make bread to feed hungry addicts.

It's like Barron says: the negatives always equal the positives. It's like some sort of pendulum, he says.

Every person he sees with those never-ending smiles on their faces, he knows that sometimes at night they get morbidly depressed. Or they cuss people out if they get cut off on the road.

In order to get in shape, he says, you have to go through the rigors of running and lifting weights. What goes up, Jibba, always comes down. It's a law of science.

Newton.

Everything has its counter.

So now it's come down to staying upstairs with a girl whom I might be able to love one day, an emotion that has escaped me for so long, but will only turn bad because I'm leaving anyways. This euphoria I feel now will only be counteracted when I get back down to the phony state school run by fraternities and alcohol. I'll be sitting in some lonely dorm room thinking about Nikki, remembering how close I was to loving her, and it will all be so overwhelming. This euphoria replaced with a morose void. Depression for days.

Downstairs, two of the sexiest girls I've ever seen are reenacting pretty much every fantasy from my masturbatorial pantheon. My best friend is drunk downstairs wondering if I'm coming back down to find out just how incredible life can get.

What is regret when you're too busy living?

Barron hurts himself to feel pleasure later. I hurt myself because I should not be forgiven.

I took Nikki by the hand, looked in her eyes, took a deep breath, and realized that as much as I might love this girl, she will be gone, and I will be full of regret when I'm some machine in a dorm, so I might as well live while I can.

How right I was. How wrong I was.

I kissed Nikki and apologized. I told her how great she was but her tears said she was done listening.

Regret later.

Lesbian fuckfest now.

I was never good with departures, but I didn't need any skills because Nikki walked out the door crying. The regret could wait.

I made my way downstairs.

* * * * *

To go into details about the night would be nearly impossible, in the same way that a person cannot describe the taste of milk.

I have only a long string of mental Polaroid pictures, some of which include:

Samantha with her hands all over Jenna's body, and Jenna with her moaning mouth around my me. Barron laughing in the background.

A toss of blonde hair and a pink pair of hips gyrating wildly against my crotch, my dick in all the way to the hilt, grinding so hard and fast to the music outside and within.

Barron getting Samantha from behind as Samantha licks between Jenna's pearly legs while I slug from the communal bottle of vodka and watch the bass of the loud music send ripples across the smooth pane of liquid.

All these red-tinted photographs of a night that never should have happened so beautifully.

There was so much wonder being totally obscured by these fucking red lights in the corner of the basement. It felt like a cheap skin-flick on the movie channels late on a Saturday night.

It was just this giant release for four young horny creeps. Livin' while livin'.

It was just this pure and absolute picture of our deeply indulgent lives. Dirty stinking teenage life. Because this is the time that many teenagers or freshmen in college get to experience things like this, and damn right it was our turn. It was like a living porno, only with louder music. And I'm pretty sure incredibly lovable and sensitive sweethearts aren't crying in their car outside during pornos, but I might be wrong.

Barron lying on his back with Jenna riding him facing away with me on top of Samantha, hammering away, working hard toward soiling my sixth condom of the night. And to think a week ago this girl was telling me she just wanted to be friends.

So much sex. It filled a void in my life that I had never filled before. I'd had sex twice before this, and now I'm living the role of pre-AIDS John Holmes in some wild orgy.

So dirty. So much happening with loud music and red lights and two blonde beautiful girls drunk and horny as hell. My best friend getting blown by the same girl I'm fucking from behind as another girl (it doesn't even matter who at this point) is getting a drink of water.

But like I said, it's useless to try to put it all into words. It was heaven in hell. Or hell in heaven. But nowhere that night was earth a part of the landscape.

And somewhere along the line, as a faint light broke through the tiny basement windows, the girls got up, got dressed, and left. I was lying somewhere next to the couch down there with no shirt on but pants but no boxers and went to get a drink of water. "Bring me down some too, eh?" Barron said in this odd voice.

I said sure thing and got two glasses from a white cupboard upstairs. As I filled the glasses at the sink I looked out the window just above the flowing water and saw the thin light sliver of the rising sun breaking onto the horizon. It was so beautiful. This orange hairline becoming a fingernail and a half circle and this bird was chirping this song and oh how majestic it all felt. I just wanted to stay in that moment forever. Because no matter how

how great what I just lived through was, it was not pure. The red light still lingered and burned. Barron was not pure. Birds and the fingernail-halfcircle sun in the kitchen window were pure. But not me.

I am Jim Carroll again. "I just want to be pure."

I decided it was time to move on, so I blinked, looked at the glasses of water, and brought them downstairs.

* * * * *

I WAS twelve years old playing Wiffle ball with my best friend when this little brown squirrel bit through this big black wire. And when the squirrel sank his teeth into enough power to supply the neighborhood's energy needs, there was no hope of any chance for survival for him. The small brown squirrel died instantaneously.

One of its little legs was so jolted by the charge that it flew off the body and hit the side of our house. Then my best friend ran over and looked at it, picked it up, and threw it at me. My little best friend thought it was funny. But I was twelve years old and that was my first encounter with death. I really didn't think it was funny.

I shrieked when he threw the leg at me. I jumped wildly out of the way. I didn't want to touch the dead leg. I'd never thought about the difference between life and death.

I jumped back and had to look away from the charred leg of the squirrel. The skin all cooked and fried and crispy, the muscle darkened and soft. I jerked my head way from the wretched death.

In the house my brother's room was completely dark in the summertime shadows. But I saw this blinking red light in the corner of the room.

The red light blinking in the dark again and again and again. Who said it was all a warning? The red light was just the adaptor of my brother's charging phone. But death was all around me.

I stared at that red light blinking in the corner in the summertime shadows and everything fell away. I got away in my head, wondering about that light.

I was twelve years old and that light has been blinking ever since.

* * * * *

NOT EVERYTHING is adding up at this point.

I brought the water downstairs and really couldn't talk to Barron about what all we just did. I don't think there are words or a real conversation that could fit that type of undertaking. I mean, what was I supposed to be like, "If either of those girls ends up pregnant, I call I'm not the father"? So we just sorta sat in two different parts of the room and basked in our own sense of the all.

My hands kept shaking, and I was cold.

Not everything was adding up.

Why had Samantha flipped out like that? And in turn, why did she agree to get into some crazy foursome with me and Barron and her friend Jenna if she was so upset? What was all this?

My confusion collapsed within itself because I really didn't want to think about all that. I just had some serious fuckin' sex.

But what of Nikki?

Nikki who?

It would have been something I would have done in the past, hanging on and giving myself a chance to love some perfect girl named Nikki, even though I'd be going back to college in too short a time anyway. I guess I'm the heartless bastard I always wanted to be. I'm not the nice guy. I don't care because caring hurts too much. Sex is immediate and feels good now.

Drugs feel good now.

Pain hurts so nice now. That bright flash of white, the complete lack of conscious thought. Just the action and the result—no middle ground or grayness. Every action has its reaction. Every reaction is a result. Every result carries with it a lesson.

Nikki feels terrible because a guy she really liked completely turned her down to go have dirty sex with her friends. That pain will give her strength for later. I remember seeing those T-shirts that said: "Pain is just weakness leaving the body." Well, maybe what we did was something like that, only different. Soul-pain. Soul-strength.

Eventually, after sitting there for a while, nodding back and forth, I bummed a few painkillers from Barron, popped 'em down with the rest of my water, and made my way upstairs and out the door for the walk home.

As I stepped outside, I noticed how abnormally warm the late-December morning was. The snow under my feet was sloshy and when I made my way to the street, it was just wet. There was no standing snow. In fact, little birds still sitting in trees were making little chirping noises. The noises made everything feel like spring. All of a sudden I'm humming "This Magic Moment" and I'm smiling at the gray-blue sky.

Right now I can see Nikki in her room. She's just waking up from a terrible night. Her pillow is still stained from tears. Her nose is all dried up from where it was running. The birds singing outside her window mock her sadness. She hasn't felt this bad . . . ever. I guess she really liked me, and I guess I really liked her if I'm thinking about her after that night.

But then I'm walking home, whistling, kicking up my heels because I just got a lifetime of sex in one night from two of the hottest girls I ever done seen. Life is . . . well, it's not good. But it's not bad.

I guess life is what you make of it.

Or what it makes of you.

I guess life is an adventure—as long as you make it. If it makes you, it's a nightmare.

I need this to start adding up.

* * * * *

BY THE time I make it home the euphoria has worn off. The exhaustion sets in and I unlock the front door to see my dad sitting at the table reading the newspaper. He looks up with these wary old man eyes, doesn't say a thing, just nods in my direction as I slip off my shoes. I walk by and pat his broad shoulder. "I'm gonna get some sleep."

"You do that," he replies and looks back down at the sports section. "We need to have a talk later," he says as I make my way upstairs. I was going to pretend like I didn't hear him but I just mumbled something like a yes and moved on up the stairs and into my room.

I closed the blinds on the windows and sat on the edge of

my bed. My computer across from me, standing proud in its technological fineness. My lifeline to the informational reaches of the world. The reflective black monitor making me stare back at me. It's like I was never gone. But the computer knows.

The computer knows what I did last night. I left a great girl for some great sex. I never would have imagined that there would be that much greatness in my life at once. The computer knows my hesitation and excitement for this big plan of Barron's that makes me so nervous. The computer knows everything I've written. Frue at sea. Rows and rows of desks at work. Pretty Samantha's white smile. Nikki's button nose. Barron laughing. Masochism in the afternoon. Sharp pain. The unnamable it. Dull pain. Death in everything. Power of will. Self-determination. Emotional pain. Beauty and longing. The white purity of clouds riding oceans of air. The black glistening shafts of icy streets at night. The red lights of sex. An orgy in the basement. Colors and memories. Barron with sweat and diamond mud down his face. A dark shadow crouched below a window. Snapshots. Polaroids of life's story. Orgasms into and onto and unto. Acronyms for days. Tears in other rooms. The numbing buzz. Relief or pain. Beauty in the small things and the big things. Everything.

I put on The Beatles because they seem to fit the bill of what I'm feeling right now. I really was never a big Beatles fan until I left for school. Frue had one of their albums sent to me the day before I left. If it was good enough for Frue, it was good enough for me and certainly anybody else.

Then I lay there on my bed and stared out through that same window I'd stared out so many times before . . . thinking about baseball or school and all that other shit. The branches outside shivered in the breeze and clacked against the pane. They held time for the songs coming from my radio.

The white walls became whiter. My bed swallowed me whole, leaving just my thoughts and consciousness. And soon I was walking along some winter landscape, feeling the cold wind bite at my face, and I would kiss back with frozen lips and be warmed by my capacity for its natural splendor. Then small animals would scurry at my feet and climb to my shoulders. I would cry with them about all injustice. They told me all about what was to happen.

Yes. I was dreaming.

I was clairvoyant in my dreams. I knew what was going to happen.

Yea though I walk through this snowdrift valley under the shadow of death, I will fear nothing because the Dalai Lama told me so in a letter to someone else.

And I slept and dreamt further.

* * * * *

I WAKE up and my mom's horrible music is playing downstairs. It's thumping through the floor of my room and the drone of the vacuum is adding another hideous layer to the sissy-rock songs. I sit up and open the curtains to feel the energy of how uncommonly beautiful it is outside. Then I stumble over to the computer, flip it on, and put on some music to cover mom's shit while the computer boots up.

I lean back in my chair, still waiting, thinking about the first time I ever had sex, and how that the first time I hurt myself was so much more important and better. You see, I was drunk and high at a party at Greg's. I was in high school, I'd had five too many, and so had this girl named Carmen.

Carmen was a hottie cheerleader slut—the stereotypical gum-chewing, mall-shopping, hip-hopping, panty-dropping, cum-guzzling type of lovely fuckpig you see in every teenage genre movie.

I was sauced and blown.

I don't even remember how it all started. Oh shit, yes I do. We were playing this drinking game and she was sitting on my lap because there were no other seats available. We were slamming down drinks, she was chewing gum in my ear, and I was laughing at Barron who kept taking giant swigs from this kid's liquor bottle every time the poor fucker turned around.

Pretty soon Carmen is chewing my ear. Licking all around, making me think dirty feelings. Carmen was just using me; I knew this. I was nine sheets to the breeze and fucked on all fronts. Was I really saving myself for marriage, like I'd been taught? For the right girl? For it to mean something?

Carmen took me upstairs.

Now what I don't remember is how it all started there. I couldn't tell you who kissed whom or what color her panties were, if she was even wearing panties. All I really saw, again, was just little snapshots of my beer dick slapping around with her on that bed. We must have been going at it for hours. When Carmen was done, and I was done, she took off. Of course I felt guilty as fuck.

It's hard to feel cheap and used when you're a man, but I'm not really much of a man, am I? But it's not like I regret anything, or at least I try not to. As was said before by someone with less shit in their brains than me, I do not regret the things I've done, but those I did not do. My first time just didn't mean anything. After that night Carmen was the same to me as she always was—some dumb cooze who was eye candy. No emotions. No real existence beyond the portrayal of fantasy in my eyes. But I was goddam glad to have that virginity monkey off my back.

My first fuck was nothing like my first dose of pain. Pain gave me meaning. Salvation. Substance.

At least I could remember all of it.

So by the time I finally got my email inbox open I'd gone another tour through thoughts of last night. Sickeningly wonderful. Everything gained with nothing gone. It all depends on how you want to look at the situation. You can convince yourself anything is right if you look at it right. Look at racism. Look at sexism and nationalism. Look at it under your own sympathies, and it will look right to you, if you want it to.

And just as I was under the impression that today was going to be all right, I received the one email that could change that. The type of news that is only the opening inhalation of a goddam tragic opera.

* * * * *

I HAD one email in my inbox, and it was from Cornelius. I still hadn't stopped by his office yet so I was expecting it to read something along the lines of: "Dammit, Jibba, we really gotta chill before I leave, man."

Assumption is the mother of all asses.

It actually read:

Sender: Corn5150@aol.com
Recipient: Jibbawocky@aol.com

Jibba, I'm typing this with my left hand because last night as I was closing up the shop I was attacked in my office and beaten unconscous. The attacker was a pretty big person, but he was wearing all black so I couldn't see him to good. Face covered with duct tape. Scary as fuck. Never been so scarred before, Jibba.

You'll never believe what he did next. Fucker took spray paint and destroyed my art. The fist, the bumper, all the photography, my paintings, stuff I never showed you. That's not all the stuff I have, but it was my best stuff.

Jibba, when I find this fukcing cocksucker I'm going to kill him. I'm going to bury him. Im going to fucking bury that fucker—believe me.

Call me man. I'm in a lot of pain right now. I just need a calm voice of reason in this fuckign shitstorm. Please.

And with that he ended the email and sent it.

I can still remember how confused I was, looking at my computer screen, with all these thoughts colliding in my head—this anger and disappointment took over the area where my greedy thoughts of lust and sex had just been dancing. I was a walking contradiction of emotion.

I was slackjawed.

I was morose and confused.

I was angry.

But what could I do?

* * * * *

I WAS thrown into a spiral of thought, lust, and exhaustion. I was still tired and groggy and now I was anything but feeling the euphoria that should have been radiating through and out of me.

I closed out of my email account and headed downstairs to have my talk with my father. I was expecting him to be like: "The next time you sleep over Barron's house ask us or call" or something like that. I don't know.

I assumed that's what it would be all about.

When I got downstairs, I saw my mother at the kitchen table.

"Mom," I said, trying to get her attention away from the bills she was working on, but she obviously couldn't hear me over the shitty music. "Mom!" I shouted and she turned, holding some papers with her chin to her chest.

"Hi, honey," she took the papers from her chin and put them on the table and smiled her mom smile. "How was your night?"

"It was all right," I played it off. "Pretty fun."

"What did you do?"

"Not much, really. Me and Barron just played some video games and stuff. Same old stuff. I got a headache from this weird red light he refused to turn off in his basement. You know Barron."

"Well that sounds like it was fun," she said, barely listening, her attention back to the bills. She trusted that I'd never do anything wrong. I'd never smoke marijuana. I'd never take part in teenage orgies. I'd never burn myself with a lighter and throw myself off a roof.

"Where's Dad?" I asked, trying to keep her attention for a moment more. "He said he wanted to talk to me."

"I think he's out in the garage. He's taking down the Christmas lights because it's so nice outside. You should go talk to him now. He probably needs help."

Shit.

"Okay."

So I threw on some shoes and headed outside to find my dad hunched over his work table full of tools and other metal refinements, humming "What a Wonderful World," and it looked like he was trying to change the bulb of one of the lights on a long string of them.

"What's up, Dad?"

"Hey, James. What's going on? How was your night?" He squinted as he wrestled with the jammed bulb.

My father was limited with words. Like I said our conversations never lasted longer than pragmatically needed. His style of conversation was a quick greeting and then he'd lace into whatever point he set out to make. If you interrupt him it's like a frog trying to cross the freeway. Your whole objective is to listen, nod your head, and then leave when he is done.

He was an old-school father.

"Not much, really. We just played video games and stuff. It was kind of fun doing that stuff like we hadn't done since our freshman year. You know, just playing games and talking about girls and stuff." I smiled to reassure him.

"Is that it?"

"Pretty much."

"Well what I wanted to talk about was—"

Here we go.

"When you came in this morning, you smelled terrible. What were you doing? You smelled like sweat, sex, and shit. I don't know what kind of shit you and Barron have been up to but if it was anything stupid you'd better fucking knock it off. I don't want you doing anything you'll regret. You have too much talent to offer the world instead of wasting your life doing stupid shit like hurting yourself drinking or smoking that shit."

Holy shit.

"Don't think I didn't know what you were doing. Your old man ain't as stupid as your mother says he is. So I just need you to know that you can tell me anything that's bothering you or if you have any questions because I know at your age I did stupid stuff. And maybe when you're a little older I'll tell you about it, because I don't want you thinking what I did was acceptable. But never, ever think that you can outsmart me. Never think you can pull the blanket over the old man's eyes.

"I'll turn my head on the drinking and smoking weed because stupid kids do stupid shit, and it's all part of it. I get it. But I don't want you losing your ambition. Your mother and I love you and want you to succeed. You have so much potential. Hey, I might not understand that contemporary weird shit you write, but I know what I like, and I like your weird contemporary shit. It's honest. We need more of that.

"But I won't tolerate hurting yourself. Masochism is not a way of life. It's a sick affliction that can only lead to bad things. It's a sick way of going about finding yourself. There are millions of other ways to do it. Because I can see where it's leading you and Barron, and I'm concerned. I can see the more pain and the more pleasure means more of one of two things. From that type of garbage you can get either get more life or death. It's like that movie I like, uh, where the guy says, 'Get busy livin', or get busy dyin'.' The pain and the pleasure . . . yeah, I've been there, James. Only in my day it was carving shit into your arm to be part of some gang of five kids who stole shit from stores for the rush, or played chicken in cars on long roads. And I understand that kids will always be idiots. But all those friends I did that stupid stuff with are complete wastes now, or they're old boring men like me. Some are unemployed, some are living in sick poverty. I had one friend kill himself, and it fucked me up bad. Yes, all that pleasure and all that pain will either lead to life or death, but there are many more ways to live that don't also risk death. I thank God for all I've gone through, because I don't regret anything I've done. It was all a learning experience. But the difference between me and those so-called friends of mine was that they never learned from the shit they were doing to themselves, and to others. James, I need you to be smarter than that. I need you to learn, always, and grow stronger. Never stop learning, because knowledge knows no age, and it is all we have in this world besides our time.

"Just please be smart. Make good choices. Drink. Smoke. Have a good time, but be smart about it. Because if you aren't making good choices, or being smart about your life, I'll beat you stupid, and so will life. Life will beat you down.

"And please, Jib, pay attention more in church. I can tell you're going through a lot right now; you could probably benefit from listening. Your soul is worth saving.

"Now go get that ladder from out there and remember that we're having a rosary today at three. Your aunts and uncles are coming over, so be ready."

We looked at each other, and then I went to get the ladder.
The old man knew all along.
The old man used to hurt himself too.
I am my father's son.
But why do I find that so disturbing?
He is a good man.

* * * * *

So I finish up with helping my dad and I go back to my room to call Cornelius. He wasn't at his office and I didn't have his home phone number, so I just put it off. I mean it's not like I've known the guy for all that long. Instead I went downstairs and talked with my brother about girls and our father and life in general until three o'clock rolled around.

Now my aunts and uncles are coming in the house with their "*Helloooo?*" calls as they peer around our door, bearing small finger foods and such. Gelatins. Aunt Irene's cookies. Aunt Sarah's taco dip. Uncle Robert's shrimp.

We eat well, then we pray well.

If there's one thing that I feel obligated to do, and feel good about, it's saying a rosary with my aunts, uncles, mother, father, and brother.

We're done with the small talk and we're starting in on the rosary. I sit within the soothing hum behind the collective voice of my family as we tranquilly go through prayer after prayer. I can close my eyes and be enveloped in such peace and calm. Hearing each individual and then the whole family praying as one, saying our Hail Marys and our Our Fathers and all the glorious miracles, the memories of so many years that have gone by, sitting on this same spot on the carpet, praying with these same people. Until that moment, I had never really appreciated how beautiful a rosary is when said amongst my loving family, with the low vibration of my voice sort of massaging my spine-soul.

Sure they're stuck in the '80s. And sure they're incredibly corny at times. But sitting here with them, I could love nobody more. They're praying with, at, and for me. And I'm praying for, at, and with them. It's a circle of love and prayer and no stress. Only the goodness of better hopes.

There is no stress in a family rosary.

It's catharsis. Like pain. Life is pain and prayer.

Life is the result of God's odd joke.

I can hate these people so much at family outings and I can love them so much at family rosaries. I can believe myself and my friends to be original in our quest of life through pain. The pendulum swaying back and forth. I can think I was the first to think that, but my father did it so many years before. I am my father's son. I pray for my father and his struggles with his youngest son leaving for college. No children left in the nest.

I pray for my mother and her struggles with bills and how her youngest son has left for college.

I pray for my aunts and uncles and their myriad stresses.

I pray for Nikki and hope that she does not hurt like I have hurt before, and I pray that my prayer can help alleviate whatever pain she feels.

I pray for Barron, for too many reasons to list.

I pray for Samantha and Jenna, that hopefully they can rise above being used by older boys and find real inner value.

I pray for Frue out there in a metal ship, in distant waters, away from us.

I pray for everyone but myself, because that's how rosaries work. But I also pray for myself.

And then the final prayer is said, the tranquility of the moment settles around us like incense in the air, and everyone opens their eyes. We all look around at each other, that slight buzz of goodness shining through our open eyes and ringing through our spines.

Now I'm exhaling and sighing, but slowly as my hands fall to my sides. I rise slowly. I walk over to my aunts and uncles and hug them, kiss them, thank them. They hug, kiss, and thank back.

It's how these things work.

Now they're leaving, carrying with them their Tupperware and plates and dishes in the paper bags they brought them in. I'm saying goodbye, thankful to see them go, as I have no use for them now that the rosary is done. My brother goes back downstairs to talk to his girlfriend on the phone. My mother cleans up all the dirty dishes and vacuums the floor again. My father is asleep fifteen minutes after they leave.

Everything is so interesting now. And I have a little more than two days until I have to leave for school.

Which, after the last six weeks, is the last place in the world I want to be.

* * * * *

THE ODD thing is that Barron told me that the plan was going down tonight, that that night I'd find out this whole big deal and all my anticipation over his first ever act of overt secrecy to me would be assuaged and I'd find out what the hell this kid was all about. I'd find out why he was being all cloak-and-dagger about this whole deal.

I sat in my room on the computer but he never signed on. I sat in my room reading a book but he never called. I sat in my room reading another book but he never stopped by.

I tried to call him after I ate dinner but nobody answered.

At like nine o'clock I got sick of waiting around like an asshole so I drove over there. The shades, drawn; the windows, dark; no cars in the driveway.

WTF—what the fuck?

So I just drive around for a while listening to a compilation I made earlier that afternoon while I think about a monkey that has been rattling the bars of the cage ever since my family left after our last prayer sesh. The monkey keeps asking me, "Jibba, how can you enjoy saying rosaries when you hate going to church?"

I sedate the monkey with my eventual reply. I tell him it's because I already learned the church lesson: life is filling time until you burn. Like making tapes, or driving around waiting for your friend to call, or playing Wiffle ball, always in anticipation of some big event coming up. Biding time until it's there.

And then it's gone.

And then it's just been replaced by another avalanche of trivia.

Until ten years later you're sitting at a desk with a cold drink listening to the same music wondering where it all went and why you couldn't appreciate and savor your moments when you were just a little idiot with nothing to do. Far from the inevitable burn.

You pull up to the same stoplight you pulled up to every day before school, with Barron riding shotgun, waiting to make a right. You see the wet concrete road from all the melting snow. You see brown piles of snow that didn't melt on this beautiful, temperate day. A long white car pulls up next to you waiting for the left-hand green arrow to glow so they can head somewhere you're not going. You wonder if you could just maybe follow them, to see if they know where Barron is.

But you just make a right and head over to the high school, driving down the same road you drove for so long, so many repeated years. But now you live at college in a dorm full of losers. The concrete glistens with moisture and streetlights arc above it, reflected on it, wide halos of light. And now in a little bit you'll be making a right into the main drive of your old alma mater.

Tomorrow night is New Year's Eve and tonight you're driving around aimlessly, pulling into your old high school, taking the big looping drive around to the back by the baseball field. The pavement ends like halfway across the back of the property at the school, becoming something like a loose rock path leading back to the small rocky parking lot for the baseball field.

You ask yourself, *What am I doing here?*

Now you're stepping out of your car and walking down the smaller rock path that leads to the bleachers on the visitor's side. Sitting down and looking up at all the stars the suburbs can provide. Just first and second magnitude stars. But it's beautiful.

There is a certain sanctity all around as you look in through the fence at the baseball field where you spent the last four years. Playing such a beautiful game, so perfect, so just. Little insignificant memories slide by your eyes as you look at the outfield and remember tracking down fly balls in practice. The silence is overwhelming.

It's still so unusually warm outside. You probably wouldn't be here otherwise.

You look at the pitcher's mound and remember the first game you ever pitched, how poorly you performed, how upset you were. Then you compared it to the last game you ever pitched there, how you threw a two-hitter and broke the school record for career wins. It looks uneven and not ready for any games, but that's all right. It's December.

You look at the old dugout and the sanctity and safety of being in there for so many games wraps you up with more warmth. You remember the big orange water cooler on the far right side, polishing off a quick cup of water after sliding into home on a single by this kid who's a janitor at the high school now. You were only a freshman then.

Now you're a freshman again. But you're not playing baseball. All you've really got is all right here. Right on this little patch of land with some fences and some grass and some chalk and some dirt. Everything and barely anything.

Somehow this tear appears at the corner of your right eye. It's not that it's over—that you can deal with. It's just all those insignificant memories, all those little tidbits that you have no idea why you should remember them.

Standing in the outfield during practice, playing home-run derby, seniors versus lower classmen. You were a senior. The sun was shining down on your cheeks and sleeveless arms, so hot and beautiful. There's this innocence.

All those masochistic memories and the drugs and all that stupid and useful and victorious stuff is of no matter now.

Right now all you can feel is that sun on your arms, the leather on your left hand, the rough, solid feel of cleats on your feet, shouting trash at all the little underclassmen fucks. You can see Barron laugh behind his catcher's equipment. His old black catcher's gear.

One tear becomes a heavy breath and a sigh, looking up into old stars' million-year-old light.

Everything is so insignificant and hurts me.

"Life only sucks as much as you let it suck, and you can only die when your time has come, and everything you've needed to do has been done. If you realize that, you will have no fear of death, and in that you will have no fear of anything."

Barron told you that one day as he stood over you with the paintball gun pointed at your forehead. You couldn't move. And it's never really made sense until now.

Everything is so insignificant. How can anyone know when their moment has come, or will come, or if it even matters?

What's the point of anything when everything is nothing?

A breeze kicks through your hair and howls by the grated metal roof of the dugout. The grass is pressed down by the wind. The tear becomes cold in the breeze. And you sigh, look up at the faint stars again, and try your hardest to remember those insignificant times. Throwing batting practice. Learning how to throw a better changeup from your pitching coach. Spitting seeds through the holes in the fence between doubleheaders.

Another heavy sigh becomes a shudder.

Just memories. Not even tangible.

Just insignificant memories.

The sun beating down on your old, dirty, four-year-old hat. Squinting in the glaring sunlight.

Standing around in the locker room listening to music and getting in that game mindset.

So this is crying.

So these are the times you'll cherish forever and never forget.

And then you stand up, take another one of those big breaths, wipe red watery eyes, and walk away, up the same path you'd taken after every game, with your jersey off but your lucky undershirt on, bat bag slung over a tired shoulder, clowning with Barron about what you were gonna do that night.

But instead you're getting into your old car with its blue interior and broken dome light. You start her up, look in the rearview mirror with your sad wanna-be poet eyes, and drive away, trying to shake the feeling.

A passive attempt at something like being okay. Something like complacency. Something like copacetic.

And then you're home. It's a little after ten-thirty. Still no word from Barron. No call from Nikki. No more emails from Cornelius. And it begins to feel like you're the last person in the world who will ever know what this big plan is.

You dial Cornelius's office but you don't even get a ring. Maybe it's worse than you thought. But how can you look up the number for a guy when you don't even know his last name or where he lives?

And how important could you be to this guy if he never told you his last name? It's a fine line.

But you've never been a big fan of fine lines.

So you go into your room, somehow avoiding your parents who were down in the living room. They're so old now.

Then you lie down on your bed and read this old book of diaries written by some poet from what seems like a long time ago. And it seems like so little amount of time but all of a sudden you've read the whole thing and it's one in the morning.

You decide sleep is better than concern about your friend or the girl of your dreams, or baseball, or all those little insignificant memories of a time when you were just a different version of you. So you fold into the fetal position and listen to the wind howl off your roof until you don't remember finding sleep.

* * * * *

"SEPTEMBER MORN, WE DANCED UNTIL THE NIGHT BECAME A BRAND-NEW DAY," Neil Diamond croons up the stairs, down the hall, and through my door. Below that I can hear the sound of a mixing bowl as my mom seems to be making something in the kitchen. My second-last time I'll be getting out of this bed for six months.

I sit up and rub itchy sleep eyes with the palms of my hands. I can't remember a time when I've slept better than that in a long while. It was this deep, cool, cave-like sleep and I can't remember a solitary moment besides the blankets of darkness and the enveloping rest.

I wish I was still sleeping as I set numb feet on the plush carpet, tiny thick carpet strands packed close together massaging me as I walk. It's the kind of thing you never thought you'd miss. But self-imported dorm carpeting is nowhere near the level of quality of the carpet in the room you grew up in.

It's not like I really hate college. It's all right, I guess. It's just so predictable. "Whoa, man, let's drink tonight. Then we'll meet some fat girls and take them back to our room." Every night it's the same. I remember looking at my time there as just this learning experience by seeing how everyone else in the world lives. How other unremarkable people fill their unremarkable time. Try to live a life with their sanity. Or maybe it's me and Barron who are the insane ones. We hurt ourselves, we do drugs, we commit crimes, we steal painkillers, we smile all the while, believing ourselves to be enlightened because one of us has dreams that he thinks prolong his life and the other just wonders and worries how much longer his life will be.

There's something about playing with the idea of mortality that I've avoided for so long . . . ever since I was twelve. And I realize that the less I know about Barron's plan the more I'm in anticipation about it. I just know that I'm going to be doing something I really don't want to do tonight. I mean, I know that everything I stand for tells me to just trust Barron because he's never steered me wrong before, but I really can't.

So instead of even worrying about it anymore, after the red basement orgy I really have no expectations out of anything, especially Barron. So anticipation has subsided, and all I'm really concerned about is getting my mom to turn her music off and maybe get something to eat. It's New Year's Eve. It's a big important date on everyone's calendar.

Lots of people are probably setting disposable tablecloths on tables in suburban basements, buying paper napkins and matching paper cups, setting out two-liters of soda, little festive confetti strewn about all around. There are other people scoring some heavy shit for the evening, buying cocaine, ecstasy, weed, peyote, opium, speed. They really don't need any disposable party supplies like napkins and tablecloths. They just need good drugs and the company of some of their fellow cosmonauts.

Teenagers are looking for alcohol and condoms.

The elderly are looking for a phone call.

I'm looking for my best friend. But nothing. So I get up and check my email on the computer standing proud across the room.

The computer whirs on and goes through its little warm-up routine. This usually takes a minute or two so I head downstairs to get some food and turn the music down. My mom is cooking and running around the kitchen like crazy talking to herself—reciting the recipe—and saying good morning to me.

I say good morning with my groggy morning voice and she smiles and I grab some cookies and some orange juice and head upstairs to my waiting computer.

I open my email account and feel myself become much heavier in my chair as I see emails from Cornelius, Barron, Frue, and Samantha. I don't even know which one to open first. My mouth is dry so I take a swig of orange juice, bite into one of the cookies, and take another drink from the bottle. What to do. . . .

I felt like torturing myself so I decided to leave Barron's for last and opened Samantha's for groinular reasons.

Sender: HEYTHERES&MANTHA@aol.com
Recipient: Jibbawocky@aol.com

James,

Hey I just wanted to let you know what I was doing tonight in case you wanted to come. I'm going to be at the back of The Park. I want to see you there. See you then.

—S—

Then I opened Frue's email.

Sender: tsquir@us.navy.etau.mil
Recipient: Jibbawocky@aol.com

Jibba,

Sorry – couldn't make it for x-mas. Busy as a bee's wing. Best to our dusty family. Don't be stupid.

Frue

Man that sucks. I wanted to hear all about how he'd been doing. I could almost call Frue a better friend than Barron. But what can you do when Uncle Sam won't let you communicate with your family? Nothing at all. Just grin and bear it and hope he survives.

Two down, two to go. Of course, Cornelius's was next.

Sender: Corn5150@aol.com
Recipient: Jibbawocky@aol.com

Jibba,

I realy don't have much time to write this. I have a lot of calls to make. I'm not going to New York. I'm never going. I'm still to injured to do anything. I was just wondring where you've been the last few days. It's alright, I know your busy and your headed back to school soon. Just call me later, I've got some weird news about tonight.

I got this strange phone call that said tonight I was going to find out who fucked me up and runed all my art. Do you know anything about this? If you do, let me know, I don't know how much I can do so I might need your help, this is some weird stuff. I'm confused as hell. But I want revenge, that guy took almost everything from me. Everything I cared about . . .

Call me later man. See ya.

Cornelius

I already knew what was written in the next email. I didn't even have to open it. Barron was better than I thought.

Sender: BJ_Lover6969@aol.com
Recipient: Jibbawocky@aol.com

Jibba,

Sorry about last night. I'm sure you'll understand. Tonight be at The Park. Or I'm sure youv'e already figured that out by now. Knowing you I'd say you saw Samantha's email and opened that one first. Tonight's the night, playboy! Big surprise for you! All our friends! Take care o' your badass self. Will see you then.

Barron Justiculator, Stretcher of Holes

And so there it is. With a sour aftertaste comes the close of the four short emails, and it's all conveniently coming together on a night like New Year's Eve. What is this, a movie? Some stupid Hollywood script where the two best friends come together in some spooky parkland during New Year's Eve with the people who've affected their lives in the last six weeks?

No matter. What can I do—ignore all the invitations?

In one of his better moments, my fucker older brother once said, "Humans and events make for a curiously led dance."

He's right, which means he had to have taken it from someone else.

So many questions. But for now I go pack my bags, because in less than twenty-four hours, I'm gone from here for a long time.

* * * * *

I LEAVE myself a change of clothes for tonight and all the rogue boxers that I never liked and the oversized tube socks my mom bought before I left for school on the ground in the closet. Other than that, I'm all packed up for another six-month stretch at my state school run by fraternity fucks and psychotro-nico-alco-liberista freaks and forced attempts at cultural diversity and enlightenment that end up sounding like parrots doing impressions of the forest.

Looking through all the stuff I'm leaving behind, little knickknacks I couldn't possibly take to school with me: trophies, rocks, game balls, old papers, and all that stuff that's more than clutter but less than worth bringing. That stuff used to matter so much. Or at least more than it does now. The little dust mites stuck in crevices that can't be reached with a dust rag or one of those feathery contraptions. Dust is just old skin particles which in a way used to be me when I was old enough for this trophy to mean something. But I've left my skin back then, on this trophy, and there I sit.

Like a man losing his hair can look at it as if to say he's left a trail that could lead him back to where he began, to see his way back if necessary. It's like that, my old dry skin is packed under the knee of the catcher applying the tag to the runner sliding into home. I am in this trophy in the smallest of ways, which is all I'm looking for as I set it down and sit on the edge of my bed, staring at the screensaver on my computer, just thinking over all that's happened in the last six weeks, my goddam life. And with all that in mind I walk over to the computer and turn it off. It's time to pack this up as well, heading down to college again with my big, proud computer. This big towering machine that's my instant link to anything I'll ever need. But then again . . . who am I kidding?

* * * * *

AFTER MAKING another call to Cornelius's office, and getting no answer, I decided there was nothing I could do. The computer was packed so I couldn't send a reply email, which I should have thought of but didn't. There wasn't really all that much else I could do, so I left a message on his machine that said my phone number and that I didn't know his number so I couldn't reach him at his house and all that jazz.

The day slips by as I sleep and talk with my brother and mother and father. These little I-know-I'm-leaving-so-let's-spend-some-"quality"-time-together conversations. The type of thing I know I'll miss in four months. The kind of thing you'll always look back on and be glad you can see it, unless you have a stroke or something.

The day slips by as I get all my bags into the garage, shower up because my aunts and uncles will be here in a few hours, and I get one last nap in before they arrive.

It's so warm, so beautiful. The man on the television says he's never seen anything like this before. He says fifty-five-degree days with no clouds and subtle winds have never been seen this early into winter. He says something about pressures and unnamed Spanish children. I wasn't really paying attention. It's what I woke up to on the television after my nap. I was too groggy to really get it to register. And besides, I heard the hellos and how-are-yous coming from the living room, followed by the deep voice of my Uncle Robert. He was a big, burly man of about fifty-seven. He was talking about the fine weather.

I walk out and exchange in hellos and how-are-yous with the steady trickle of old family members coming in through our front door. They're asking me what I'm doing tonight and I'm telling them I'm going somewhere with Barron and they're smiling and asking how ol' Barron is doing, saying how they always liked him, how they're happy we're still friends even though I'm going to college now and he isn't. I'm smiling back. Everyone has such grand feelings on nice days.

I take everyone's coats into my parents' big bedroom with the big mirror attached to the big dresser. One of those real fancy fuckers with a real oak finish, real dark brown, lacquered heavily, and I remembered something that happened to me when I was thirteen years old.

* * * * *

SIX YEARS ago I was a horny thirteen-year-old kid looking for pornography in my parents' bedroom. Nobody was home, as it was summer break from school. My brother had a job but I was too young and both my parents were at work as well. I was looking for some cranking material and I'd used my brother's stash the day before and I wanted something new. I figured maybe my parents confiscated some of my brother's stuff at some point. As quickly and thoroughly as I could, I opened each drawer of that big dresser and jammed my hand in through all the shirts and socks and pants to feel the bottom and see if anything had been hidden in a corner.

I'd made my way down the left side and was searching my dad's sock drawer when my hand came across something heavy and metal. If there were a camera over my shoulder, it would have looked like the turning point in one of those after-school specials.

Jibba Got His Gun.

I gripped the object by the heavy handle and pulled it out of the drawer. It was dense, and so beautiful and sleek, with a polished-platinum look to it all around except the black grip. The gun was a work of art, so overbearingly impressive and scary. The potential of this heavy-ass piece of dead weight kept me in awe. Its silence was deafening.

I looked at myself in the mirror with the gun. I looked so out of place with this beautiful firearm in my hands, and here I was this wiseass thirteen-year-old kid.

I don't fuck around with guns though. I put it back where I'd found it. I just liked knowing that I knew where my old man kept his gun. I felt like a sort of adult then. It made me feel good. Like I was extra cool and grown up for that. I was a kid, what could I say?

I never found any porno, though. Stupid religion.

I shouldn't say that. Those religious assholes out there, including my parents, are a lot better than I am when you really break it down, but that's not saying much. I just have a real problem with people who can be so sure they are right about something so fuzzy. The only thing I really know is that I don't know much. I know that sounds like something an old fisherman would tell his apprentice, but it's true, so what of it? Intelligence I could do without. Life is too short to go around thinking about it too much. That's what people who are paid to think do so I just say go out there and kiss the girl you want to kiss, hurt yourself, smoke weed, drink alcohol, get in a fight, whatever. Just do it because it'll make life fun maybe. Don't ever think your opinion is correct. Mine isn't. Not usually, anyway. I'll be the first to tell you that I'm full of shit. I learned this because my parents haven't yet, and I don't want to be like them. They still listen, but I've stopped listening to the people they listen to.

Actually, I should say this, to be more precise. I don't know much, but I do claim little slices of knowledge. Not nearly enough, though, to make a cake.

* * * * *

SO ME and my family all sat down to this really impressive potluck dinner. Everyone made all their best food, my parents to boot with their famous lasagna and breaded chicken breast. So much good food. I thought to myself that *This was a great last meal*. I wouldn't be eating like this again anytime soon.

So I actually had a good time when I was at home. Everybody arrived around six and we ate at six-thirty, and then for like two hours we just sat around and had one of our family discussions/arguments. All in good fun. All in togetherness.

I come from an incredibly intelligent family. All my aunts and uncles are graduates from prestigious colleges, or alternatively they're uneducated autodidacts who started their own businesses. It's great listening to the ideas and thoughts they've accumulated over their stressful lives. They've sent children off to college who aren't here tonight. I asked Frue's mom about the email he sent me and she frowned and said she understood, that it was horrible we couldn't keep in better contact but that she herself had trouble keeping in touch with him. She said we should expect that at least for another year.

The conversation varied from religion to politics to the unfortunate undertakings in a high school out West, where a year ago some kids, armed with bombs and guns, entered their high school and attempted to murder as many of their peers as they could. That one was a conversation you had to step softly around to make your point. And I just listened to everyone. Sometimes they'd ask for my opinion, my having just graduated last year, and I'd chip in with the ol' two pennies. But mostly I just sat back and observed my conversational family. My own opinion, the real one I kept from my family, is that I can't believe the trend didn't start earlier.

And then it was around nine o'clock and we broke out the board games just like old times.

And then it was ten-thirty and my brother took off to the party at his friend's house. It was around that time that I excused myself also, because it took fifteen minutes to get to The Park and I wasn't sure how easy it would be to find everybody.

I felt really guilty leaving my family for the night, but I was a teenager and a freshman in college so it was expected of me to leave around that time so that I could go party with my friends. They all like Barron, would never suspect him of anything but laughs.

I liked Barron.

I'd only suspect him of almost anything.

And anyway, I feel guilty about everything as it is. To pile it on is to become morally richer, according to my beliefs, as long as I beg for forgiveness.

But I said my final goodbyes and hugged and kissed and wished happy-new-years to everybody. I felt so empty for whatever reason I don't know. I guess like I said I'm always sad when something ends.

I can usually gut through the feelings of guilt. And besides, I had shit to take care of. This promised to be one hell of a night.

* * * * *

So I hopped in my car and drove the fifteen minutes to The Park listening to a compilation I'd found that immediately brought me back to the spring of my sophomore year. I love when a song can almost make you feel exactly like you did some time way back when. But even that is wrong because you never really remember all the bad shit that was going on at the time that bothered you. It's like this one girl told me down at school, "Sure you miss your friends from home, but are they as perfect as you remember them? Just because you're in this situation where you're around people who aren't like them doesn't mean they're as great as you remember." And that's true, too.

Nothing was as great as you remember it, except those moments that were truly exceptional. And they are so few and far between. Your face is bathed in the light of exploding fireworks, and it's just so right, only so often, maybe once or twice ever in your life.

All this stuff passed through my head as I made that drive, cruising under the white streetlights as they climbed up my windshield and over the top of my car and off into the past. Always heading towards the end.

The Park is this giant plot of land that is under state protection and cannot be developed on or bought by commercial enterprises wishing to expand their corporate campuses. I used to come up here all the time in high school with dates because it's really romantic at night walking along this trail that goes around the lake at the center. Where you pull in there are these places you drive farther in towards the middle of the park. To the left are the biking and running trails, to the middle is the waterfall where I'd always make my first kiss with my date, feeling scared and excited, and to the right was the Park Lodge and where the park's police horses were stationed.

I drove straight ahead because I figured I knew what Barron was thinking. He knew how much the waterfall meant to me and anyone else in our town. It was the place where I first kissed Belle. I shut off the car. The last line of music I heard was something like "of laughter and soft lies," which seemed right.

And then I got out of the car.

This is it.

It all comes together.

* * * * *

I DIDN'T even expect to drink on this fine New Year's night. But when I got to this clearing something like fifty feet from the overlook of the waterfall I saw Barron sitting there with a bottle in his hand and a case of beer at his feet.

He stood up and gave me a hug. He said, "Good to see you, man. Have a drink, eh?"

And I sat down and we just chilled there for a little bit. The breeze was so nice, in the cool air all blowing all around the moonlit clearing, with the leafless limbs of the trees and shrubs swaying and whistling to me and my best friend. It almost felt religious.

And then Nikki appeared.

I said to Barron, "What?"

He laughed.

"Not bad, eh? She's here for you, kid."

"What?"

"Yeah, man. She was crying and crying and Jenna wanted me to do something so I called her up and told her to come tonight. That you'd be here. She said she had a lot to tell you."

"What were you thinking, man? And for God's sake, what the fuck is the whole plan here? Where is the guy? Why are you being so cool about this?"

He had a big laugh. "Easy, man. Have some drinks. Have a good time. Everything will reveal itself when it needs to be revealed. One step at a time. You know that."

Samantha winked as she walked by. I nodded.

Then Nikki was nervously walking towards me.

I took her by the hand and led her to the observation deck of the waterfall. The water sounded so powerful that night, with the wind and the march of a few dry brown leaves on the ground. The whole town had been blanketed in snow, but this warm weather was melting everything, and it all trickled toward the waterfall, which thundered below. Such beauty. I stopped right at the edge, with my right hand resting on the wooden fence they'd built to keep people from falling in.

After a moment or two of silence, I was too nervous to just go without doing anything any longer. "Barron said you had something to tell me," I said, and as I talked she changed her standing position and she leaned out of the shadows into the moonlight, and her *face*! I stammered and said, "Jesus, look at you."

She looked at me for another awkward moment. A wind kicked up and rustled her raven hair. She stared at me with something in her blue eyes. Something like sadness and longing. I couldn't pinpoint it.

She didn't say anything.

I started to talk again. "Nikki—" but before I could finish my thought she kissed me. The kiss was warm and wonderful. I was locked in this moment of perfect purity, what I'd been looking for. I was lost in this moment of everything I wanted. Belle couldn't fuck with my mind here. Cornelius's problems weren't shit. College was for the birds. All that mattered was that this perfect girl was kissing me on the overlook of a beautiful waterfall in a moment that has meant so much to me in my short, useless life.

And finally after a moment much too brief, she pulled back. She looked at me with that look again. And she walked away.

Now she was gone forever. It was a goodbye kiss. And there was no reasoning with it. There was nothing I could do. Lost and gone forever.

I stayed in that spot for around ten minutes in silence, both forearms resting on the fence, watching the branches and remaining leaves shimmy in the breeze, listening to the water make its final jump off the cliff and roar into the lake below.

I was shocked to find the girls had somehow snuck up behind me while I was lost in some thought I couldn't really figure out. They were drunk and trying to be quiet but one of the girls slipped on a stick and said, "Ow," and my moment alone was broken.

Barron lobbed me a bottle of beer and I opened it up and took a big swig. I needed to get intoxicated, real quick. I asked him for the bottle of vodka and he laughed and handed it to me happily. I brought this on myself. All of it.

"What about the cops? What if they come around and see us with all this?" Samantha asked, an actually valid point I'd been wondering.

"Don't worry about them. There's one dude working tonight, and he's getting drunk at the Lodge. I made sure of that."

"How?" Jenna asked.

"I bought two bottles of wine and left them for him with a kindly worded note," Barron said matter-of-factly.

"You think that'll work?" I asked.

"We'll be fine. Trust me, Jibba."

So I nodded and took another swig from the bottle, already starting to feel the warm numbing effects of the alcohol. I felt so bad, the way Nikki left me. That was such bullshit. She shouldn't have done that. She should have just called me and yelled at me, or spit in my face, or slapped me, or never seen me again. Anything but what she did. I already missed her.

"Fuck it, man. It's over. Live for the moment. I thought you knew that already. You're oh-for-two tonight, Jibba," Barron said putting a hand on my shoulder.

I knew. I just couldn't.

It's all coming together.

A decision is made.

I took another drink and looked at Samantha, who winked again. I walked out of Barron's grasp and grabbed her by the hand and led her back towards the parking lot.

On the way back, not sure why, I wondered where Cornelius was. I hoped he was finding his answers. Forget that, though. I took Samantha into my left arm. She didn't say anything. She smelled like candy.

We got back to the parking lot and I looked at my watch. It was eleven-twenty. It was time to fuck this girl in the back of my car.

She was drunk and leaning against me by the door. I led her directly to the backseat. She knew the plan. She knew the deal. I justified it in my head. *If I can't have the one I've been looking for all my life, I might as well have the one I can have. Fuck all this guilt.*

She backed in through the door and started taking off her shirt. I followed her every move as I climbed in the back with her, my shirt coming off with hers, my pants, her underwear, our everything. I took her into my arms and after some quick foreplay we were going at it like jackrabbits. It was that hot, vibrant, drunken sex. She was panting and moaning and it looked like we were clam baking the car up real bad, real good. She was great. It was great.

But it wasn't perfect. It was great, though.

And then we were done. We found a comfortable position and held each other for a little bit, still not talking. It was eleven-fifty. As I finally got my shirt back on, along with my pants and my hat, I said we should get back to the waterfall and celebrate the New Year with them. She agreed.

The night was cooler now that I was all sweaty and I could tell Samantha was cool too, so on the walk across the parking lot I put my arm around her and brought her in close to me. My New Year's fling. Kill them with kindness.

Or so I always thought.

We got to the top and Barron had also just gotten his shirt back on. He knew we were coming and he'd already had a beer cracked for me and Samantha.

This was to be my first ever New Year's where I wouldn't see Dick Clark counting down and watching all the little people in Times Square get half as wasted as I was. I always loved being warm when they were cold. High when they were drunk. I felt this nice distance between us. Anyway, my own Dick Clark just enjoyed a balls drop.

I thought about all the different people in my life and how they were welcoming this arbitrary holiday of the earth's latest revolution around the sun. I thought about the parties of the past and present. I missed random people I used to know a lot better. Old high school friends I never see anymore, old random hookups from back in the day, all sorts of folks . . . I missed them all. I realized that I'd made one final decision, and I'd brought it all on myself. I'd let it bring itself to me. I looked at my best friend in the moonlight and he drunkenly laughed at something he'd said and I saw Samantha and how impure everything was.

Barron held up the Indiglo face of his watch. We started the countdown.

Then it was three.

Then it was two.

Then it was one.

Then it was Happy-New-Years all around. I kissed Samantha again. I hugged Barron. I kissed Jenna. It was a great time. Two sets of best friends starting a new year together with the interesting cool people they'd just met and began fucking recently.

We partied together, drinking and laughing up a good time, feeling the new-possibility groove of the new year. The old footprints rising as we were drinking. The chemicals in our bodies becoming moisture as we replaced them with new ones. For old times' sake me and Barron burned each other with a lighter, but we were too drunk for it to hurt much.

Then it was two in the morning after no time at all. I was so happy. But it wasn't perfect.

Then the girls were telling us they'd arranged to have Nikki pick them up and they were heading out. I said my final goodbyes to Samantha. Told her I'd see her in six months and she smiled and said goodbye back. Then we kissed, and Barron kissed Jenna, and Nikki drove them all away.

Barron put his arm around my shoulder.

"Our night is just beginning."

* * * * *

"Have you ever seen a grown man cry?"

"What? No. Well, probably . . . Yes. Why?"

"Do you want to?"

"What do you mean?"

"Check this out."

He pushed a button on the keys in his hand and the locks popped open on his mom's truck. He then pulled the back door open and unveiled the tied-up figure of a middle-aged man.

"Getting him in here was fuckin' hard."

I couldn't believe what I was seeing. So this was the plan.

"This fucking guy's a fatass. You hear me, fatty?" he said and punched the bound man in the kidney. There was no response from the body, so Barron pulled some smelling salts from his pocket—what's weird is that as this scene unfolded I almost had a bigger unbelieving reaction to the fact that Barron had smelling salts in his pocket than a passed-out grown man in in his trunk—and waved them in front of the man's nose. *Is this really happening*, I asked myself. But by then Barron was pulling the bound man out of the back and standing him up. He was a large, middle-aged man, still hunched over in pain.

"So this is the guy?" I asked, trying to make it all out.

"Yup. This is the sick-fuck pedophile."

The man finally stood up. His eye socket was swollen almost shut, and his ear was bleeding. A black streak of bruise ran down his cheek.

It was Cornelius.

"Cornelius?" I asked.

"Ji'a?" he asked, both of us paralyzed with confusion. I saw blood in his mouth.

"Small world, huh?" Barron asked. "Now get up that hill, fatty."

I tried to stop him. "Barron—"

"It'll all be fine, Jibba," Barron said. "Trust me—you'll see."

"Are you okay, Cornelius?"

"He's better than a casket full of kittens, Jibba. Let's just do this."

Barron marched Cornelius up the stairs and to the platform by the waterfall with Cornelius shuddering in pain with each step of his right leg, the leg Barron had obliterated with the bat.

I'd never seen Barron like this before, with this kind of focus and intensity, at least outside of a sports field.

Barron shoved him onto one of the benches on the overlook. Then he punched him in the side of the head. I followed.

It clicked on some deep level. Barron had a plan for everyone tonight. But I was still forced to ask. "How do you know for certain it was Cornelius?"

He laughed. "I promise there's an electrifying explanation, kid."

"Okay," I said more confused than ever, reluctant to experience whatever this plan was now that it was right in front of me and I could feel its breath on my face. Cornelius's breath.

Barron looked wild in the face, in the eyes. It's like they didn't even blink. His brain was whirring with life, and I mean that. The gears of his brain were usually well-slicked and silent, but now he was like a computer that's got too much porn on it, whirring loudly as it endeavored to function normally while being overloaded by complicated excesses.

I was still pretty shitfaced, and ungodly confused, and my stomach was doing somersaults of anxiety. I could barely breathe, you see.

And then Barron spoke.

"Of course I arranged all this, Jibba. It was my planning, my doing, because this is it. This is my night—my last night. You see, I'll try to clear things up for you, Jibba, my friend."

"This sick fuck," he motioned to Cornelius, whose hands were still tied, "is Cornelius Pout. I don't know what kind of wild designs the Fates or Karma has created for us in our little existential cat's cradle, but Jibba you have been hanging out with and befriending the man who ruined my life."

I stirred as I stood, more than uncomfortable. "Barron—"

"Do you remember me, Cornelius? Do you remember little Barry? Little Barry the scaredy-cat? Remember what you did to me?"

"Barry the scare—?" and then Cornelius stopped, because he did remember. He remembered something, and his eyes filled with even more fear. And then the fear disappeared and his body relaxed, like he'd finally been allowed to give up.

"Yeah, I remember you."

"Shut your mouth, you motherfucker," Barron said. He pulled out a shiny, platinum handgun. "Or should I say kidfucker?"

"Jesus Christ, Barron, what the fuck are you doing?" I asked, terrified. *This isn't real*, I thought to myself. *I'm still at home and I'm still in bed.* I pinched myself but I couldn't feel anything. I was in shock. I was shocked.

"This isn't a dream, Jibba. You're not asleep, and yes this is me with your dad's gun. It's all real. It's real as hell. And it's all just a matter of time. All things will be explained.

"You see, James, when you were gone I went into another depression—thanks for calling, by the way. You were gone, my girlfriend was gone, everything was taken from me. So as bad you felt sitting in that dorm, I felt worse, brother. And that is all I have to look forward to for the rest of my life. I have nothing, will have nothing, and I don't even want anything anymore, besides vindication. Salvation. Besides an afterlife. Besides something completely different than this.

"So I'm incredibly alone one night, contemplating suicide because that's how I am, how I've always been—I had some *trauma when I was younger*—and I have this plan. I've had this plan all the while. It just came together like this, but it could have come together differently and still been my plan. You were sitting in your dorm room drinking a beer and I had this plan. Sure I didn't know it would be Cornelius here—but it's perfect, isn't it?—and I knew I could stave off my depression for this moment of perfection.

"I knew that I'd find someone who really made me sick. That was no problem. I just needed time to find him. And I did. Absolutely I fucking did.

"Jibba, do you remember my aunt who died?"

"Y—Yeah . . ." I struggled to make the word.

"Well she didn't die of any disease. She killed herself in that church. She had some *trauma* in her youth, you see. My mom cries every time she thinks about her, and that shit gets to me too. So now I have this sick bastard to finally complete my little plan.

"You, James Bentley, are here because you were meant to be here all along, to watch me in my moment, as my best friend. You are my best friend, Jibba, the best friend I could ever have, and I want nothing else than to have you here with me in my best moment. And this is your best moment, too! It was all in that goddam poem you sent me. Do you remember that? Your offering? Something somehow closed your Catholic eyes, Jibba, and I can't close mine.

"Cornelius, you're going to free yourself when I tell you." He pointed the gun at Cornelius's head. "Understand?"

I knew where this was going, and I knew what I had to do as well. Some things you just can't fight. Some battles aren't meant to be won. Can't be won. Not when you're me, at least.

"Yes. What are you going to do to me?" Cornelius asked stiffly.

"It's not what I'm going to do to you, asshole. It's what you're going to do to me."

He punched Cornelius in the gut again and then turned to me.

"Jibba, I love you. You are the greatest person this world has ever known. You have been the best friend anyone could ask for. I just can't take it anymore. We've had to overcome too much, Jibba. This is your last lesson from me."

I couldn't talk or swallow because my heart was in my throat, because I knew what was happening . . . a tear rolled from the corner of my eye. Finally I coughed out some emotion and said, "I love you, too, Barron."

"Fag," he said and laughed.

I laughed and cried.

"Cornelius, here's the knife," Barron said and threw him an unopened pocket knife—it landed on his lap. I looked over at Cornelius but he didn't look at me. He just kept staring at the ground.

Cornelius kept that look. Barron had the gun.

"You see, I've always been suicidal. I mean I've had my moments of happiness and everything. I've always had a good time, but I also knew that I'd kill myself. Like it was in the cards or something. The suicidal tendency is so tempting. It's always there, like a bass line in the song of my life. It's the answer to all problems. So clean, so perfect, just death, just the answer to the cosmic questions of whether there's a god and an afterlife. No more waiting. Which means no more living. Because that's all life is, waiting. And I'm sick of it, because my wait has sucked the biggest dick. I'm sick of everything and everyone, and everything everyone represents. I'm sick of not having my best friend around anymore, even though it's perfectly his right to better himself, to get away from this goddam shithole. To get smarter. I fucking miss him though. I'm sick of idiot girls who don't know what they want. I'm sick of my unhappy mother and son-of-a-bitch father and their mindfucking beliefs and bitterness. I'm sick of the sad memories I have outweighing the possibilities of the future.

"I need to free myself from desire.

"And it's never been done this way that I know of. This will also answer the question of whether if you are willfully murdered if it is suicide. I'm just a big lab rat. All three of us are rats. The lawyers in the afterlife are going to love us. God's hysterical witnesses. And I say fuck it. Either I'll be a martyr for my own cause or I'll just die and whatever happens is fine with me. I don't care anymore. And there's no way I'm changing my mind. Not after all the thought I've put into this. So don't even think about it, Jibba. I can't be convinced of anything anymore. The trap is closed.

"I just want you to really understand what I'm doing here. When I turned ten years old—a few months before I fell into the hands of this sick fuck—I had this thought in church that maybe my whole life is a prayer, and I started it off, at that age, with this big In-The-Name-Of-The-Father-The-Son-And-The-Holy-Spirit, and I thought, *Well at the end of my life, the prayer will be over, so I'll say 'Amen' and that will be the documentation and reflection of my life, this big prayer.* And that's what I'm going to do now.

"Cornelius, when I say 'Amen' you're going to cut the tape on your wrists and you're going to grab the gun and you're going to shoot me. I really don't care where as long as you do it until I'm dead.

"You'll free me from desire, you worthless fuck."

I can't really describe what I was. Fuck it. I'm sick of explaining everything anyways. I felt exactly how you'd feel if you knew your best friend in the world was about to die. Because he was. And I could see it coming now.

"Cornelius, it was me who put you in that cast and broke your nose and destroyed your art. I did it because you are one sick piece of shit and I hope that you die, you unsuccessful fuckup drunk unhappy motherfucker. You are scum, and my last laugh in this fucked life will be to die at the hands of one of the many people who fucked my life."

Cornelius looked surprised at first, something like *Is he kidding*, but now he was more serious, this look of *I have to do this* came over his face. It all dawned on him.

"Jibba, I want you to learn from all this. You've always been with me in the past and I've tried to never steer you wrong. I cared for you like a brother. My brother. And now is my final lesson. I'm just wondering if you're willing to learn it. If you have the capacity at this point in your life to understand how much it means to me that I die like this, at the hands of a man who makes me sick, to a man I hate more than life itself. It's so perfect this way, kid. I am so Zen right now. Knowing you're right here, and nothing else matters in the world. Because Jibba, you gotta toss the cone—gotta make the little bitch cry. And once that's done, you know that it'll all make sense. I love you, man.

"Cornelius, you morose fuck, it's time. Now cut that tape and pick up the gun with a glove or something because my prints are all over it. It'll look like suicide, pal. Plus I have a note in my pocket. Don't worry about Jibba. I can guarantee Jibba knows what he's doing and won't go to the police. He knows how badly I want this, and he has a lesson to learn.

"She's offering it to you, Jibba. It's in your hands, kid.

"Now come and get me, Cornelius. Make me an angel.

"God, forgive me for my sins . . . Amen."

The world was in this slow motion as it felt like everything and nothing happened all at once. I never saw anything happen. I just saw this scurrying and Barron smirking and looking skyward with his eyes on the stars and the last thing I saw was his face in the moonlight before I turned to my left and threw up.

Then I was running down the stairs and I heard a gunshot, and another gunshot, and I stopped at my car and puked again. I turned around and looked up the hill. It was the same brown hill it always was—it didn't care. The dirt was still dirt, the few plants still shimmying in the night breeze. I went back up.

What I saw when I reached the top of the hill kicked me in the stomach. Barron, my greatest friend, was dead on the ground in a fatal pile of himself. There was no romance to it. He was himself like an empty shell casing. Cornelius was dead, too. Barron had been shot through the heart, and Cornelius had shot himself through the temple—the gun on the ground between them, glinting in the moonlight.

My father's gun—I picked it up and rushed to my car.

I don't remember driving home and I don't remember coming in if I was quiet or not. My parents were still downstairs with their guests and it was late but they had a life. The music and the clatter were loud—I hoped loud enough to muffle the sounds of my entrance.

I staggered through the halls, finally coming to my senses a bit. Realizing who and where I was. I was walking down the hall, into my parents' bedroom, thinking about all the lessons I'd ever learned from Barron. All the important things he'd taught me about how being truly happy could never happen because it would never be appreciated until being truly depressed took place. That perspective was needed. Pure depression was suicide. So maybe for that last glimpse of time I'd looked at him he was truly happy before he died. Was that what he was trying to teach me?

I was entering the house still wondering what Barron was trying to tell me about everything. Was everything worth it? Was my shitty dorm and my loss of my best friend the path to total happiness? To purity? My total depression . . . could it be worth it to go on? How could I have befriended the man who ruined my best friend's life?

Panicking, pulling the gun from my pocket, I was opening my father's sock drawer, to put the gun away, and then thinking that maybe Barron wanted me to join him like I'd always done—that that's why he'd used my father's gun. We hurt each other together, we fucked girls together, we were friends together, so were we to die together? Was that it? Was that his whole plan, to have me kill myself like him? He'd been so strange lately. I am thinking about this but there are many more feelings than thoughts.

I am standing in front of a large mirror with a gun in my hand, looking myself in the eyes wondering if I'm going to kill myself because I'm crying and I miss the greatest girl I could ever imagine and I blew it all through my stupid choices and my lack of whatever I am. Barron believed in himself, and then he killed himself. After the death of my religious convictions all I really believed in was Barron, so should I wonder why I still have this gun in my hand? It doesn't even feel like he's dead and still I'm here. I'm looking at myself in the mirror and I'm much older now than I was back then, when I saw myself before. I'm crying. I'm thinking. Or maybe I'm only reacting. Maybe Barron's action is causing this reaction—Barron's pendulum swinging back to wherever it's going next.

Right now.

I'm standing in my parents' room with a gun I found when I was so much younger, its barrel is kissing my temple, I'm looking myself in the eyes in the big mirror, the metal of the gun glinting softly in the lamplight from my parents' pathetic nightstand, and I'm sobbing and I'm thinking about my great friend Barron.

I'm crying—I have my answer.

And Jibba

I THINK I have cancer. Cancer or Multiple Sclerosis. Or Amyotrophic Lateral Sclerosis. Something fatal. Scleroses. Degeneration. Worried sick. I get these weird headaches, and sometimes my vision is blurrier than other times, and it feels like one of my legs is weak and numb, and sometimes my muscles fasciculate like rats under blankets, or sick musicians tapping out some sad death dirge. I think they're trying to warn me. I will awaken alone in the middle of the night, and my hands will still be asleep, with the pinpricks and the pain and the numbness, and I have to consider that it means there's something wrong in my brain. My brain or my spine. I've either got a tumor growing in there or plaques developing—I don't know exactly how MS works, but that's probably what I've got. Whatever would be the worst. I'm pretty sure there's definitely something wrong. The universe throws itself on top of me, and grinds me to nothing, unaware of its crushing bulk, like a friendly retard.

I can feel this anxiety growing in my stomach, and I start to feel cold (like I always do—I always feel cold), and I can feel little vibrations in my feet, and when I try to forget it, that's when it gets really bad. Distractions don't take. My breathing is so shallow—it shouldn't be this shallow. I'm still a young man. (Not that young, though.)

I've been dying for as long as I can remember.

When I was a kid, I spent at least a half-hour every night before bedtime praying that when I awoke the next morning—some unremarkable day in my youth—I would be protected from the vile sad-makings of the ever-present agents of Satan, who were forever chasing me through the halls of my suburban safety and trying to corner me in despair, aiming to infect me with beguiling diseases and snap important bones at crucial moments when I could least afford the loss or stand the pain—and shake my faith!

Like the time I broke my arm just before summer break from an awkward first year in public school, and I had to spend the glorious sunshine days inside with my itchy-sweaty arm propped on a pillow while I watched mind-rotting television programs and ate chocolate/peanut butter/caramel/pretzel bars by the handful, the healthy cut of my body turning blubbery and pale—and muscular atrophy was my summer babe.

I'm looking up brain-cancer symptoms on the Internet right now, and they all seem to fit. I can see how I've recently felt all of these harbingers. Nausea, blurred vision, strange neuropathies. I can see it now. "Well, Jibba, it's probably nothing, but let's get you an MRI anyway." Then it's, "Please call us back, Mr. Jibba; Dr. Greenstein needs to see you concerning your test results." Then it's cancer or MS, crying, surgery or daily injections of wild chemicals, then a slow or rapid deterioration from cachexia, the further disintegration of my pathetic will to live, and then, when the cancer returns, or when the MS gets really bad, or when I'm whittled by Amyotrophic Lateral Sclerosis, I'll have to kill myself.

The phone rings.

"Hi," my boss says. "Come see me."

My boss is a tall, ugly cunt. She started this company when she was my age, and she's made it into one of the most successful businesses of this sort in all of Los Angeles, but that doesn't change the bona-fide fact that she's an asshole fuck.

I push myself away from my desk, which is situated in the middle of a large room full of congruent cubicles, and walk past the poster I put on the carpeted half-wall that shows a police photo of a young suicide victim who hung himself in his dorm room, across the bottom of which says, "Hang in there, baby!"

My boss's office is, like her, insipid, inane, and cold. It's boring, yet pretentious. As described by one of our designers, "It's very 'come in' but also 'leave.'" It's the nest of a bird situated in a very high tree, a bird with no predators, the cock of the squawk, a long-necked, hideous griffin. Fuck her.

"Hey, I need you to get me two more reports by tomorrow

night," she says, preening herself with talon fingers. Her hair is fake—we can all see that—but she preens her fake feathers anyway, because for her the illusion is more valuable than the truth. She's one of those people.

"Yeah," I say, looking at the books on the wall next to her, a Gatsby-like collection of wonderful titles—their spines crisp, their page-corners unturned. "That shouldn't be a problem at all."

"Good," she says, reclining. "How's things going?"

Ha! I'm sure my condition is right up there on her mental checklist of things to give a shit about. This is a woman who asks for my opinions and then cuts me off to give her own opinions, ending the conversation before briskly walking away from my desk, uncomfortably eyeing my inspirational poster and other effects, like the copy of a bound Pejorative Dictionary I co-wrote in college ("Mexican: see Spic, Spick, Beaner, Wetback, Donkey Cowboy").

"I don't know," I say. "Fine, I guess."

"That's not a very positive answer," she says.

Fuck you.

My boss oozes positivity. Always positive. It's obvious to me that these layers of optimism are a necessary compensation to disguise the fact that she's pregnant with self-doubt.

"Just been doing a lot of thinking lately," I say.

"I've been there," she says. "When I was your age . . . ."

At this point she begins another ten-minute monologue. This is the sort of cooze who tells stories for herself—stories that begin, proceed, and end entirely in the middle, and which last for as long as the expediency of the moment permits—not because anything within them has anything valuable to offer, but because it is her turn to talk.

"Yeah," I say, thinking to myself as I look at an untouched volume of James Joyce's *Ulysses* that James Joyce is one of those writers who had everyone fooled, that his almost incomprehensible prose was necessary, like my boss's positivity, to disguise the fact that he had nothing new to say. He had everyone by the thumbs, including my shit-for-brains boss—him and Faulkner. What's so genius about writing like an idiot?

"I guess that makes sense."

"Now go get 'em, Jibba! Get positive!" she says, leaning forward with a dismissive smile that's supposed to inspire me but which makes me want to retch into a potted plant and then throw my dirty puke in her pockmarked face.

I walk out of her office and fantasize about punching through the wall-glass and using a sharp window shard to cut long, jagged, vertical lines up the veins in my arms, the blood pumping out so fast there's nothing any of my horrified coworkers could do except watch me die with a coy smile on my face.

The only reason I don't is because I haven't written the letter yet.

I sit back down at my desk and return to my anxiety.

This website says anxiety is one of the symptoms, too.

My phone rings again. I look at the display and see that it's Rachel.

"Hello," I say, pinning the phone to my ear with my shoulder while I type into the search engine "blurred vision + anxiety."

"Hi," Rachel says quietly. "I'm going down for a smoke. Want to come with me?"

The search doesn't yield anything useful—nothing I haven't read already.

"Sure," I say and hang up.

While I wait for her to find me at my desk—she's a girl, after all, and standing when they say they're ready is an exercise in futility, so I usually wait for her to come to me because I don't have patience for that feminine mystique shit—I open my notebook and carve a few more words into the worn pages.

. . . a trek, a trudging march down into the fire,
my head ablaze, my eyes roiling coal, the puffs of my breath savaging the air in this lonely cellar,
I cannot outdistance this far corner.

It sucks.

Rachel is wearing a red skirt and black blouse today. She must have shaved her legs last night, because today they are on full display—haunting, taunting, tantalizing, and tempting me. Begging me to caress them with my hot hands and greedy wet tongue. She has her arms folded across her flat stomach, which pushes her delicate breasts to a salacious new perkiness, and she's looking at me.

"Ready?" she asks in her sultry voice as she gently strokes a few strands of hair from her eyes.

I close the Internet browser and stand. "Sure," I say with a grin, catching her seductive glance. She smirks back and turns with a twist of her hips that spins the hem of her skirt into a wide circle, revealing for a brief moment (unintentionally, mind you, as her spin was more to be cute than anything) a winking peek at her black panties, and instantly I have a rock-hard erection pressing uncomfortably against the teeth of my zipper.

She walks down the hall, past the office tenements of my coworkers all gazing slackjawed into their computer monitors. My hard sensitive dick, like a divining rod, follows close behind her close behind. Every now and then she turns back and catches me looking—eyefucking her—and she smirks again. She knows exactly what she's doing to me. And I hate her for it.

We get outside, and it is powerful heat and unbearable brightness. It is my oft-repeated theory that Los Angeles is the world's foremost producer of glint. Everywhere you turn, the magnificent sun spits glints and glimmers off of the galaxy of metal and glass that comprises this city, damaging your eyes (the cause of my blur? Not likely, but noted) and leaving smudges across your field of vision. The trend of movie starlets wearing massive sunglasses could only have started here, because there's no such thing as a sexy squint.

I turn and face Rachel and the building, where there is relief from the sun-trauma, and where Rachel is making a lovely O with her mouth as she places the slim little cigarette between her sweet pink, shiny lips.

Obviously, my mind is on something besides the cigarette.

"God, this job sucks," she says after her first toke on the butt.

"Yeah," I say, watching her lips as they gracefully push the smoke into a wispy stream that floats into the glass behind her. "It's a job; of course it sucks."

"Yeah, but not every job sucks," she says.

No shit, Rachel. Wow, great insight. Just take your panties off and let me be done with you.

"That's true," I say. "Our jobs do, though. That's for sure."

"What's wrong?" she says. She can tell when something is wrong. She can tell because lately there's always something wrong with me.

"Same old," I say.

She playfully rolls her eyes. "What is it this time?"

"It's gotta be a tumor, or MS," I say. "Fuck, I don't know."

"You have to learn to relax, Jibba," she says with an unintentionally condescending smile—like I'm six years old and have scraped my knee. "I get really worried too, sometimes."

"It's not that easy," I say. "I try, you know. I really try, but when I wake up, or when the slightest inconsistency arises, it's back."

"I know exactly what you're talking about," she says, even though she doesn't have a fucking clue. "Every time I get worked up, Taber reminds me to close my eyes and repeat my mantra." Taber. Rachel's doucheboyfriend whom I'd like to watch drown in shitty piss. He reminds her of her asinine "mantra," as if either of them even had a third eye to open. *Taber* reminds her to relax. Taber can die of Hepatitis AIDS for all I care.

"That helps, I'm sure," I say. I don't want to argue; I just want to lay this little girl down on the grass and fuck her for the ten seconds I'm good for and then clean myself off and go back to my desk and fret. Instead, she just sucks in another toke and looks me up and down. She does this every now and then to keep me interested. Like everything else she does, she just does it so I can lust after her and she can feel like she's still "got it" even though she's been with Taber since Hannibal crossed the Alps on an elephant.

"You look good today," she says, approving my choice of clothing and hairstyle. Apparently, today I am hiding my pudge well.

"Thanks," I say, all of a sudden nervous. "You . . . ah . . . You too, for sure." I later add, "You look great."

She smiles. "Thank you," she says, looking down, a touch of rose spreading across her cheeks—she's a living poem of exotic flirtation, and like a poem she is something I can contemplate but never touch. But I don't want to touch a poem. I don't want to spew my semen in a poem's mouth.

"Your legs look really sexy in that skirt," I say honestly, though playing it off playfully. "Shit!"

"Really?" she asks, again blushing. "Thanks, Jibby!" The condescension has returned. The beast of the ego she so vehemently denies exists has been sated, so she quickly returns to her throne, having slummed long enough to excite the fat muck-covered vassal at her perfect feet.

I kick around a pebble while she smokes. I turn away from her briefly to swing my erection up behind my belt, which usually serves to drain the blood out so I can face her again without her knowing just how . . . prominent . . . the lust I can barely disguise from her is. I read somewhere that this maneuver is called a "German Soldier," probably owing to the Nazi salute my prick is now exclaiming.

"Did I tell you what my grandmother did?" she asks, sucking the cigarette right down to the butt. (I've got something she can suck down to the butt.) "She's getting a lawyer now."

Ah yes, her grandmother. The soiled cunt. A woman who married into money (no doubt her granddaughter's secret ambition) and who then took on the airs of a completely different person—someone who acted as though she herself earned the fortune that was a supposed corollary benefit of her true love. I have heard so much about this grandmother and her battles with her own family that I am half-tempted to find this woman and suffocate her with her own fecal diaper. Instead, I get to talk Rachel through her problems with her vexatious family, problems with her idiot friends, her unconscionable metrosexual boyfriend, and the people who don't like her stupid art. In return, I get distracted insights into my anxieties and not-so-secret million-dollar sexually frustrated hard-ons that die lonely deaths tucked behind a five-dollar fake-leather belt.

"I guess that makes sense," I say. "Considering everything you've told me, that's the obvious next step."

"Not really," Rachel says, ever the contrarian. "She could drop the whole thing."

Does this girl ever listen to herself? Or think? Dropping the whole thing is the last thing someone like her grandmother would do, and for Rachel to think that makes me wonder what I find so attractive about her.

But then she bends over to stub out the cigarette on a low foot-rail and my mind blanks out. I become a caveman, my hands twitching considerably in witness to the battle as the bastard ethical part of my brain holds them back from grabbing her hips and using her hot wet vagina to masturbate myself to satisfaction.

We both head back inside, me refusing to hold the door for her as my erection goes back down and I hate her again.

"Dropping it doesn't sound like something she'd do," I say. "Not after this long, and not after burning this many bridges. Napoleon and Hitler invaded Russia for the same reasons. What makes you think your grandmother is any different from those maniacs?"

"You shouldn't say stuff like that," Rachel reminds me. I say stuff like that all the time, and she usually laughs. Nevertheless, her insights and ethics are typically determined by the necessities of the moment, and her brain must have had a burst of some chemical or another that made her feel bad for agreeing with me, so instead of facing her own reality she had to chastise my observations.

"Sorry," I say, because I don't want to argue with her. Arguing with Rachel—and most women, in my experience—is like playing table tennis when the other side of the table is stood vertically—whatever spin you put on the ball, no matter how expertly you do it, the wall just puts the opposite spin on it and sends it back. You're always wrong. Her ethic is to always be correct in the moment, no matter how wrong she is objectively. Probably because an objective universe is a scary universe (I know because I believe in an objective universe, and I'm scared), and Rachel, who has made men's heads turn since she was twelve, has always been "right," and now that she's facing the sour side of maturation, she needs to cling to the feeling that daddy's little girl is still always "right."

When I get back to my desk, I have several work-related

emails to go through. A couple of shit-wits from our legal department need my help with structuring the company's contract boilerplate. It takes me a half-hour, after which I still have three hours of "work" remaining in the day, which I spend on the Internet, trying to figure out if my blurred vision is optic neuritis—a sure sign of MS.

* * * * *

THE DAY ends at exactly 5:30 pm, when my chair spins around and around from the haste of my exit. I hurry downstairs to my motorcycle, fire up the engine, and lay another rubber patch on the pavement, zooming off to my apartment, which is only a couple miles away. I break every speed limit between work and home, zooming through red lights, my blood with a thousand eyes in every direction, feeling for danger while my brain and hands and rocket bike create it and revel in it like a pig in hyperslop. The rush and release and my greed for speed—I need to get away from that place. I need to get away from Boss Bird and Rachel's pleasing, teasing knees and all the rest of those fuckfaces.

I park at my apartment and see that my beautiful new neighbor—a young blonde named Wyldflowyr, who obviously has revolting hippies for parents or had her birth certificate filled out by an illiterate nurse—is checking her mail. I decide to check mine, even though I never get anything except unabashed reams of junk mail.

Wyldflowyr closes the small metal door to her mailbox and turns in my direction.

"Hey," she says.

"Hi," I say, and I can't think of anything else to say. She's obviously looking for eye contact, but it just doesn't happen. Like there's a pile of bricks on my eyebrows, holding my gaze on the pavement. My breathing goes even shallower than normal. I can smell a faint hint of a scent my ex-girlfriend used to wear back in high school emanating from this lovely dish. A dozen memories of awkward sexual incompetence hurry to the fore of my mind, and I see her curly blonde hair and her smooth skin, and now she's walking by.

Shit.

I walk upstairs, enter my mediocre apartment, and plop on the couch. There is a half-hour until my roommate gets home. This is my favorite half-hour of the day. It's the longest possible time before I have to go back to work, and I can revel in long-sought silence. In the wonderful quiet, broken only by the whir of distant traffic and the occasional poo-too-tweet of summer birds, I open the book I'm currently reading—a soldier's history of World War II—and I let the words in, and the images, and the stories fascinate me totally. I am above all things a bibliophile, with a specialization in the European theater of WWII.

A half-hour later my roommate unlocks the door and walks in. My roommate is my brother—Vernon.

Vernon walks straight to his room; the two of us don't even acknowledge the other. No need. He emerges a couple minutes later, having replaced his work clothes with a worn pair of shorts and a sleeveless T-shirt. His arms are striated—"ripped" as the kids say out here—like the rest of his body. Vernon clangs around the kitchen for a few minutes. I barely notice because the one world I have free from my fret and hate is the faculty of my mind when it is reading. To borrow a joke stolen from Jerry Seinfeld, "I could read [the sports page] if the plane were going down."

Vernon pops on the TV and places his tuna sandwich and salad on the coffee table. Immediately there is the yammering chatter of two sports commentators arguing the finer points of which one of them is more full of shit. (The catch is that they're both full of shit. It's like what my father used to say about sports writers, "They're always right about yesterday and wrong about tomorrow.") I return to my reading while he flips through the channels.

"You talk to Mom today?" Vernon asks after a while.

"No," I say, putting the book down. "Why?"

"It's her birthday."

"Oh."

"You gonna call her?"

"Maybe," I lie. I'm not going to call her. I only call her when it's completely necessary. And because I'm a radically independent person, that's not often.

"You won't," Vernon says, chewing his tuna.

"Did she call me on my birthday?" I ask.

"You told her not to, dude," Vernon says. He's got a point. My mother and I had just gotten into a big fight over the fact that I was thinking about quitting my job. Turns out I was right, in that I quit that spirit-raping job, and it was the best thing I ever did. That was more than six months ago. I soon thereafter found my current job, which also sucks, but which is at least tolerable—twenty-five steps ahead of the indignity of writing copy for those shitheads. Shows what a fuck-all cooze of a parent she really is. Now that I'm out from the suffocating cloak of her whorish idiocy, I am free of the tumor that birthed me. Today, I am expected to call and celebrate its birth? NUTS!

"She and I have nothing to say to each other," I say. "Nothing that hasn't already been said."

"She misses you, man," Vernon says. "She was really hoping you'd call."

"I was really hoping she and Dad would stay together, but then there's no pleasing that poisonous woman, and that sort of ended that," I say. "So I guess we'll both have to live with the disappointments she created."

"It's not like that, Jibba," Vernon says. "And they ended up back together, didn't they?" Vernon's always cool. He's been Californicated for real.

"Whatever," I say, picking up the book. He drops the subject, which I appreciate momentarily before I am back again in a ditch in Holland, hungry and cold, preparing myself to take a German machine-gun nest two hundred yards to the east.

That's how the night proceeds. My phone doesn't ring. I don't get any email. I am left alone to my own devices, and I spend this and most evenings in the minds of the poetic and literate and interesting, free from the boring tedium of the forgettable majority of the so-called people around me. I have grown to read about and love war. It is life distilled to its most basic and overpowering aspects: the mind and body desperate at their respective peaks, a man fighting for an idea, and for his brothers around him, and women helping those men return to battle, or return home as wounded heroes. If he is dying, he can die for a reason.

If only I had a war!

* * * * *

I AWAKE in the middle of the night. It's only been three hours since I fell asleep, and I need to use the bathroom. Frequent bouts of urination—did I read something about that before? An early indicator of Parkinson's? At this point it's all a bit muddled. It's too late. The apartment is silent and dark except for a few bands of moonlight streaming in through the large window in the living room. I piss on the inside of the bowl, not directly into the water, but rather down the inside walls. Even the gentle hiss of my piss is thundering in this midnight silence. I don't want to wake up Vernon.

Walking back to my room I think I see something on the couch. Is that a person sitting down? A murderer? I see some sort of form.

It's a suit coat.

I return to my bed, collapse on my stomach, and lay there in the suffocating silence. I can barely breathe.

Fucking Rachel. How can someone do that to someone else? She must know that the animal lust booming from my planetary testicles is slowly driving me into the basin of the damned. Were I doing that to a fellow coworker, I would not provoke their lust with flirty tricks. I would maintain a normal formal distance—physically, emotionally. I would not torture. I would not look for little victories over my obsessive's libido and revel in the crunch of their broken, natural desires.

But all of that is merely a work in supposition, because in truth there is not a woman who works there who could possibly find me attractive. Not only am I a fat tubbo, but surely they can see what I can feel: atrophy. Disintegration. Disease. No woman would willingly pair with the fat and dying unless possibly she was severely abused by a fat uncle who later died of lymphoma in her crib. I would set such a foundation myself—I'm probably not below such cruelties—but I don't have the time or patience to wait for my abuse to turn into something resembling consensual ass-play, and I don't find children particularly attractive.

Cursed, I tell you!

I think about Rachel's legs wrapped around my waist, her moaning mouth breathing hot on my face as she reaches a shaking cascade of sweet orgasms, and I fuck my hand to completion. In the midst and mist of my personal pillow talk, I fall asleep again.

* * * * *

IT'S FRIDAY now. The long-awaited end of the work week. I've just gotten back from my lunch break, which I spent under a tree in a park near our building. I go there every day. Most of the time it's just me, my food, and my book, but sometimes a Mexican nanny will push a stroller laden with blonde-haired/blue-eyed children across the lawn, or a homeless bum will be reaching his diseased hands into the gaping black maw of an overstuffed garbage can. Possibly looking for bottles or cans or something. I don't know. I can barely look at them, and I simply cannot talk to them. It's not that I hate them for being homeless, but I've read enough medical periodicals and seen enough medical dramas on television to know that homeless people could be carriers of drug-resistant diseases and not even know it—infecting people left and right while being cried over by liberal coozes for exhibiting a quiet homeless dignity that is actually the stifled monologue of the clinically insane.

I'm slightly sweating from the vigor of my plodding pace (I've really got to lose some weight) as I sit back down at my desk and open my company email account to find five more requests from the idiots in the legal department (ah, yes, law school, the proverbial parachute cowardly students take up to the high-dive because they're afraid of the splash when they hit the water after graduation) who need me to once again fix the wording of an important letter our company is sending to a client in Australia. As always, time is pressing. (It really isn't, but stressing the importance of haste is an easy way to lend credibility and importance to the hastener's cause, and by extension, job.)

Rachel is wearing some ugly frock Taber bought for her last year. It makes her look like she's on the losing end of a Native American beauty contest. Not only on the losing end, but also slightly offensive. The one benefit of whatever that is (a shirt? a dress?) is the fact that when she raises her arms to fix the ponytail at the back of her head if I stand at the right angle I can see down her sleeve and to the warm peach hug of her bra and tits. I take a mental snapshot of this lovely Friday treat and file it away in my extensive mastur-bank, out of which I will be taking copious withdrawals tonight.

Time flies by while I catch an embarrassing number of gaffes in the legal copy, and soon it's time for another of Rachel's smoke breaks. Her woman-sense is on high today, because she shows up at my desk just as I send the file back to our lawyers and am open for distraction.

I look her up and down, and I really hate that thing she's wearing. She can see I'm not as impressed today, and the little imp smirk at the corner of her mouth—that smirk of ownership—disappears. I can see she knows this because she breaks from the pattern of our daily interactions by stepping into my cubicle and feigning interest in one of the files on my computer. "What's this?"

As she steps forward, her leg touches mine, and it's immediately countdown to ignition. I can smell a light fruity scent. I want to bury my face in her stomach while my fingers manipulate her clitoris to full stimulation. I want her delicate hand down my pants, jacking me off eagerly while she moans in my ear, trying to position herself so that nobody in the office notices our fuck-play.

"It's a book I'm writing," I say.

She can sense the magnification of my lust. She must be able to see the twitches in my forearm. I know this because she backs away to her normal distance, coolly satisfied.

"Ah," she says, as if waiting for me to finish a thought I thought I'd already finished. "Can I read it?"

"I don't know," I say. It's dangerous for her to read it, and it's not really done yet. If she read it at this point, she'd think I was obsessed with her, and she'd fail to recognize the fact that I'm only obsessed with her body.

"I've liked the other stuff you've showed me," she says (a poem I had published in a fourth-rate literary magazine and a short story that was wordlessly rejected by the faggots at *The New Yorker*). "I'd love to read your book sometime." Oh, how she gives of herself! The saint!

Rachel is one of those girls—one of those people—who thinks that the deep desire she feels to do better for this world makes her a giving, liberal, helpful person. People like Rachel see the old adage that "The road to Hell is paved with good intentions" as something that only applies to other people. I have an uncle who says simply awful things to everyone. "You should lose some weight," to my still-baby-fat-laden young female cousin. "If niggers had any work ethic, they'd be Mexican," to me in front of my old friend DeLane. The only difference between girls like Rachel and guys like my Uncle Rayford is that Rachel feels that the love in her heart somehow magically bursts forth from her chest and warms the world with its delightful intention, while my uncle feels nothing in his heart but honestly believes that the things he says are for the good of the person listening. They both believe themselves to be helping other people, but are they right? You could argue that Rachel's unfulfilled intentions are less harmful than my uncle's forked tongue, but I don't see it that way. Aristotle's concept of ethics begins with the idea that everyone is trying to do good. No matter who they are or what they're doing, the vast majority of people are endeavoring to make themselves, their world, and those around them, better; nevertheless, the trouble begins when one tries to define what is good. Rachel does nothing, but intends to do everything. The world at large remains the same. The only thing that changes is a feeling within Rachel that allows her to believe herself to be an altruist. A so-called good person. Like she has sacrificed herself for the greater good of humanity, while in reality she has done nothing but satisfy her own ego—an exercise, ironically, in selfishness. My uncle does something, and many times he makes things worse by sacrificing whatever point he had to the terribly negative connotation that goes with it. But sometimes his observations plant a seed that later flowers into a maturation point for the listener. I know because it happened to me. And Rachel has never done anything to make me a better person.

Nothing.

"It's not really done," I say, standing. "And it's bad luck to see the bride before the ceremony." I smile, and my fat cheeks balloon like blushing floats.

We go downstairs.

It's sunny and hot again—Los Angeles summer. On the coast here it's not so bad. The fresh Pacific wind cools over the cold water and takes the edge off the heat. Ten miles east of here, the air has already been soaked in urban mire and the wind turns hot, and it's ten degrees warmer and a thousand percent shit.

It feels good here right now. Invigorating and bright. In the distance, a rare Los Angeles sight: billowing white clouds ambling across the sky. Today, Rachel's little girl-mustache is ambling across her lip (she must have a beauty appointment this weekend, the monkey), and her clothes look like hell, and I'm not that impressed. I'm also tired from the night before—I haven't been sleeping much lately—and my brain is unfocused. (Symptom?) Rachel puffs and we talk about our weekend plans (I have none; she *es la bella de la fin de semana*), and our conversation again slumps over to our loathing of our jobs and the wonderful fact that it's finally the weekend again.

Near the end of the cigarette, I am sitting on the grass, not looking at Rachel, and she asks me, "Do you think I can get a ride home after work?"

"You can do anything you set your mind to," I say, not really listening.

"I need a ride home, Jibba," she says, this time looking at me directly.

Oh.

I feel like I'm falling. I can't breathe, and I feel like I'm going to shit myself.

"Sure," I say and put my head between my knees as the blood rushes out.

We walk back upstairs.

Rachel looks like hell today, and I'm cold and anxious.

* * * * *

I THINK I might be gay. Gay or just completely fucked up. Possibly perverted by Catholicism. Probably perverted by the bizarre sexual backwardness of Catholic ethics and the slutorious adventures of my whore mother and pious father (Catholics, both).

But I don't know if it's gayness. I'm physically attracted to girls—
God knows that (and damns me for it)—but I don't feel anything
else. I don't want to be with them. I don't want to be with anybody. I am seized by lust from time to time, and I struggle inwardly against the straitjacket of civilization, and then it passes
and I am somewhere else, probably playing video games or
worrying about the different ways I might be dying.

* * * * *

Rachel needs a ride home.

A supple, writhing girl-ape naked on my bike, pressing her
hot clitoris against the vibrating seat while I enter her from
behind and we rocket around the streets of Los Angeles and
fuck like demons in a shit-show. The two of us bursting into her
apartment and me pressing her against the wall grabbing her
hair and pulling it so she's looking up, and I softly drag my teeth
across her pulsing neck while she hurriedly undoes my belt and
unleashes the monster and bends down and greedily puts me
deep in her mouth. We fuck for hours, and she grunts dozens of
orgasms into my flesh until the summer sun slips and smolders
behind the Pacific curtain, and when it is dark, I dress and leave,
Taber arriving a half-hour later to find his girlfriend fucked to
deep sleep.

* * * * *

"Thanks for the ride," Rachel says awkwardly, keeping a sober
distance and popping my thoughts as I drop her off at her apartment. "I'll see you Monday, bucko!" she shouts over the roar of
the bike as I wave and rocket away into the early Friday evening.

I ride to the beach and watch the sun slip and smolder behind the ocean, and then I ride home to where I will masturbate
to the fantasy I have of what my life would be like if I weren't a
fat, depressed, loser faggot.

I ride home in the quickly fading post-sunset pink air. I feel
now, after my good deed, I have earned a reward.

* * * * *

Vernon is at a bar, no doubt. Friday evenings are his golden
hours. Lots of women trying to have fun and drink and play away
the pain of their banal lives. Vernon, a real rake, a real snake,
gives them everything they think they need. He's like an oil der-

rick that always strikes pink.

Which leaves me alone.

So I get the drugs out of my case in the closet, I put on only the best music at only the loudest volume, and I set fire to the forest in my brain, and this is the highlight of my week.

* * * * *

HOURS PASS. I sit almost motionless on the balcony, stretched out on a lawn chair, the music bouncing off the walls of the apartment and finally escaping through the open glass door before singing to me and then shooting out into the Santa Monica evening. My downstairs neighbor is striking the ceiling with a broom handle—a subtle way to tell me to turn down my music. At seven o'clock this morning, while I was trying to get back to sleep, her precious little snowflake baby was crying like a raped seal for the fifteenth consecutive day, so fuck her and her broom and baby.

Eventually, the album ends, and as I sit lost in thought, pen and paper in hand, a few more lines of an uncertain story etched darkly into the white, I hear the apartment door open and the sound of Vernon and some lithe vagina fill the air. I turn my head slightly and with my peripheral vision see a woman in her mid-thirties. Tall, blonde, tough-tanned skin. A seven. Vernon's average.

They are soon in Vernon's room. Door shut. Giggles and laughter and then quiet, and then music.

I do more drugs and sit in front of the mind-numbing television, and the injuries of the week are dissipated and soothed as I feel the great slabs of my mind float and separate, only to crash together later.

These are our golden hours.

* * * * *

I HAVE a dream that night.

I am walking down a street from my childhood: a long line of suburban trees leaning into each other's arms, creating a bright green canopy that is broken now and then where the hands of the trees have yet to grow, and through those gaps shoot golden sunrays that paste themselves to the street concrete. There is mournful bagpipe music playing somewhere—an old church song I can barely register, soft at this distance.

An image flashes into my head—an old cardboard box—and the box appears on the street.

I am thinking about how everything you put in a cardboard box in an attic is changed somehow. It just becomes the hidden content in a dusty cardboard box in an out-of-the-way place. Kind of the same way the digestive system chews and digests matter. What it was is no longer what it is. Corn, chicken, a human heart. It's all the same in there. Just calories.

These are my thoughts, but I do not feel like I am authoring them as I walk along the shady street.

There is a cardboard box on the ground—the contents have been spilled onto the grass, against the curb, and some sit in the puddles of sunlight. I begin to pick these items up, and with every grasp (in this case a dull trophy) a memory of my youth is triggered: being ten years old, sitting in the shade of a gazebo, wearing a flag-football uniform, surrounded by my teammates and our families, waiting for our next game of the weekend tournament. So young, so simple, the memory is so clear and wonderful the version of myself in this dream begins to well with tears. I grasp at an old album, and I'm twelve years old, lounging in my best friend Brian's room, with the window open and a light breeze tumbling through. There are storm clouds in the distance, but for now it is still sunny, and we are letting the day stretch out before us—the long summer day—and I can remember how secure I used to feel in that room with my friend. We are listening to one of our favorite bands. I can hear the lyrical wail, "I miss the comfort in being *saaaaaaad*!" I pick up a dark-blue hooded sweatshirt, and I'm walking home from school on a crisp autumn day that is rapidly turning into evening. The taste and smell of firewood flavors the air. The clouds are heavy and gray, but they do not spill. They press themselves against the tops of the deep green trees that have not yet begun their annual smolder. The air feels so cool.

I start to cry. On all three layers: myself in the memory, myself in the dream, and I can swear I feel myself—the part of me still mildly conscious in this light sleep—sobbing on my bed.

I am picking these things up and putting them back, but not

before their personal importance washes through me like a cleansing tide. For a time, I can feel the warmth and goodness of the days of my life when I was . . . accomplishing something, even if they were trivial accomplishments.

It is such a beautiful feeling, within the feeling I knew before this new feeling, that I am sobbing as I'm walking down this beautiful street and picking up the memories of my life, one by one, and placing them back into a cardboard box, to be altered and forgotten again.

* * * * *

I WAKE up, and I still feel like crying. My life. What a joke. Like the day: beautiful at sunrise, but now, with the sun searing the span of my head and shoulders, it is an endurance.

Everything seems like it was so much better in the past, with the mercy of selective memory holding onto only the strongest impressions and letting the everyday worries fall into the void. All my life, however, is everyday worries, so I'm not even sure if what I remember is true.

I do more drugs.

Saturday bleeds into Sunday. I barely leave my room. Vernon is at a writers' conference, teaching. All day I splay out on the puffery of my soft mattress, ingesting soul-numbers, packing away boxes and boxes of soft memories and endeavoring to trap and discard the old, bitter regrets that scurry between them.

The regrets mount as I rearrange the attic, and soon I can't see the boxes of tender memories any longer, so I turn on my computer and distract myself with pornography and my ongoing onanism.

Immediately after I finish, I am disgusted with myself.

Ten minutes later I am ready to do it again.

Then it's Monday.

* * * * *

I WAKE up sad. The weekend has played out, and not at all have I grown other than older and closer to the day I will die. (*Oh, the day!*) My heart is heavy—mourning some lost love I cannot name. Vernon is out the door early. Mondays are pitch-days. He writes for a sitcom in hellish Burbank. A long drive. The apartment is completely silent, with the only movement being the line of light-bands slowly crawling up the couch and the wall across from the door to my room.

I put my drugs away until next weekend.

Like the light-bands, I make my way slowly around, and I try not to think about where I have to be soon (work, work, work!), trying, honestly, to discover what it is that causes this blanket of sadness that leaves my throat tight with emotion.

It never works, so instead I pull out a pocket knife that was given to me by my father before I moved out here, and I turn on one of the gas burners on the stove. The blade comes to a perfect point at the tip, and this tip I hold to the blue flame. I pull off my shirt, sit down at the kitchen table, take a deep breath, and press the knife's tip into the inner part of my upper arm, near my armpit.

The pain makes me drop the knife, which clatters to the table, and my brain releases its lovely endorphins, and FUCK! It feels good. It fucking hurts so good.

I don't feel so bad anymore.

I press an alcohol swab against the burned skin and it's round two—FUCK! Yes. I can breathe. Today, this morning, I can breathe again.

Mmmmmm, I mumble into my forearm, head down on the table.

I throw some disinfectant cream on the wound, bandage it, and then get dressed for work. For the next three or four days, every time I move my left arm, it's going to release the hounds, and my brain will get me high.

It's funny, I know this is completely fucked-up behavior, but it works.

It works, doctor.

* * * * *

IT'S CLOUDY. Rachel wears jeans and a modest shirt. We're busy, so there isn't much time for her.

Mondays are nice.

* * * * *

MY PHONE rings. It's Vernon.

"Hey, man," he says. "Wanted to know if you're coming

tonight."

"Tonight?"

Vernon laughs. "Yeah, the premiere."

Then I remember. "Oh yeah, I thought you were talking about something else."

"So are you coming?" he asks.

"Of course, man."

We figure out the details and hang up.

"Who was that?" Rachel asks. Unbeknownst to me, she has been hanging over my shoulder the whole time.

"My brother," I say.

"What's tonight?"

"He's a staff writer for *Stomach Punch*, and the episode he wrote premieres tonight. They're having a sort of viewing party at their offices in Burbank, and he wanted to know if I was coming."

"I like that show," Rachel says. "I didn't know he wrote for them. That's awesome." (I've told her a number of times about Vernon being a writer for that show.)

"Are you asking if you can come with?" I ask.

Rachel smiles, flattered. "I wish I could, but Taber and I have couple's yoga tonight."

"Okay," I say, turning back to my desk. I don't find her that interesting today, and every mention of the word Taber makes me a little sick. She raps me on my left arm, which pushes my burn into my torso, and there's the pain and endorphins again, *Hooooeeeeeee*.

"Whoa," she says, seeing the flinch in my face. "You okay?"

"I'm fine," I say.

"You look like you're in pain," she says, with her eyebrows furrowed.

The creature stirs.

My phone rings. It's my boss. Rachel, afraid of her, quickly disappears. The first time I've ever been glad to hear from my boss.

More banal bullshit to begin with, then she tells me that an email dispatch I sent to one of our clients happened to impress the CEO of the very same broadcast network that airs my

162

brother's show. My boss is glowing with praise for me and my work. The praise does little to endear me to her, and I feel as though she is a mother bird regurgitating chunks of worm into my mouth. I get out of there as fast as I can, but not before using the opportunity to ask about leaving work early so I can make it to Burbank in time for the start of the party.

"Absolutely, Jibba," she says.

I leave an hour early.

* * * * *

TRAFFIC.

Los Angeles is one of the greatest places in the world to live. The unfortunate thing is that's not a very well-kept secret, which makes it one of the worst places in the world to live. I would guess that in Los Angeles county alone, there are probably somewhere between ten- and twenty-million people sprawled across this seemingly endless urban desert. Which means millions and millions and millions of cars, cars, cars. I sit in traffic and it's cars, cars, cars, cars, cars, and trucks, and cars and trucks and jeeps and sedans and honking and the shimmer of heat rising from the pounded pavement (I am going for effect here).

Even as I lean between the traffic on my bike, the pace is a snail's race, and it takes me about an hour and fifteen minutes to travel fifteen miles. During this time, I am thinking about North Korean nuclear explosions leveling the city, and me speeding around, kicking up the ashes on my rocket bike, disgusted with myself about how happy I am that so many millions of people are dead and I can finally stretch my bike's legs.

Eventually (and I mean eventuallyeventuallyeventuallyeventually BEEP! BEEP! BEEP!), I am at a major studio, parking in a visitor's lot that is about three-hundred yards from the lot where I eventually find the main door to the studios where they write and film *Stomach Punch*.

A fat Mexican guard scans a list for my name with all the haste of the aforementioned traffic, and soon I am leaning over his clipboard and pointing to my name. "*¡Aqui! ¡Aqui!*" He lets me through with an unimpressed frown.

The first thing I see when I walk inside is a girl so beautiful she makes Rachel look like a toilet. She's walking along, talking into a cell phone.

"Like, you know? Like, he said that; he totally said that. You know? Like, can you believe it?"

"Read a book," I say through gritted teeth as I walk past her. I don't think she hears me. Fat pieces of shit like me don't exist to women like her.

The next thing I see is Vernon, in all his glory. The man is beaming. His breath, however, smells like vomit.

"You nervous?" I ask.

"Puked three times already," he says as he escorts me through a rather boring corridor. Vernon is cooler than dry ice, but, God bless him, he's also got the extraordinary ability to turn that chillational bullshit off and focus all the energies of his brain to a single task. The last time he threw up that didn't involve drink or malaise was before our high school football games. He was a maniac, all-state. I was eventually kicked off the team.

"It's exciting, man," I say. "What does Randy think of how it turned out?" Randy Miller is the executive producer of the show.

"I don't know, man," he says. "Guy is hard to read. But I think he's happy with it. He didn't fire me yet."

"Right," I say as Vernon pushes open two large wooden doors.

A large, largely empty studio. At the front of the room is a big white screen. The seating for the audience is folded up. Some chairs have been brought out, and some people are milling around, pecking at a craft-service table loaded with delectable victuals. Having not eaten dinner, I make my way over to that table, where two women, one of them plump, the other a spidery-looking Jew, are noshing.

Vernon introduces us.

They are uninterested in me, and they are soon back to their gossip. Vernon is called over to another private group—they all work here—and I bring my sandwich over to one of the padded audience seats, away from everyone. A few chews into my first bite and I hear Vernon say something, and then the entire group laughs. They all seem to like him.

Nobody here wants to talk to me. And why would they? They

all know each other. I'm the younger brother of the youngest member of the show's writing staff. Professionally, I am at the very limits of the periphery of entertainment, and when I am asked what I do for a living, I lie. I tell some that I panhandle. They don't think that's funny. I tell others that I work for the government. This, they believe. Then they walk away. Nobody wants to talk about the government. Especially not these sundry go-go-go people. I tell some people the truth—that I am a proofreader and writer for a multimedia firm—and these people are unimpressed.

The truth is I don't know what I am. I'm nothing, or something. I'm still trying to figure it out.

What I am now is throwing away my paper plate and standing in the corner of a large room, pretending to be reading a sign while I just wait for this whole thing to be over with. I know Vernon wants me to get out and be more social, but I have nothing about which to have a conversation with any of these people who are never listening anyway. Most people don't find me very endearing.

The unmistakable voice of Randy Miller—nasally, nerdy, pregnant with a caustic wit—calls everyone's attention to the front of the room, where he has his arm around my brother.

"Everyone, we're about to start the show, but before we do . . ." Randy says.

"Let's get drunk!" one of the writers yells, followed by a smattering of laughter.

"You've been drunk since this morning, John. Anyway, I would like to congratulate our new friend Vernon on his first broadcast episode!" Randy says. The crowd cheers and applauds—me included—and Randy continues. "He wrote a wonderful script, and we're all glad to have him on the team. And ladies, he can make his cock vibrate." The cheering resumes, and then the lights fade.

I find a seat, far from the others, and settle in.

The episode is funny. I can tell which jokes are Vernon's. The performances are acceptable, with the exception of the role of "Vanessa"—the blonde 36-24-36 knockout the network crowbarred into the cast in an attempt to shore up their prime demographic—played by an actress named Kelsey Scott, whom Vernon refers to as "just another super-hot, dismissive bitch." Kelsey is somewhere in the audience—I saw her earlier—and I cringe when both of her big punch lines only get forced chuckles from the already biased audience. She is simply not funny, but I would still hole her out like a pick-ax drilling into a pastry.

The lights come up, and there are applause and cheers. Vernon is congratulated again, and the crowd slowly dissipates.

All in all, I am proud of Vernon, and seeing as how the five or six jokes from his first draft are about the only things that have made me laugh (intentionally) all day, I can't help but feel concerned for him. I am a lone comet, and my opinions are usually far afield from those of the greater planets, so the idea that I like Vernon's episode/jokes can only mean he's destined for anything other than longstanding success. Seems like every time I like a show, or a potato chip flavor, or a girl, the show is soon canceled, the chip company gives up that flavor, and the girl either already has an unbearable boyfriend, or she physically couldn't be less interested in my fat belly, sweaty armpits, and blotchy face.

Yes, I control the universe.

The last time I watched sports on TV, my old favorite team was making a run for the championship. They lost. I wanted to stick with it, having put so much time into caring about the team that just lost, so I cheered for a different team that had some players I respected. They lost. The next team I cheered for: lost. In the championship round, I had a fifty-fifty shot. My team lost.

Oh, my negativity!

I think perhaps people can tell. They stay away. "He controls the universe, you know—but he's terribly negative. Let's go suck someone else's cock."

Indeed, they stay away. Like now in this studio.

Except . . . .

"Who are you?" a female voice asks. I lift my gaze from my hands—my hands! I exist! I never seem to get over this—and turn my head. It is Kelsey Scott, eyeing me like I'm a potential rapist. "Do you know someone here?"

I look her up and down. Her skin is perfect. Smooth, unblemished, I can't even see any pores. Her lips are full, womanly, red. Her eyes are sky blue, made all the more profound by the perfect pitch of her platinum-blonde hair. My thoughts are not lust but a wandering wonder. She is physically flawless. Even the gape of her unthinking mouth sparkles like wondershine.

"I own the building," I say, gesturing with my hands in an all-encompassing motion.

"No, you don't," she says, getting all the more nervous. "What are you doing here?"

"Relax," I say, trying to smile, but failing. "My brother wrote tonight's episode, and I came here to celebrate with him."

"Your brother is Vernon?" she asks, literally unable to make the mental connection that we could possibly be brothers.

"I'm afraid so," I say.

"I don't like Vernon," she says with all the tact of a lewd graffito on a bathroom mirror.

"Me neither," I say jokingly, hoping she'll join the mirth. She does not.

"He thinks he's so cool, and he's not even that funny," she says.

"That's what I keep telling him," I say, just going with it. Here I take the initiative from her. "Let me ask you something: what are you doing?"

"What do you mean?"

"Well, let's see, you're a successful actress, and I'm a fat piece of tubbo shit. Why are you talking to me? If I were you, I'd be . . . I don't know, masturbating in front of a mirror or something. I wouldn't be rudely telling some fat idiot about how much I didn't like his brother."

"You looked sad," she says, almost hurt by my rude question. This hits me in the chest.

"Well . . ." I say, and laugh one of those you-have-no-idea laughs. "You're right. I am sad. Got a cure for depression?"

"What are you depressed about?"

I take a moment to think. What am I depressed about?

"You know how pretty the sky looks on a clear night? How you can see billions of stars up there, twinkling and pretty?"

"Yeah," she says, mouth again agape, picturing a star field

behind her perfect eyes.

"Well, those stars are all alone. When we look at them, they look like a beautiful, dancing, shimmering team, lighting up the night, right? But if you think about it, there are unimaginably dark and cold distances between them—literally millions of light years. They're alone, burning with bright intensity, but unable to see anything. Stars have no eyes. They live these singular lives. They just burn until they burn out, and then they collapse upon themselves, and the universe grinds on forever without ever knowing anything else about them, barely warmed by their one-time existence, expanding in perfect indifference."

"That's beautiful," she says.

"Yes, it is," I say. "And it's also the saddest fucking thing there is."

As much as I'm enjoying this, I have nothing else to say, and I'm already beginning to worry about the silent diseases that are hastening the burn of the star of my body and soul.

"I have to go," I say. "It was nice talking to you . . ." (I pretend not to know her name).

"Kelsey," she says, extending her hand.

"Kelsey," I say. "Right. I knew that." I shake her beautiful, delicate hand.

She smiles. I feel nervous. I feel a pang in the lower-right quadrant of my torso—possibly the first flare of appendicitis, or something worse. Pretending to be scratching an itch, I feel for a lump.

"And?" she asks

"And what?" I ask.

"What's your name?"

She wants to know my name? Nice!

"Jibba," I say.

She furrows her brow. "That's a weird name."

"My grandmother was a Zappa," I say.

"Really?" she asks.

"Nah," I say. "But best of luck this season, Kelsey," I say, "or break a leg . . . or . . . shit, whatever's good."

She laughs, then frowns. "Good luck yourself, Jibba."

It's getting late, but Vernon and the others are planning on going to some "actor bar" where he and the others can use their "producer" status to talk to and hit on the universe of unbelievably sexy women who are so prevalent here in the valley.

I hug and congratulate my brother and then make a French exit (slinking off without a goodbye—I hate goodbyes).

I emerge outside, and it is dark. The edge has been taken off the heat of the day, and the night air is refreshing. I waddle to my bike and cut a razor path through the highways that bring me back home.

Where I again masturbate and think about rubbing my engorged monster up and down Kelsey Scott's hairless perfect skin as she thrusts her hips up against mine and we fuck until I finish inside her and we both fall asleep together just like that.

* * * * *

AN EVIL man invades another country, and then another, and then another. His menace grows to where dark masses cloud the horizon of a distant continent. Young men are called into a battle for the future of the world. After two years of training to fight in the biggest and most advanced combat in the history of mankind, these young men who enlisted to defend their home and an idea . . . they are standing on the precipice of war.

They depart in boats and planes laden with weapons and survival tools and the knowledge that they're already dead.

They land upon a rocky shore, and many of them are torn apart by gunfire and explosions, but there are many more who survive the invasion into the heart of darkness, into the European Theater of Operations, and they push forward.

They fight bravely, their entire beings crackling with the intensity of mortal combat, and they rise to their purpose.

* * * * *

I SOMETIMES picture myself on one of the hundreds of C-47s hurtling through the flashing sky, my heart pounding, looking out into the night and seeing colorful tracer fire from anti-aircraft guns cutting the night sky like glowing sabers, turning some of the planes around me into dive-bombing caskets that plummet into the massive ocean or crash and explode on land in a final fireball. The green "go" light goes on, and the soldiers in front of me hurriedly file out of the back of the plane, their parachutes popping open as they drift into the mouth of Cerberus. And then I too am drifting down, hearing more anti-aircraft ordnance whizzing by my face and feet. Landing with a thump, I hastily strip myself of my parachute and affix the bayonet to my rifle and am set upon by a charging enemy soldier. He knocks me to the ground, but I swing my rifle around and cut the artery in his leg. He falls and I pounce upon him and push the bayonet into his heart, and he dies. I don't enjoy it, but I don't feel bad about it either. It needed to be done. I crouch down and try to locate anyone friendly, but right now I am alone, beset on all sides by one of the world's largest fighting forces.

* * * * *

THIS THOUGHT-BUBBLE is popped by the sound of my company's IT guy sharing a dumb joke with one of our designers, who forces a laugh. And then there's the quiet of daily toil.

I return to my work, finger my pudge, pop a couple potato chips into my mouth, and sigh into the insipid ether of the workday.

I finger more pudge, pop more chips, write more emails, and listen for Rachel as she goes hither and thither. She's wearing a smooth pink skirt and sleeveless white blouse today, and she smells magnificent. She washed her hair this morning—I try not to think about the fact that the shower was probably due to a morning romp with Taber—and when she leans over my desk to grab a stapler a light waft of her conditioned hair tickles my nose, and were not my hot hands chained to the desk by the villain of my ethical control, I would have groped her until I was fired and sued.

My stomach has been hurting lately. When I eat, or just after, I get a rolling pain. My stool has changed color. It's lighter brown. Lighter every day. I look up hepatitis symptoms and eat potato chips and feel sick.

* * * * *

THAT IS my week. Or at least, that is my week until Friday afternoon.

Friday afternoon, after a long lunch alone in the park (Rachel had a hair appointment), I am sweating back at my desk, watching an animation Vernon made a few weeks ago. It's very funny, and I'm enjoying myself, which somewhere in my brain makes me nervous. It has been my experience that all my joy is the doorway to doom, depression, and my damning.

And then that sinking feeling is confirmed when my phone rings. For a moment I am thrown off because the phone on my desk doesn't appear to be ringing, and then I feel the vibration in my pocket and realize it's my cell phone that's ringing. I look at the caller ID and see that it's my mom.

"I'm working," I say. "Can this wait?"

There is no sound on the other end. Then there's a sniffle.

"Jibba," she says, whispers actually. "Have you talked to Vernon?"

"No," I say, barely listening, still watching Vernon's cartoon. "Is he okay?"

"He's fine," she says. "It's your father. Jibba, honey, your father's dead."

I hang up.

* * * * *

IN HIGH school, we were being prepared for some national standardized tests, and one of our assignments was a full dip into the literary exercise of "description."

I described My Father.

"If a comedian scientist were to take the best elements of an unabashed, unedited raconteur and combine them with the vulgar appearance of a real-life Ignatius J. Reilly—a chubby, sweating man-pig, with big paws that attach to arms that were made for hugging tight the loves of his life . . . If one were to see a plumber lean below a sink and emerge with a rose in his teeth, greasy black streaks across his face, humbly handing the American Beauty to the woman he adores . . . If one were to pull to mind the idea of a man who could outsmart the devil even if he could barely sign his own name . . . a devout Catholic with the vocabulary of a drunk pirate, and as brave . . . .

"Objectively, my father is the usual. He has worked a menial job for many years, and some might argue he has squandered the full potential of his unusual mind, but nobody in our family sees it that way. He's like one of those paintings where you can see an image, but if you look closer, it's just dots.

"He gambles, he watches too much football, he snorts and hocks gross loogies and spits them out open windows (sometimes onto a neighbor's windshield "accidentally"), and he cuts gas and tells stories that have entire neighborhoods rattling the panes of their windows with howls of laughter. He lives big. He spends big, drives fast, eats gluttonously, chain-smokes menthol cigarettes, and loves my brother and me perfectly. He loves his family in a way that is simply perfect.

"When the sun rises, it rises on his serene eyebrows, and when it sets, it sets on his slumbering toes."

* * * * *

THE NEWS of my father's death doesn't hit me immediately. In fact, I go back to my work.

Then Rachel is over my shoulder, and she's frowning. "I hate my grandma so much! Just wait until you hear what she's done now."

"My father's dead," I say. "I think I have to go."

"Oh, my God," Rachel says.

Not intending to be rude, I walk past her, toward my boss's office. As I walk, my phone rings again. It's Vernon. I pick up.

"I already bought us tickets. We're taking the red-eye tonight," he says. "You doing okay?"

"Kind of numb," I say. "I'm about to tell my boss. I'll call you later."

The door to my boss's office is closed, which is rare. I sit down on the loveseat by her lovely secretary Ms. Cummings—a kindhearted woman of extremely advanced, yarn-cloaked years—who reminds me, "She's in a meeting right now, but they should be done any minute."

I nod a thank you and sit and think.

The door opens and a tall, mustachioed creep walks out clutching a briefcase and sharing a forced laugh with my cunt boss. He eyes me briefly on his way out, and his gaze goes to the exit when he sees me and my heavy shit. Without being prompted, I walk in and close the door.

"Brynn, my father died today," I say to her. Her eyes widen. "I'm going to need some time off."

"Oh, my goodness, Jibba," she says. "That's terrible. Do you know what happened?"

Strangely, I feel like opening up to her, if only because I finally have her undivided attention. Nevertheless, I look at that wall of unread books and am sobered.

"No, I don't," I say. "My mom just called; she could barely keep it together."

"Take as much time as you need," she says with the first touch of warmth I've ever seen cross the field of her usually cold eyes.

"Thank you," I say, standing.

"Actually, Jibba," she says before I reach the door. I stop and turn. "I know this is terrible timing and all, but I wanted to be straight-up with you."

Oh, shit.

"As you may have noticed, we've lost a few accounts lately," she says. I have noticed, indeed. The whole world's headed down the shitter, and we're at the foremost tip of the swirl. "Well, yesterday we lost the Palisades account, and we're going to have to lay off that whole division."

"What?" I ask.

"I'm sorry," she says.

Before I leave, I hock a horker into a vase on her desk and dismiss myself with a surly, "You suck. The real crime here is that we get laid off because you're incompetent and condescending. Go fuck yourself."

* * * * *

NUMB, I pack my few work-belongings into my backpack. I don't remember any of this, really, but presumably I walk downstairs, get on my bike, and somehow make it safely home.

There, I pack more belongings into a suitcase and lay down. But I'm not crying.

I think about my dad, but I can't cry. There's nothing there yet. In older times, a traveling Russian prince's baggage would arrive at a distant manor a full day before the prince himself arrived; though the gates of my castle are open, it is still empty for now.

The sun goes down, I force down a few bites of food, and eventually Vernon comes home. We hug, and then he packs his own suitcase, and we lock up the apartment.

I toss my suitcase into the back of Vernon's Jeep, and soon we are rumbling through the calm nighttime summer air of this sprawling desert in a shocked state of unbroken silence. No radio. Just the rumble of the engine and the wind whistling off the edges of our ears. Across the windshield I see the soft, fragile, twinkling beauty of the city, and I try to concentrate on that, on those lights and the way they shimmer. The hills roll for miles up and down, dotted with white-yellow specks. Vernon drives mournfully, the heavy hammer of the family lead foot lightened by the distracting largeness of our loss.

We eventually find a spot in the long-term parking lot and take a terrifying shuttle ride to the airport. Our driver, a turban-wearing Hindu mystic in his mid-forties, ululates a strange song as the transport clatters over speed bumps and into potholes. Vernon and I make trivial observations to distract ourselves from this newfound terror. Yet somehow we safely arrive at the terminal, where we are herded into a very long security line. Like cattle, we pack together and shuffle slowly toward the front. My anxiety grows with every five minutes that pass. I can't bear the thought of missing our flight and having to do all of this again in the morning. Our plane's loading time is quickly approaching. I'm surrounded by unhappy families, busy businessmen, and a smattering of others, some of whom look scary, and most of whom look stupid.

The illusion of security.

A modern building is built to a code that leaves it five times as strong as the structure needs to be in order to remain standing and functional. Because of the delicate nature of flight, however, the modern airplane is built to a standard that leaves it only 1.4 times as strong as it needs to remain functional—any more reinforcement and it couldn't leave the ground.

I have a double-edged anxiety going now—one half worried that we'll miss the flight, the other half worried that we'll make it. For this and many other reasons, I only travel when it is absolutely necessary.

The people around me smell. All their faces are dead.

Vernon is way off his game. We've usually got each other

howling with hysterics, but now we're just two more sour-faced travelers ever shuffling towards a pathetic future.

Somewhere behind me, I can hear a couple arguing. It's an invasively petty argument. I turn around and give a shut-your-fucking-mouths look, but they're in their own universe right now, and I'm just more static. The noisy waiting continues.

A shadow of a thought crosses my mind: I don't have any drugs with me this time. Usually, whenever I go home, I make sure to smuggle some with me. This isn't that kind of trip, but on that front it appears to be the kind of trip where I'd need more drugs, not less (and especially not none).

But here I am now at the front of the snake-like coil of the security line, being waved forward by a Mexican in his fifties. I slide my possessions into the X-ray machine and shoelessly and beltlessly step through a metal detector and am given a hard up-and-down look from the short-haired grump. I don't even bother to look at him, already hurrying to retrieve my things as they line up at the far end of the luggage procession.

Everything I do feels plastic and scripted. There is no feeling to it, which to me feels plastic, and scripted. A going through the motions. It's muscle memory now.

* * * * *

VERNON AND I trudge to our gate, lay down our bags, collapse into the stiff, shitty seating provided, and wait to hear the boarding call that eventually comes forty minutes later. Over the course of this wait, Vernon has his eyes closed, not sleeping, just resting, and I am looking around at all the faces around me: a fat man and his androgynous-looking middle-aged wife sitting in a wordless and spiritually defeated comfort; a traveling Asian businessman wearing a smart suit, clicking around on his computer, probably delicately avoiding an accidental click into the sordid underbelly of the machine's copious, possibly illicit smut; the petty couple that was behind us in the security line, who are both younger than I, probably recent college grads, he looks like he was the best athlete in his frat, and she looks like she's reached the peak of how she'll ever look (which is, at best, a seven), and I think about how she'll look in ten years, when she looks twenty years older, thirty pounds heavier, and twice as unhappy as she appears now.

I scan all these people to look for possible security threats.

Between faces, I think about how Vernon and I must appear, at least to the people out there whose inner spectator isn't exclusively reserved for observing itself. I wonder how we appear to those who look around in order to see what's out there (as opposed to seeing how what's out there is reacting to them). Ultimately, I think we must look like exactly what we are: two brothers (we don't look that much alike, but there are trademark similarities in the facial triangle) in their late-twenties waiting silently (mournfully, for those with extra perception) to go somewhere they both consider unpleasant.

A voice announces that it's time for us to get on the plane.

As I stand and grab my bag, I see a group of people gathered around a television. People around a television isn't surprising, but what grabs my attention is that they are all standing. There are chairs provided, but everyone's on their feet. Very Un-American.

"I'll be right back," I say to Vernon and walk over to the group.

They're glued to the news.

"—making this the first aggressive act on a scale this size in decades. We don't have much detail for you as of this reporting, but our experts are calling this an unsettling—"

"What happened?" I ask a short woman next to me.

"It's on the news . . . China just invaded Japan," she says and turns back to the television.

"The hell they do that for?" I hear her ask someone else as I walk back over to Vernon.

"Dude, you're not going to believe this: China just invaded Japan."

"What?"

"I don't know. They're talking about it on the news right now. That's what all those people are doing over there."

"That's fucked," Vernon says. "Shit."

"Yeah," I say.

The boarding continues. Nobody wants any hitches. We all want to get on the plane and be off toward our plans.

*****

I DON'T know where the notion of sexy stewardesses came from, but it certainly wasn't from anyone who's flown recently. Perhaps all the sexy whores are just going into porno because at least then they're making money for all the fucking they'd be doing anyway. I don't know. What I do know is that I was once again let down by the two mid-fifties-looking women (tops topped by androgynous mom chops) and the young, utterly homosexual male who comprise this flight's attendance crew.

Because we ordered the tickets so late, Vernon and I aren't sitting together. I find my seat between a walrus and an Indian restaurant. Nestled in their fleshy spillover, I soon sleep.

*****

ABRAHAM PETER 'Heck' Bloom and I were born in the same hospital on the same day. We discovered this fact during our birthday at school in Kindergarten. When the teacher announced our mutual birth anniversary, obviously Heck and I had to size each other up. He looked like a cool kid (it woulda been shitty if it were Garret Penny, as he remains the only kid I've ever seen who'd frequently blow his nose into his mouth), so I wasn't upset with the coincidence, but I have to admit Heck looked enormously disappointed.

Normally, people don't like me. I can tell. I have a lot of experience watching people, and I can read the stuff they don't want read. They don't like me, but at least most of the time they try to hide it somewhat. I don't know what it is about me that they don't like, but I generally receive what the objective observer would call a negative response from people. Fortunately, the people who like me are so cool they more than make up for all those shit-fer-brains bitches and bastards who don't like me. It's the ten percent. It's always the ten percent. We float on very little.

That day after school I went up to Heck as we unchained our bikes.

"Hey, Heck?" I asked.

He stopped and turned. "Yeah?" he asked quietly. He looked kind of sad.

"Do you think I'm a loser or something?"

Now he looked genuinely confused. "What? Why?"

"Today when the teacher said we had the same birthday, you looked like you thought I was a loser."

Heck smirked when he understood. Then he laughed. "Oh, no. I was just sad about something else. I think you're cool—you're the best kickball-kicker in school."

I smiled. "Thanks. So what were you upset about?"

In a way, somewhere in that tiny moment between when I finished my question and he started phrasing his reply in his head, our friendship began.

"There's nothing special about me," he said. "I always thought I was the only person born today. And here you were born on the same day, and you're in my same class. That makes me like super-normal. That's what I was upset about. It's not that it's you, Jibba. It coulda been anyone."

"Yeah, but . . ." I said. "What about your cool bike? I don't know of anyone with a cooler bike."

"What about Jimmy DiSanto?" he asked.

"That is a pretty cool bike," I had to admit.

We both laughed.

We were great grade-school friends.

But we drifted as we got older. Heck turned out to be special in this way: he was a genius. It started when we were in sixth grade. He won first prize in a mandatory, middle school–wide essay competition. Of all the sixth, seventh, and eighth graders in the school, Heck's essay "What I Would Do with the Go-Karts" displayed a flourish for language and a maturity of thought that so impressed the school staff that they read the essay in its entirety during a school assembly—something they had never done before. Heck's essay even outshined an essay by a then-eighth-grader named Alice Cook, who later went on to write a best-selling sex guide when she was a sophomore at NYU and who is now a feature writer for *Vanity Fair*.

Heck became somewhat of a local celebrity. Any attention brings attention from women, and soon Heck was off in all sorts of directions. While I mainly stuck with our little core of friends, Heck bloomed. It was bittersweet for us. We felt proud to count the smartest-but-not-nerdiest kid in school as our friend, but we watched with bitterness while he (rightfully) branched out.

During the summer before eighth grade, my friends and I didn't see much of Heck. He always enjoyed hanging out at the pool with us, but he wasn't around.

I found out later, much later, only a few years ago, in fact, that he wasn't around because he was receiving psychological counseling. He was receiving psychological counseling because one night, alone in a room at a relative's house in another state (he never told me who it was), he overheard his sister's rape. He never wrote about it, and besides the appointments he attended that summer, he never talked about it.

Not for a long time, at least.

His sister emerged on the other side as a bride of Christ. She endured the rape, endured the counseling, and then she ended up at a seminary. She never could let anyone touch her again. Only God could touch her, and she felt touched.

Heck circled back 'round to my friendsphere after high school. During the summer after our freshman year in college, Heck and I found ourselves co-hitting-on the same girl at the party of a mutually friendly sleazeball we knew.

The girl turned out to be a lesbian, and we turned out to be better friends than we'd ever been. I told him about my anxieties and depressions, and he told me about his depressions and anxieties. From the ashes of our mutual shit came the phoenix of our friendship.

He saved my life.

That same summer, I was out with my newfound friend Heck and our mutual friend Brian. We were at this bar called The Moneypenny, which was unusual for us because normally we just hung out at Brian's (he had his own house after his parents both died in an auto accident). However, we were at The Moneypenny because Heck was meeting some female friends of his.

The night was moving along pleasantly enough. Brian, a shell within a shell within a shell, even more than I, was actually chatting up one of Heck's female friends (who turned out to be Brian's longtime girlfriend's old tennis rival). Heck himself was chatting up the friend he was doing at the time (a stunning model named Gloria, whom we serenaded a number of times that night with our awful renditions of Van-and-Jim Morrison's howling caterwauls: "GLOOOOOORIA!"), and I was, of course, sitting outside of the general conversation in a corner of the bar, unable to talk to anyone even after singing so raucously.

My friends and I jokingly refer to our hometown as "Fight Town," and near the end of the night, some fight-lookers descended upon the largely empty bar.

Ours was the only corner with any females in it, so the guys worked their way over to our direction, where they set up at the next table over.

Everyone at our table, besides myself, hadn't even noticed that they'd entered. I noticed because I notice everything.

One of them recognized Brian, who despite being an introvert was the best baseball player on our team back in high school. Brian could field, throw, and hit, but he couldn't hit for power. He'd always been very slight. And he spoke softly. Unfortunately, Brian's full name didn't help with his seemingly unmanly aspects: Brian Gary Fogger.

One of them, whom I recognized as Carl Wenderschmidt, who played against us back in high school, called out, "Hey, Fagger, why don't you introduce us to your pretty friends? Might as well point 'em in the direction of someone who can get it up!"

It was one of those moments where everything stops. But nobody wanted the hassle. Not at our table, at least. Awkwardly, the conversation between my friends continued; nobody made any mention of what was said. Best not to feed the monkeys.

Obviously, that wasn't going to be good enough.

A handful of peanuts lofted through the air and skidded across our table.

"I said, 'Hey, Fagger!'"

Brian Fogger was many things—a tremendous person, a refreshingly reserved conversationalist with a charming reticence, and a loyal friend—but one thing Brian was not was a fighter. He always reminded me of one of those guys who would never raise his fists to fight. He would take his ass-kicking, and then he would wait. Brian was smart. He would get his revenge, and it would be exponentially worse than the offense that triggered it.

"Carl, please just leave us alone," Brian said when Carl jerked his shoulder. "Please."

"Shut the fuck up, Fagger," another one said—Carl's older brother Mark.

"Let me get this straight," Heck said, standing up. "You guys aren't going to leave us alone, right? You're just looking for a fight?"

They looked sarcastically taken aback. "No, Heck," Carl said. "Nobody here wants a fight. What gave you that impression? Is your pussy starting to pucker?"

Heck laughed. "Something like that," he said. "Here, let me buy you guys a round of drinks. We don't want any trouble."

"Good," Mark said. "Jessie! Heck here's gonna buy us a round of shots and beers."

"And an order of wings," Carl said.

"And another order of wings," some guy I didn't know added. Jessie looked over at Heck. Heck nodded.

The fight-lookers sat down and laughed when Jessie brought over their drinks. They started horsing with her as she tried to balance the tray. The one I didn't recognize playfully tugged on her elbow, and the tray slid from her hands—the bottles breaking on the ground and the shot-glasses screaming as they clattered on the table. The table began bleeding liquor to the hardwood, shard-strewn floor, and I could see the pretty Jessie Sloan's lips begin to tremble. She was the only one working.

"Whoops!" Carl said. "Hank, why'd ya have to yank her arm like that? Now we need another round on old Heck over there, Jessie. I'm real sorry about Hank. He can be a real stumble-bum—can't ya, Hank?"

"I got problems," Hank said, and they all laughed.

I glared at them all. I hated them. I know I hated them. Mark, Carl's brother, noticed. "What the fuck're yew lookin' at, homo?"

"I'm still trying to figure it out," I said. I don't remember thinking those words, but that's what I said. I stood up to help Jessie, but Mark interpreted it as my standing to fight.

He lunged at me, and while I tried to disengage from him, little Hank blasted me across the side of the head. When I fell, I

I landed on my side, on a broken bottle. I passed out for a few moments, but I came to when I felt a heavy boot crunch into my ribcage. There was action going on above me, but all I knew was that I was about to pass out again, and my torso felt like a broken accordion. Another foot kicked me in the chest, and the pain that spread from the contact point to my broken ribs was like an acid thunderstorm under my skin. I let out a vile scream and passed out.

This is what happened when I was out cold: as unluck would have it, I re-landed on the razor-sharp edge of a broken bottle.

Brian got the girls out of the action and to a safe corner. Heck was dealing with three of the guys himself while the other two were dealing with my lifeless lump. Brian tried to separate us, and soon they were pummeling him. He let out his own din. "Heck! Help!"

"Jibba," Heck said when he told me his side of what happened, "in twenty years of our being friends, I'd never heard Brian like that, and I don't know, man . . . I lost it."

He knocked Carl out with an open-palmed smash to Carl's nose, picked up a shot-glass from the table, and crunched it against the side of Mark's head. It shattered in his hand. Mark's face and Heck's hand started bleeding. He wheeled, picked up a discarded pool cue, and broke it across the third dude's knee. He raised the splintered cue over his head and used it to break the arm of one of the other dudes. When Hank heard the broken-arm guy's scream of pain, he saw that his friends were defeated, and he raced out.

The girls rushed over to me, turned my body, and were sprayed by the blood pumping from my arm. The cephalic vein of my left arm had been cut by the bottle.

"Holy fuck!" Heck let out. "Gloria, get your car!"

* * * * *

I AWOKE in the ICU. There was no one in the room. It was four hours after the fight—around five in the morning. There was nobody in the bed next to mine. I looked around the room. It had that hospital sterility, both metaphorical and literal. There were purple clouds floating in the night air outside. I watched them for a while.

Eventually, I noticed a note had been left on the table next to me.

Jibba—
Had to take Gloria home. Could not reach anyone at your house.
Will be back soon. Get better, pussy.
—Hecktor

* * * * *

THAT WAS Heck.

That was nine years ago.

We hang out every time I go back to my hometown. He's a millionaire now. He's written one novel—published four years ago, *A Brief Crack of Light*. It was a national bestseller.

Over the course of the night of that red-eye flight, as Vernon and I flew across the wide belly of our homeland, towards our hometown, my great friend Heck pulled a noose around his neck and leapt to his death.

* * * * *

BUT HE didn't die.

I would get the full story from Brian later.

It's weird how sometimes we feel the early warning tremors of life's horrors, and sometimes we don't.

I had felt neither my father's nor Heck's. I felt only the doom-signifying wobble of the massive aircraft in flight—built to be only 1.4 times as strong as necessary—as the dreams in my sleep kept breaking up into incomprehensibly jangled shards, as my mind tried to synthesize the understanding that my father was being prepped to be buried in the ground forever.

* * * * *

WHEN MY ears begin to pop, as we make our final approach to land, I half-open the window-shutter next to me, and the whole sky is dawn-golden. The sun is a half-inch over the horizon, baring its naked best.

By the time we get our luggage, the sun is well up, and we wait outside in the early morning heat. Heck is supposed to pick us up, but I can't reach him, so Vernon and I rent a car. Neither of us wants our mother on the road right now, in her condition.

On the highway back to our house I get the first text from Brian: "You back yet? Heck in hospital. Tried to kill self last nt. Visiting hrs 2-6. Call me."

"Goddam," Vernon says when I tell him. "Goddam."

I text Brian back, "Just landed. On our way home. You hear anything new?"

Brian texts, "Nah. Going at 2. Pick u up?"

"Ya."

* * * * *

OUR HOMETOWN isn't that bad in the summer. I think about that as we drive down the highway in the sterile-smelling rental car, about how I'm at least glad all of this is happening here, now, in the bearable summer, rather than during the unendurable winter, which is just around the corner.

As we whip down the freeway, we wind through a mix of farmland and forest, and I gaze at the golden fields of wheat and the cool green shadows of the trees. The sky is blue and densely populated with great white puffs that look like animals and nations.

Vernon doesn't say much, and neither do I. He, the elder, is driving, and I, the younger, am passenging.

He does say one thing of note, though, a few miles from the off-ramp—something we were evidently both thinking.

"Mom better have a goddam good explanation for why she hasn't told us how he died."

* * * * *

FORTY-FIVE MINUTES after leaving the rental lot, we pull onto the long driveway of the one and only house our family has ever owned. There is one car in the driveway—not our mother's, which is in the garage, but our cousin Tina's.

It's Tina we see first when we walk through the door. She is in the process of standing up from a chair in the living room, and she says, "Ah, just as we thought: you boys are here."

Vernon makes a beeline for our mom, and Tina approaches me with an austere smile, and we hug.

Our mother weeps into Vernon's chest.

"I'll see you soon," Tina says quietly and heads outside.

"Thanks, Tina," I whisper.

Then the Vernon-and-Mom hug ends, and my mother and I observe each other. I don't like her, but I don't hate her enough to deprive her of love in such a dark hour, so I walk over and accept her hug hello. She cries into my chest, too, but nothing seems to be able to affect me.

Afterwards, Vernon guides her to take a seat on the couch. He and I sit on a pair of recliners.

"Mom, what the hell happened?" I ask.

"Whoa, Jibba," Vernon says. "Mom, do you need anything to drink or anything?"

"Sure," Mom says, "I'll have some water."

"Jibba, get her some water."

He goddam loves that older-brother card.

As I get a glass from the cupboard and fill it with cold water, Vernon says, "Mom, it's been killing both of us not knowing what happened."

I hand her the glass, and she thanks me and drinks a drag of water.

"I can't," she says. "I can't say it. I asked Tina to tell you. She's waiting outside. I'll be here."

"Mom, what the hell—" Vernon starts.

"Just talk to Tina, Vernon!" Mom snaps.

He looks at me, and I look at him, and we both agree to just go with it.

Vernon shrugs. "Be right back," he says.

Outside, Tina is smoking a cigarette. She's one of the more appreciable members of our family, and while we all get along, this is certainly awkward. As Vernon and I step outside, a large cloud passes in front of the sun, and the whole neighborhood is temporarily shaded.

"Okay, guys, I wish there were an easy way to tell you this, but, well, maybe this is it: have you ever heard of David Carradine?"

"Oh, my god," Vernon and I say simultaneously.

I can't seem to synthesize what I've just put together.

"Tina, is this a fucking joke?" Vernon asks, legitimately pissed.

"Yeah, Vernon," Tina says, "that's exactly the kind of person I am—a person who'd joke around like this. Why do you think your mom didn't want to tell you herself?"

"Good point," I say.

Vernon tries to accept it. He struggles with it, but eventually he does accept it.

"Jesus," he says.

"Your mom found him—in the bathroom."

The three of us stand there on the driveway, with Tina's cigarette smoke circling between us as it rides a lazy breeze. The cloud unwraps the sun, and as we begin to squint from the return of glaring sunlight the three of us turn back toward the house and walk inside.

* * * * *

"Okay, Aunt Sylvia," Tina says, "I'm gonna go."

"Go, then," Mom says. She is sitting in the corner of the couch, at an angle, rigid in the protective shell of proper posture.

None of us is acting naturally; we shuffle stiffly and don't know what to do with our hands.

Tina leaves, and we return our attention to our grieving mother—Vernon sitting next to her on the couch, holding her hand, and me sitting on our father's favorite recliner, facing a painting of Jesus.

"I'm so sorry, Mom," Vernon says.

"Don't be," Mom says. "He died doing what he loved, apparently."

"So you didn't know about this?" I ask. "About this . . . idiosyncrasy?"

I can't face her as I ask this; instead, I ask this to Jesus.

"Of course I knew, Jibba," Mom says. "We argued about it, but who could talk that man out of anything?"

"Isn't what Dad did kind of un-Christian?" I ask Jesus.

"God the fuck knows anymore, Jibba," Mom says. Vernon and I exchange a shocked look, because that was maybe the third time in our life that we'd heard our mother utter a cuss word.

"Did you hear about Heck, Mom?" Vernon asks.

My mother seems to register this question with a visible

surprise—like she thought that her grief was so powerful that nothing else in the world could have happened since it began.

"No," she says. "What happened?"

"Got a text from Brian when I landed—said Heck's in the hospital. We're gonna go later. Still not sure what happened."

"Oh, how horrible," Mom says. "Is he okay?"

"No idea, Mom," I say.

"What?" she asks. She's going deaf.

I straighten up and turn to her. "I don't fucking know, Mom."

Vernon sighs. "Jesus, Jibba . . . ."

"Oh, let your brother be," Mom says. "The Lord will forgive him."

"That's rich," I say. "And what about Dad? Will The Lord forgive him?"

"Yes," Mom says. "And so will we."

We sit together for the next few hours, quietly discussing family matters. There is a moment when I look at the television my father was always watching when he unwound after a long day, and I can picture him sitting where I am sitting, contented and tired and drifting peacefully, and the memory—this stacked pile of similar, specific memories—punches me in the stomach, because there he was and here I sit and he's not here to move me and he never will be again. It's what we're all thinking about. Even in death, in this room my father is a slumbering gorilla.

Eventually, we reach a lull in our tepid talk, and Mom stands up. "I can't sit around all day frowning again. You boys must be starving after that flight. Let me make you something to eat before you go to the hospital."

"Sure," Vernon says, not looking hungry but looking to make her feel at ease. "It's about time you started mothering up around here."

* * * * *

THE FIRST visitor arrives just after the water comes to a boil. It is Uncle Rayford—our father's brother.

Some siblings look alike, and some look nothing alike; Uncle Rayford looks so much like our father it's somewhat unsettling. In fact, when he walks through the door, for a moment I think this whole thing has actually been a prank, but then my brain registers the subtle differences between Uncle Rayford's face and my father's.

"Hi, Uncle Rayford," Vernon says at the door, and they shake hands.

"Vernon," Uncle Rayford says as a hello and walks past him, toward the kitchen, where my mother is stirring an already-prepared pot of pasta sauce. Before he reaches the kitchen, he says over his shoulder to Vernon, "Suck any cocks yet?"

I laugh as I'm sitting in the living room flipping through our father's well-worn *Holy Bible*.

"That goes for you, too, Jibba," Uncle Rayford says. "Try not to shame your family while you're out there, huh?"

Without waiting for a reply, he addresses my mom.

"Sylvia, the people at the funeral home told me they're almost ready for tonight. They need us there a little early."

My mother doesn't say anything. I look up from the book in my lap and see that she is nodding to the news Uncle Rayford gave her and absentmindedly stirring the sauce. Uncle Rayford has his arms folded and is leaning against the counter by the refrigerator.

None of the words in the *Bible* offers any solace or wisdom to me, so I dismissively close the book and put it back in its little shrine on the coffee table and head into the kitchen.

"Need any help, Mom?" Vernon asks. He's just emerging from his old room, where there's still a bed but which is otherwise occupied by a desk and our parents' computer and other office-type stuff.

This breaks Mom's occupied thoughts, and she returns to the reality of the situation. "No, thank you, honey," Mom says. "Actually, yes, you can set the table."

"Jibba, help me set the table," he says. Fucker.

"Sure."

Vernon grabs the plates and napkins, and I grab the glasses and silverware, and we begin setting the table.

"How are things with you, Jibba?" Uncle Rayford asks.

"You mean besides this?"

"Yeah."

"Besides this, things are even worse," I say.

He is just making conversation; he doesn't want to get into it. I don't blame him. It's difficult enough for me to go anywhere with this yoke of loathing across my shoulders.

"I'm sorry to hear that," he says with a look of helplessness, which makes me feel bad.

"Don't worry about it, Uncle Ray," I say. "In all good stories, the main character has to go through some shit before he can grow."

"We're all going through some shit now," he says.

"Indeed," Vernon says.

And this is when the first plate of pasta is placed below my face, its sweet-smelling steam dancing up my nose.

It's my dad's recipe—this sauce.

With the first bare whiff of this old, memory-inducing smell, I am brought back to this same room when I was three years old, hugging my father's leg as he dragged me around the kitchen as he prepared his special pasta sauce. It's winter outside, and Mom and Vernon are at the movies with Vernon's friends. My father is humming a song I don't recognize—perhaps a song of his own invention—and his hands are a galaxy of smells, from mixing and combining all the ingredients that go into this starburst of flavor.

Before I realize what's happening, a tear falls from my face into the very sauce that provoked the tear.

"He made this sauce, didn't he?" I ask, my voice wobbling. Evidently, this hadn't hit Vernon yet. He drops his fork to the plate and looks at Mom for an answer.

She nods, unable to speak.

"I can't eat this," I say.

"Don't be silly, Jibba," Mom says. "Do you think I'm eager to finish off one of the last true signatures your father left us? But he made it for us, so eat it!"

Vernon picks up his fork and starts eating again. His face is more serious than I've ever seen it.

Nobody says anything else as we eat. For me and Vernon, this is our last kiss goodbye to our father—and from him a warm hug within.

After we finish, we sit around the table with Uncle Rayford

while Mom cleans dishes in the sink.

"How are you doing, Uncle Rayford?" Vernon asks.

Despite the fact that they look so much alike, our father and his brother have very different mannerisms. When our father was putting together an answer to a question, he often preceded it with an unbroken tone of thought, "Mmmmm—pretty good considering the fact that I'm dead now."

But Uncle Rayford, when dredging up an answer within himself, rumples his eyebrows and looks at the floor. "I've . . . I don't know, Vernon. I haven't cried this much since I was a kid."

Mom, by now, is finishing the dishes—is down to, in fact, the last dirty dish: the sauce pan.

With the hot water running, and steam rising up to her face, Mom looks at that jet of water and at that dirty pan. That water would erase that signature forever.

"OH, GOD—I CAN'T DO THIS!"

She turns off the water and begins swooning to the ground. Uncle Rayford, Vernon, and I pop from our seats and catch her before she passes out on the hard kitchen tile.

We slowly lower her to a sitting position on the ground, where she begins hopelessly weeping, her sobbing shudders shaking all three of us.

In my pocket, I begin to feel my phone vibrate, but I don't check it. Mom cries.

We all cry with her.

* * * * *

THE VIBRATION signifies a text from Brian.

"Be there in 5."

"Mom," I say to her on the couch in the living room where we brought her, "Brian's on his way over to take me and Vernon to the hospital to see Heck."

"You go ahead," Vernon says. "I'll stay here with Mom. Uncle Rayford has to get back to work."

"Is that okay, Mom?" I ask. "You want me to stay, too?"

She seems to have returned to a grieving normalcy. "No, honey. Go see your friend—try to make something good come from all of this."

I head upstairs and shower off the grime of the flight and

my overall feeling, but I don't feel all that much better afterwards. I feel dumb for having expected a change in demeanor; as if a stream of hot water could wash off an internal rot like it can the last remnants of my father's spaghetti sauce.

By the time I get back downstairs, Brian is in the living room, hugging my mom and telling her how sorry he is.

* * * * *

BRIAN LOOKS like an older version of the boy I grew up with—where once there had been the smooth skin of youth, now there was stubble and the swarthy complexion of a landscaper. He's driving what would be described in a screenplay as a "blue car." Nothing fancy, just four doors and a kiddie seat in the back. It coughs and sputters as he starts it.

The midafternoon sun is cooking everything with its long hot stare. The sky is white-blue, and the puffy clouds have moved off and been replaced with rippled sheets of clouds much higher in the sky. All around us, everything is verdant green or Earth brown or wheat gold or fence-post white.

"How's Vicki and Aletta?" I ask.

"Both good," he says. "Vicki said to tell you how sorry she is, and Aletta said, 'Gockle, Daddy,' so obviously she's torn up, too."

I grin.

"Tell them I said thanks."

"What about you, man? What's new in your world? Besides the obvious."

"A few minutes after I found out about my dad, my boss told me I was being laid off."

"Jesus Fuck," Brian says. "So you moving home?"

Brian has made it no secret that he wants me to move back, and over the years he has kept up his enthusiasm for the prospect. Usually I would make a joke about it, but today I just can't.

"I'm not taking any options off the table right now," I say. "I don't goddam fucking know what I'm going to do."

Brian doesn't reply other than to nod his head.

Soon, we are pulling into the parking lot at the hospital.

* * * * *

AH, YES, that awful hospital smell—a revolting mix of antiseptics, feces, human decay, and the stale air of a building without hinged windows. In this madhouse of disease, I begin to worry that my hypochondria will flare up. I keep my eyes to the floor and follow Brian's lead. Knowledge is power, but medical knowledge is crippling.

We get in an elevator with a shrunken old woman and an overweight orderly—all of us reach for and hit the button for the third floor: ICU, post-op, and radiology.

Brian says, "It looks like we're all having a bad day."

The old woman does not give a response; the overweight orderly smirks. When the doors open, the old woman heads toward radiology, the orderly heads toward post-op, and I join Brian as we head toward the ICU, where another overweight orderly points us in the direction of Heck's room.

* * * * *

THE DOOR is open, and so are the shades, revealing the high puffs and the blue-white sky. The walls are lime green, and The Smell is here, too. There is only room for one bed, which we can't see as we enter the room—immediately to our right is a small bathroom. But after we pass the bathroom we see the cottony-white sheets of the bed and two large rumples in the shape of a leg each. Then we see two hands folded over a blanket-turned-down stomach, and then we see Heck, with his eyes closed and his head back on the high pillows, sleeping or meditating. There is an ugly injury across the front and sides of his neck.

I clear my throat, and Heck's eyes open.

As Heck registers recognition of his two friends, not only do his eyes open, but they brighten.

"H—" he says, barely the faintest squeak at all, and a pang of pain rips across his face, which proceeds to fill with a just-remembered frustration. His hands briefly move up to the source of his pain: the injury across his neck.

The rope.

Right now, I think, *there's a mortician applying makeup to my dead father's similar injury*. Then I see Heck reach for a notepad and pencil on his desk. He quickly scribbles something and shows us.

"*Can't talk.*"

"Right," I say, and take the pad and write, "What happened?"

He looks at me with crossed eyebrows and scribbles a reply.

"*I can hear, you retard.*"

Brian and I both laugh, and I feel guilty that it was the guy in the hospital bed who had to break the tension in here.

"I have an idea," Brian says, and he walks out of the room without explaining himself. I stay with Heck, who can't seem to look at me, like he's embarrassed.

"Did you hear about my dad?" I ask.

He solemnly nods yes. Then he looks at me as if to tell me how sorry he is.

"Thanks," I say. "When did you get so fat?" I ask jokingly. He's put on a few pounds.

He writes, "*New book. Haven't gotten out much.*"

"A new book finally," I say happily. (Of course I loved "Crack," as we'd taken to calling his first book.) "Is it done?"

"Is what done?" Brian asks as he enters the room with a laptop computer under his arm.

"Heck just told me he's been working on a new book," I say.

"Well this should help him tell us about it," he says. "I borrowed it from one of the nurses."

Brian turns on the computer and brings up a type-to-audio program and hands the machine to Heck.

"All yours," he says and sits down.

Heck types, and a robotic voice says, "*Thank you, Earthling.*" We laugh.

Then the robotic voice says, "*How are your mom and brother doing?*"

"Mom's a mess, man, but I don't think it's fully hit me or Vernon yet."

Heck nods. He turns to Brian and types, "*How's your family?*"

"They want to know why you tried to kill yourself," Brian says.

"Yeah," I say by way of supporting Brian's bold statement.

Heck types for a while, and then the computer says, "*Tell them it was necessary for a part of me that they've only ever met in my literature. That should clear things up, no?"*

"What's that mean?" I ask.

Heck types. *"I've written three books in my life. The first was not a book but rather the accumulated three-million words I wrote before I sat down to write 'Crack.' The second was 'Crack,' and the third—which I'm calling* Two Eternities of Darkness—*I just finished."*

"Okay, so what?" I say.

"I hate to give away the ending, but in the third book, the story doesn't end. It ends by virtue of the fact that there are no words left, because at that point in the story the narrator kills himself, and there's no one left to finish the telling."

"So you had to complete the deed in real life?"

"It seemed like the right thing to do," the computer says. *"All my stories are rife with suicide—that curious existential blend of bravery and cowardice—and it just seemed fitting to end my career with my own. I have nothing left to write, and writing is my life, so I have nothing left to live.*

"The way I see it, the storyteller is part of the story."

Brian and I think about this.

"The shrinks here don't seem to understand that," the computer says, and I smirk sardonically.

The three of us are silent; the only sounds we hear are coming from the hall. Then there is the clicking of typing.

"My brother was the paramedic who came to your house, Jibba," the computer says. *"I know what happened."*

"Great," I say.

"What happened?" Brian asks. "I just heard that he passed away."

"He . . . You ever heard of Michael Hutchence?" I ask.

I can see Brian run the name through his head, find it, follow the story to the end, and then turn to me and say, "Oh, man, Jibba—I am sorry."

"Thanks," I say.

More of that hallway silence.

And again more typing.

"He's the one who kind of inspired me," the computer says. *"He was a great man."*

It takes a moment for what Heck just said to sink in, but after it does, I am looking at him with great confusion. "How?"

Brian and I both look at each other with an equal curiosity as Heck types his long reply.

"*When my brother told me what happened, it all made sense—the stuff your parents went through when we were younger. I think that might have been his thing, Jibba, and your mom found out about it, and maybe normal sex just didn't interest him anymore, so that's why she had to look outside the marriage for lovers. And even though it kind of tore your family apart, he was just being who he was. We don't always want to be the same person other people want us to be. Your mom probably realized that. I found it inspiring. For better or worse, he died doing one of the things he loved. With the way my life and my so-called art are so intertwined, I tried to do the same thing. In a way, we both failed.*"

A nurse talking to another nurse about the beach, a ringing telephone, the beeping chirp of a heart-rate monitor in another room, playing the beat of that patient's life.

"What are you going to do now?" Brian asks. "I know you can fool these clowns and get out, but do you think you'll do it again? Are Jibba and I wasting our time and friend-feelings right now?"

Tears begin to fill Heck's eyes. He looks at Brian and me, and the look says, "I don't know what I'm going to do now."

While my mind tries to fit together the puzzle pieces Heck just handed me, I add my own question. "You can't keep writing?"

He types his reply.

"*After 'Two Eternities,' nothing I write will be truly original. I've used up every convention I've invented, and from now on it'll just be an ever-diminishing echo of my two little fireworks going pop.*"

"Shit," Brian says. "That kind of makes sense, Jibba."

It's not a final decision; the conversation is ongoing, but we all step back and let each other relax for a second. I lean against the wall in my chair, and I look out the window at the way the wall frames the ever-changing sky, and the sky is so bright it makes me squint, and in squinting I see Rachel's little pretty O mouth about to suck the butt of a cigarette, and I have a flash of an idea.

"I've got it!" I say so loud it causes Brian and Heck to jerk their heads toward me and a nurse to come in and make sure everything is okay.

After she leaves, I say to them, "Reinvent yourself, Heck! Okay, so you're done with the written word, but you've still got art in you, so why not try something else? In fact, I have your next career: photographer."

Brian and Heck don't look very convinced.

"Think about it: it's not too late to learn how to take a pretty picture, you've got the money to afford all the equipment and time you'd need, and here's the goddam clincher: you're a famous writer, man! Have you ever seen the women Charles Bukowski was able to bring to bed? And you'd have a camera. Dude, just pick a new art world to dominate if you're done schooling us all on how to kill a narrator."

"*Ha ha*," the computer says.

"Maybe you'll never be the best photographer in the world—and by the way, who the hell is?—but that's not the point, is it? It's about the challenge, right? You're not just your literature, my friend—and you know it. So take a few goddam pictures. Aletta Fogger deserves to live the privileged life of having an Uncle Heck Bloom to teach her how to be excellent at everything—especially considering how very little her own father can teach her."

Brian says to Heck while motioning to me, "This fuckin' guy."

Heck smirks and types.

"*Photography is too easy,*" the computer says. "*But you might be right. I might think about buying an instrument or something, maybe some canvases and paint.*"

"Good," I say.

"Just don't draw any pictures of painters killing themselves," Brian says.

"*Ha ha,*" the computer says. "*Your poor daughter.*"

We all laugh at that, including a quiet squeak by Heck, who then shudders with frustration from the pain in his throat.

The doorway is suddenly shrouded in darkness, and an overweight nurse leans into the room.

"Everything okay in here?" she asks, responding to our laughter and the computer voice.

"Yes, ma'am," Brian says. "Just trying to cheer up our friend here."

The overweight nurse is, at best, appeased by what Brian says. Evidently she's uncomfortable hearing the laughter of other people.

"Speaking of unwanted interjections," I say as the doorway returns to normal light, "I was telling Brian on the way over here that I got laid off from that job with that multimedia firm—right after I heard about my dad."

"*Fucks*," the computers says.

"Yeah," I say. "You know what kind of made me laugh when I thought about it, though? Doesn't getting 'laid off' sound like it would be much better than it is?"

Heck smiles weakly and types while Brian chuckles.

"*Or being 'bedridden*,'" the computer says.

Brian and I laugh.

Brian sits there trying to think of one, and then he does, and it's his usual simple Brian greatness.

"Or 'jam coverage' for that matter," he says, referring to a defensive option in football.

More laughter (Heck's laughter a silent beam.)

"Well, Heck," I say, "I should probably get going; my father's wake is tonight. Do you know if or when they're going to let you out of here?"

"I'm on a twenty-four hour psych hold," the computer says. "If they let me go, I'll be at the funeral in the morning. St. Jude, right?"

"Yeah," I say standing, "at ten."

"Okay," the computer says, "maybe I'll see you there."

"I might come back later," Brian says to Heck. "You want me to bring you anything? Something to eat?"

Heck motions to his throat, to say that he can't eat, and then he motions to the tube that's keeping him fed.

"Oh, right," Brian says. "Well, you want me to blend a pizza and see if we can jam it through that tube?"

Heck smiles weakly and types.

"*Fuck it—yes, let's try it,*" the computer says.

Brian and I laugh.

"See you later, man," Brian says. "Go easy on yourself."

Brian can sense that I have a bit more to say to Heck, so he heads out into the hall with a look telling me to take my time.

"Thanks, Heck," I say to my bedridden friend. "I mean it. Thanks for your perspective on my father, and for trying to explain why you . . . did this. I know I have no right to ask you to live a life you might find agonizing, but as long as you're alive I'm going to tell you this: even if you never write another word, you will always have substance and meaning in my life, and for as alone as I almost always feel, yours and Brian's friendship means more to me than I think most friendships mean to most people—and friendships are more meaningful than almost anything else in the world, so just imagine how vast my feeling is right now."

With a tear rolling down his cheek, Heck types and the computer speaks.

"*Shut up, queermo.*"

I smile.

"I love you, Heck. Welcome back to the living."

With the tubes going into and out of his body, we exchange an awkward hug.

As I reach the doorway, I hear the computer say, "*You, too.*"

* * * * *

As we pass the nurses' station, Brian tells the only attractive one that Heck is done with the computer if she wants to go get it from him.

"Is he really the guy who wrote that book?" she asks. "He doesn't look at all like his picture."

"In a work of fiction, even the author's picture might be false," I say. "If you liked it, go talk to him about the book. Whether he wrote it or not, he's a mighty big fan."

"Of the book?" she asks.

"Of you," Brian says. "Of all beautiful women who take care of him."

The nurse blushes as Brian and I walk toward the elevator.

* * * * *

IN THE car, Brian and I talk during the relatively brief drive back to my house.

"You think he'll always have that gash across his neck, like a scar from it?" Brian asks.

"Looks like it could go either way," I say, "but if I know one thing, I bet Heck hopes it stays."

"Yeah," Brian says.

It's weird to see my old neighborhood again. It looks the same, but there are all these little indicators of passed time that remind me that this all was here while I was gone—a once-new sign now weather-worn, a scribbled graffito on a bridge abutment . . . .

"You think anything I said made any difference?" I ask.

It's a thoughtful while before Brian responds.

"Something needed to be said," he says, "and I didn't know what to say. If anyone could pull it off, if anyone could penetrate that wicked dungeon in his head, it's you."

"That's a big if," I say.

"Yeah," he says, "but I think all three of us are at least glad you tried."

"Yeah," I say, feeling unconvinced but knowing he's right.

"Can I get you or your family anything? I got all this pain around me, and I feel pretty useless."

"What have I told you about underestimating your value as a friend?" I say. "I mean, you gave Heck a voice back there. You've done a lot, man."

He applies the brakes at the end of the driveway and says, "Thanks, Jibba."

"You're a great friend, Brian Fogger," I say. "Thank you for the ride. Say hi to Vicki and the kid for me."

"You got it," he says, and I close the door. Through the open window he says, "I'll probably bring them tonight."

* * * * *

"AVE MARIA" is being sung quietly by an opera singer on a series of small speakers in the off-white ceiling. The walls are a color that is a mix of gray and brown, and the tall windows are embellished with drapes bearing a sufficiently somber yet luxurious chocolate-brown color that reaches from the ceiling to the floor. In the middle of the room is a matrix of black, empty, padded, collapsible chairs. At the front of the room is a glossy green casket, the top quarter of which is open, revealing the heavily-made-up face of my deceased father.

My mother is talking about the last pre-arrival details with the funeral director, Vernon is checking his overall appearance in one of the mirrors in the hallway, and I am at the back of the room where the wake is about to be held, gazing at that gleaming green casket, unable to look at what's inside.

Before I know it, Vernon has his arm around me.

"Let's go have a look," he says. "I'm curious to see him now that I know he's a sex freak."

Good old Vernon.

"Okay," I eventually say.

As we walk toward our father, Vernon adds, "Besides, we're going to be saying hello and goodbye to him every day for the rest of our lives, anyway."

"I think I know what you mean, but what do you mean?" I ask.

I can tell Vernon likes this question—that he's kind of glad I asked it.

"You don't see Dad every time you look in the mirror?"

"Yeah, I guess," I say. "That's true." I look remarkably like our father and Uncle Rayford.

"So every time you look in the mirror, you'll say hello and goodbye to him, and the same with me, when I jerk off."

He's gonna think about our father when—?

Then it hits me.

"No way!" I say, way too loud for being in a funeral home. I look around and nod an apology to the funeral director and then turn back to Vernon, "Dude, are you serious? You're into that, too?"

He doesn't say anything; instead, he winks.

The only reason I don't believe him is because Vernon is the biggest liar I know.

Fortunately, this talk has distracted me enough that by the

time I'm back in the real moment, we're at my father's casket.

That does it.

My father's lifeless countenance, stitched together and made up, my father unable to sit up and wipe that shit off his face and rub his hands together and say, "'Vernon and Jibba, you two are in *a lot of trouble!*' . . . is what I would say if you were, but you're not, so have a good day at school, boys!", like he always did when we were kids. (He was always messing with us like that.) My father there, unable to talk to anyone in the world about whatever nirvana he found with a belt around his neck, unable to drive me and Brian and Heck to football and basketball and baseball games, unable to sneak me and Vernon into R-rated movies when we were much too young.

This thing in that casket is not my father, and seeing it there makes me feel sick, because it's mocking what he was—it's a cruel caricature from someone with no sense of humor at all. Look at that pitiful thing—that's my father? That's what he is now? Just an ugly bag of stitched flesh in a fancy box? Is that right? This is the superhero who raised me?

NO!

THAT'S NOT HIM!

THAT'S FUCKING NOT WHAT HE IS NOW!

* * * * *

I'M COLLAPSING into a burst of tears when I feel my brother's hand on my shoulder, and then his full weight as he leans into me and cries, and he's shuddering and so am I, and goddammit I can't cry hard enough—there is no cry loud enough to give ample voice to the certainty within me that says that that's not what my father is.

* * * * *

MY MOTHER, Vernon, and I take position off to the side of the room, in a short line, to be greeted and condolenced by a procession of well-wishers.

There is my father's gruff coworker Gus, and his bird-like wife Annie, who both tell me, using the exact same words: "I'm very sorry about everything that has happened."

There is my cousin Tina, and her father, Uncle Rayford, and they are both wearing black. Uncle Rayford grunts me a "Hm," in greeting, and Tina gives me a big hug and introduces me to her boyfriend, Douglast—"yes," he tells me, "with a 't'"—and he too tells me how sorry he is, from very high above me, the fortunately tall man. I thank him. She asks me how I'm doing. I tell her, "I can see where the idea of a soul came from," I say. "Because that's not my father up there." She and Douglast agree, or at least they tell me they agree. I wouldn't have disagreed with me at the time, even if I disagreed.

I really feel like I hit something with that soul line, and I don't really feel like getting into the specifics of how I'm doing when everyone asks me, so for the rest of the night I use that reply as my fallback. It's sufficiently secular, religious, and existential enough to be politely delivered and dismissed.

Nobody really knows, so they acquiesce to my numbstruck ramblings.

Eventually, I have to pee, so I excuse myself from the mourning line and walk across the deep carpet to the brighter hallway, to the even brighter, floor-tiled bathroom.

On the way out of the bathroom, in the yellow-lit hallway, I am walking along and staring at the deep crimson carpet when I hear my name called by a woman's voice.

I look up and see platinum-blonde hair, red lips, smooth pore-less skin, and a black dress of mourning—yes, it's "super-hot, dismissive bitch" and professional actress Kelsey Scott.

"Kelsey?" I ask, as confused as she was when she saw me at the episode premiere party.

Once again I feel like I am looking at something surreal, or like she is the only real thing in the world.

"I thought that was you," she says.

"What are you doing here?" I ask.

Together we move to one of the seats in the hallway, to get out of the way of a group of mourners who've come to pay their last respects to my father.

"I own the building," she says making a wide, all-inclusive, sarcastic gesture.

"No, you don't," I say, mocking the tone of voice she used on me back in Burbank.

She playfully pushes me, and I am shocked by how much I

am relieved to feel nonfamilial human contact.

"Actually, it's partly true," she says. "This is my parents' business."

"Really? You're from around here?" I look at her with a renewed interest, which is hardly difficult.

"Yeah—well, nearby," she says.

"Really? Did you go to Walter?"

"Oak Grove," she says.

Walter High School is a windowless shithouse public nightmare at the intersection of three counties, and Oak Grove Finishing School is a state-of-the-art private palace in the middle of rolling bucolic fields.

"Ah," I say. "So why are you here now, though?"

"Our showrunner's wife is from Japan, and he put the show on temporary hiatus after the China invasion while he works with her on trying to get her family out of there. And evidently your mom had bragged to my mom about Vernon writing for 'Punch,' and my mom called me and asked about Vernon, and I had been thinking about you, so I flew back this morning."

Her penultimate clause does not escape my attention, and I suddenly feel anxious and undeserving of her attention.

"Why were you thinking about me? Is it the smell?"

Sometimes I think I smell like the fat piece of shit I am. It's hard to explain.

"What?" she asks, very confused. "The smell?"

She scoots closer and puts her hand on my shoulder and leans her face near my neck, and sniffs.

"No, you smell like a man," she says. "I like it. But I was thinking about you because of that little talk we had back in Burbank: it's like the only meaningful conversation I've had with anyone in years."

I can't think of a way to reply to this, so I just look at her pretty face.

"And it's not like it was that meaningful, really, but that's what makes it all the more important to me," she says. "I can see all the starlight, Jibba, but I can't feel any warmth."

This little speech blasts through all the inhibitive layers that keep me from existing as a physical being, and I am able to put my arm around Kelsey, and pull her closer, and sit with her there comfortably in the folds of my mourning embrace, with her healthy perfection pressed against my fat rolls, and for now I don't notice the fat rolls—only the beautiful weight pressing against them.

She takes my hand and says, "I'm so sorry about your father."

* * * * *

"Jibba?"

It's Brian, with his wife and daughter. Brian is wearing his only suit—dark blue, with a white undershirt and a darker-blue tie—and his wife, Vicki, is wearing a tasteful dark-blue dress. Two-year-old Aletta is also wearing a dress, but hers is almost the same shade of crimson as the carpet. In fact, as the family walks up to us, Aletta is flapping her dress while looking at the carpet, and laughing at how they're the same color.

"Hey, Brian," I say, removing my arm from around Kelsey's shoulders, standing, and accepting a hug from him.

Kelsey stands, too.

"Hey, man," Brian says as we disengage from the hug.

"Nice to see you, Vicki," I say and we hug. "You look younger than the last time I saw you—like an angel."

"Aw, thanks, Jibba," she says. "I'm so sorry."

"Thank you," I say and turn my attention to Aletta.

"Hey, Aletta," I say. "That's a very pretty dress."

Aletta looks up at me, laughs momentarily, and then runs behind her mom's leg before having the guts to look at me and Kelsey again.

Kelsey!

"Oh, I'm so sorry," I say and take Kelsey by the hand and have her stand with me.

"Kelsey Scott," I say, "this is my great friend Brian Fogger, his wife Vicki, and their daughter Aletta."

Kelsey greets them cordially.

"How do you know Jibba?" Vicki asks.

"I work with his brother," she says.

"Oh, for that TV show?" Vicki asks. "I'm sorry, I've never seen it. With this little bug here, the only thing we get to watch anymore is *Animal Parade*."

"Great show," Kelsey says. "*Animal Parade*, I mean. But yes, I work with Vernon on *Stomach Punch*."

"That's wonderful," Vicki says. As she says this, she picks up Aletta and holds her while Aletta plays with the necklace around her mother's neck.

"Thanks," Kelsey says. "How do you all know each other?"

"Brian and I were best friends growing up," I say. "Vicki went to the same high school as us. She and Brian started 'going out' when we were sophomores, and they've been together ever since."

"Aww," Kelsey says. "That's so cute."

"What about you two?" Vicki asks. "How long have you been together?"

Kelsey and I look at each other. She's embarrassed and I'm anxious.

"We met at a party for the airing of Vernon's first show," I say.

"And I flew out here after I heard about what happened," she says.

"Her parents own this place," I say.

"Small world," Brian says.

"Just the right size," I say and blush because it was such a corny thing to say. Kelsey and Vicki don't respond to this verbally, but there is a response from them that I can inexactly perceive.

"We're not together, though," Kelsey says. "I mean, I want to be, but Jibba doesn't think I'm smart enough for him."

"Hey, I never said that . . . to you," I say.

"Then why didn't you ask for my number after we attended that astronomy lecture we both enjoyed?"

For this I have no reply, or none that I want to admit out loud. I didn't ask for her number because I figured she'd draw up a restraining order against me.

"Thought so," she says in reply to my silence.

"Sounds like you're the stupid one, Jibba," Brian says.

"I don't disagree," I say and turn to Kelsey. "I'd like to try to make it up to you, if you can forgive me."

"In my experiences," Kelsey says, "it's a lot more fun when you're *not* forgiven."

"I like this girl!" Vicki says, and as if to add some punch to her mother's statement, Aletta jubilantly adds, "Gockle!"

* * * * *

VERNON IS surprised to see me walk in with Kelsey. He smiles when he sees us, and Kelsey, somewhat to my surprise, smiles back.

"Hello, Vernon," she says and hugs him. After they disengage, she adds, "I am so sorry."

"Thank you, Kelsey," Vernon says.

Before Vernon can follow up with any questions, Kelsey affectionately turns to our mom and introduces herself, and while they meet each other, I catch Vernon up on what's up.

"Wow," he says when I finish.

Typical Vernon.

"Kelsey, that is the most thoughtful sentiment I've heard today," my mom says. "Thank you so much."

"What'd she say?" Vernon asks—as do I, nonverbally.

"I don't think it would make sense to you guys," Kelsey says. "It's a girl thing."

As she looks at us, it is plainly evident that our mother is bursting with a quiet pride at sharing secret grieving "girl knowledge" with a friendly young Hollywood actress.

"Do you two mind if I borrow Jibba?" Kelsey asks as she slips her to-be-escorted arm into mine.

"*Yes*," Vernon says quietly, but heavily with sarcasm.

"Of course not, honey," my mom says.

"Thank you," she says, and we walk to the very back of the room, where there is an empty loveseat, and we both sit down together again.

"When do you think you're coming back to L.A.?"

"I'm not sure," I say.

"Your work doesn't care how long you're gone?"

"I got laid off right before I flew back."

"Shit," she says and frowns. "Your life's just a bowl of peaches, huh?"

"It is right now," I say.

What a blush!

She squeezes closer to me, and by the moment I feel more like a man.

For the rest of the night, well-wishing mourners visit my mother and Vernon near the casket, and, if they are so inclined, me in my reverie at the back of the room.

When nearly everyone else is gone, Kelsey stands up and says, "Do you mind if I go pay my last respects to your father?" After a moment, she adds, "And first, I guess."

"That's not my father," I say.

This gives her a momentary pause. "I know," she says, "but the gesture is still worth something, and I bet he was a great man."

"Did you hear how he died?" I ask with an unexpectedly petulant tone.

"To be honest, I'd rather hear how he lived," she says. "Have some stories ready for when I return."

She walks to the front of the room, where my father's glistening green coffin awaits her sad tender touch.

* * * * *

IT'S SO real it doesn't feel like a dream, which is what it turns out to be, but part of me still doesn't believe that, even though I swear I woke up.

I really am in a troop-deployment plane as it rumbles noisily through the air and flies low over an Asian peninsula throwing the bark and sparks of war. There are fellow American soldiers in front of me and behind me, and we're all silent in fear and anxiety as we look into the mouth of death with its millions of metal teeth, some of them already ripping into the wings of our aircraft.

There is a loud explosion—one of the engines, I'm sure of it—and the plane begins to roll and fall from the sky. Just then, the green "go" light goes on, and my fellow soldiers begin shuffling to the door and diving out of the plane. When it is my turn, I shuffle and dive the same.

As I descend, I can see that I'm falling into a jungle. A thin beam of moonlight pierces the canopy, and I can see a small spot on the ground, and as I watch that small spot, I see something unrecognizable and massive move across it.

The sudden jerk of the parachute pulls me out of my sleep and into a room that is pitch-black except for three glowing red numbers that read: 4:19.

This is the room I grew up in. Later this morning is my father's funeral.

* * * * *

My mother has dyed her wedding dress black, and has had it let out a bit, to fit better in her more sedentary old age. She is wearing a black veil and holding a black rosary in her right hand. To me, she looks kind of crazy dressed like that.

But I understand.

She can't seem to pull her eyes from the coffin in the middle of the church. The priest on the altar is giving a funeral mass, but I can't hear what he's saying. It's just sounds. I hear everything: a priest's voice, the click of those rosary beads, the hum of the air-conditioning, the occasional cough or throat-clear, Aletta Fogger letting out a brief child-sound, the atmosphere going into and out of my nose and lungs, the quiet whir of traffic on the street outside, my mother's occasional gasps and gulps as she tries not to collapse into hysterics.

Before I know it, I can understand the priest to say, "—eldest son, Vernon, will now give the eulogy."

The sound of Vernon's feet scuffling along the church carpet, then the sound of a microphone being turned on, and Vernon's throat being cleared.

"My father loved this shit," he says, which gets a respectful chuckle from the crowd. "This—being at church, listening to a priest tell him where to look for the light. And he also loved the opposite of this. He loved to watch pornography and hang himself with a belt while he jerked off."

The room is thrown into the heaviest of silences. Vernon proceeds.

"How can any brief speech possibly be a proper summation of and goodbye to such a person? And not just for my father, but for anyone?

"So let us mark this sad occasion, for one thing, as a nod to the dynamism of human life. My father was by all accounts an ordinary man. He made slightly below the national income average; he worked hard at his job and achieved satisfactory but not spectacular results; he had a wife and family and friends; and yet look at the depths of who he was: a massively devout Catholic, and a closet sex fiend; a family comedian, and an unremarkable pedestrian; a demigod descended from monkeys, and made to feel bliss and guilt for it all.

"He didn't run from it. He didn't try to rationalize the vacillations of his personality. He reached out in every direction that interested him, and he died for it.

"In a way, my father's story is a reminder to us all that we should never underestimate the depths—as unusual or glorious as they may be—of the people we meet, know, and love. In each of our houses are many mansions.

"When Jibba and I were kids, our whole family went to the beach, and while we were still setting everything up, Jibba ran off toward the water, and before we even knew he was gone we heard him come screaming back, *crying like an onion on burger day*—to put it in our father's parlance—and it turned out Jibba had come across a dead seagull on the beach. It was one of his first experiences with death, and of course he eventually asked if everyone in our family were going to die, and our father said, 'Well, I don't mean to shock you too much, Jibba, but everything that lives will die at some point.' And when Jibba asked 'Why?' Dad said, 'I don't know; it must have been in the contract we signed before we got here.'"

The audience chuckles at this line.

As well as many others, I'm thrown into a momentary vertigo, because Vernon does not continue speaking. After a few moments, he clears his throat again, and it is evident that heavy emotion will not permit him to continue, until he finally coughs it out.

"The philosopher Immanuel Kant, if I understand him correctly, stated that we are altered by the universe, and that we alter the universe—that it goes both ways, that we create the universe that created us. So, in a way, I like to think that what he was saying was that if everyone in the world tries hard enough—and I'm not kidding here—I think we can bring my father back to life."

Vernon is smiling and really trying to sell it.

"We can do it!"

I don't feel right.

Did that just happen or did I just think that?

Vernon is at the podium, crying. Finally, he coughs out what he was trying to say.

"Goodbye, Dad."

It echoes through the church, as does the sound of Vernon's hard-bottomed shoes walking off the altar, across the carpet, to where he is met by Tina, who ushers him to a seat as he breaks down.

What the hell just happened?

The priest continues the funeral mass.

At the end of the mass, the pallbearers—me, Vernon, Uncle Rayford, and three of my father's burly friends—carry the casket to the hearse, and I get in a car with my mother, Uncle Rayford, Tina, and Vernon.

It couldn't hit at a worse time—this weird feeling, like fuzzy in my head, and in the quiet of the ride to the cemetery I plow through my periodicals of hypochondria and begin to group the different potential maladies by source. The first, of course, is "brain tumor"—why the fuck do I feel this way? Did Vernon really say that Immanuel Kant thing? Is it grief? What is this, and why did I immediately begin to think of medical diagnoses?

In the car, I'm going crazy, and my family is mourning around me, and we all look the same, except my eyes are scanning back and forth in thought as we go.

"Great job, Vernon," Uncle Rayford says, "with the eulogy."

He's right enough to distract me out of my mental catalogs. Tina and I make solemn grunts of agreement, and Mom eventually says, "It was your father to a T."

Another chorus of solemn grunts of agreement.

"Thanks," Vernon says.

We are getting out of town now, into the country, where the cemetery is. The sunlight is beaming right into the core of my brain. I have to keep my eyes closed.

"I meant all of it," he says. But the sound of it is too quiet in my head—there's ringing in my ears, and it feels like it's getting louder, but it's not.

"I just wish I didn't have to say it today."

Nobody can reply to this, and nobody else speaks for the rest of the drive.

* * * * *

THE SUN shines above us, but also low on the horizon a dark gray cloud crawls forward, toward us. We'll be out of here—all but one of us—by the time the storm arrives, but it's perfect that it's there.

The inimitable Kelsey Scott catches up with the grieving family, and after she says hello to Mom and hugs Vernon and tells him what a great job he did on the eulogy, she turns her attention to me.

"Hi," she says, with a floral mix of greeting-kindness, mourning-respect, and attention-bestowing.

"Hi," I say, trying to match that sweet tone but, being otherwise distracted with medical worries, missing.

"You okay?" she asks, and it sounds like there's cotton stuffed in my ears, and a refraction of sunlight off of Uncle Rayford's wristwatch sends another piercing pain into the center of my brain. I grimace.

"What's wrong?" she asks.

"I don't know," I say, too loud.

"Do you feel sick?" she asks.

"Yeah," I say, "or something."

Why can't I think?

What am I seeing?

Is that—?

* * * * *

HECK BLOOM is all better. He's wearing a tartan kilt and playing the bagpipes—the same song, "Amazing Grace," over and over.

"Heck?" I ask.

Kelsey, following me, repeats the question and does not understand it. "Heck?"

I try to swiftly walk over to Heck, but there's something wrong with me; I feel like I'm walking somewhere else. Eventually, though, I make it.

"They let you out?" I ask.

But he doesn't answer—just keeps playing "Amazing Grace" on the loud bagpipes, filling the air with those wonderful wistful sad notes, but the sound is so loud it hurts my head.

Kelsey is tugging my arm. "You know this guy?"

"He's my best friend!" I shout to her, to be heard over the bagpipes and the cotton in my ears. Kelsey looks unsettled by my reply.

"Jibby?" I hear a voice call out.

I know that voice.

"Are you ready?"

I turn around, and people are shifting nervously, but nobody is looking at me except Kelsey, but it wasn't Kelsey's voice I just heard.

I'm at my desk at work, and I turn around, and there's Rachel. She laughs and says, "Geez, what are you writing?"

"Heck! What the fuck is going on here? How'd your neck get all better so soon?" I ask. But he just keeps playing.

"Answer me!"

Kelsey has left my side and returns with Vernon.

"Jibba?" he asks.

"Jibba?" I'm being asked. "Is that him?"

Vernon, in full battle gear, dead on the ground—six large holes in his torso. "That's him," I say, and I start vomiting on the sand.

Vernon and Kelsey are looking at me.

"Fuckin' Heck won't answer me. Is this a joke or something?"

"Heck?" Vernon asks.

"It's nothing," I say as I follow Rachel outside.

"Jibby?" the voice calls out again. "Is that you?"

"It's Rachel," Rachel says, looking at me as I plead to Heck and Vernon for some answers. She's wearing a dark-blue tank-top and a short black skirt. "My grandma died. She was from around here! Isn't that the weirdest coincidence? We're burying her at this cemetery right now!"

"Jibba, dude, you just got to chill out, bro," Taber says, with his arm around Rachel's waist and his hand down the front of her underwear. "You know, bro?" She's playfully pushing him away and bucking happily against his hands.

"Jibba!" I hear a voice above the din in my ears. "Who are these people?" It's Brian, and he's holding little Aletta, whose face is pitched in a wail, but I can't hear her scream at all.

The bagpipes go silent, and I am almost knocked over by the absence of the droning sound.

"Now do you see?" Heck says perfectly clearly.

"What?" I say.

"The storyteller is part of the story."

Rachel says that to me, too.

"The storyteller is part of the story, Jibby."

And so does Kelsey, and Vernon, and Taber, and my mother, Uncle Rayford, Tina, Douglast—they're at my desk at work, and they're crowded with me around my father's green casket, and they're at the Scotts' funeral home, by the long, chocolate-brown curtains, they're in the mists.

"The storyteller is part of the story."

I'm at my father's funeral; I'm in my boss's office at work; I'm sitting with Kelsey on a loveseat as the moon in the window outside glows coolly; I'm returning fire on all sides and waiting for the fatal thump of a bullet through my head.

But where am I?

I thought it was a medical problem—that I had some sort of vile disease—but I see now that it's something else. It's more than that. How could I have known? What else could I have done?

I'm watching Rachel smoke with her glistening little O mouth outside the office and I'm lusting for her tight body as I carry my father's coffin to its dark hole in the countryside, but where am I?

I'm on a motorcycle and in a plane and a car and on my feet in California and my hometown in the flyovers, but where am I?

I'm crying with my older brother over our dead sex-fiend father's coffin while listening to an operatic rendition of "Ave Maria," and I'm sending another email to those clowns in the legal department about their shoddy boilerplate before it's time for the sweet weekend again, but where am I now?

I don't feel right—how am I doing this?—and where am I?
Are they right?
If the storyteller is part of the story, then how would he ever know that the story is over?
He'll just cease to exist.

About the Author

Daniel Donatelli is the author of the novels *Music Made By Bears* and *Jibba And Jibba*, as well as the sundry collection *Oh, Title!* He was born in Cleveland, Ohio, in 1981.

For more information, please visit www.hhbpublishing.com.